RETURN OF THE PALE FEATHER

Return of the Pale Feather

TIME WALKERS BOOK 2

E.B. Brown

Kirkbride

Contents

Part One	**2**
1	4
2	16
3	20
4	24
5	32
6	40
7	50
8	58
Part Two	**62**
9	64
10	72
11	74
12	80
13	94
14	102

15	108
16	112
17	124
18	136
19	150
20	158
Part Three	**162**
21	164
22	174
23	180
24	192
25	198
26	202
27	206
28	218
29	226
30	240
31	244
32	252
33	254

About the Author	**266**
Also by E.B. Brown	**268**

A farther Confirmation of this we have from the Hatteras Indians, who either then lived on Ronoak-Island, or much frequented it. These tell us, that several of their Ancestors were white People, and could talk in a Book, as we do; the Truth of which is confirm'd by gray Eyes being found frequently amongst these Indians, and no others.

- **John Lawson**, *A New Voyage to Carolina, 1709*

Part One

1

Maggie

Maggie reined her mount in closer to Winn's war pony, taking comfort in the touch of her husband's knee against hers as their horses brushed together. She reached for him, her fingers sliding against the slick skin of his golden-brown thigh. It had been a long ride on a humid summer day without rest, a sacrifice made to speed their journey home, and she was glad it would soon come to an end.

"Do you need rest?" Winn asked, placing his hand over hers. She shook her head.

"No. I just want to get back. The sooner the better."

He tipped his head toward her, a slight movement, yet she felt the sudden tension of his leg muscle under her hand as his blue eyes met hers. She wanted to ask what was wrong, but if she knew nothing of his warrior ways by now, she knew enough when to keep silent. Her own body stiffened, her response attuned to his. He slowed his pony and hers followed suit.

"I think you are right. We will stop to rest," he said, his voice louder than necessary. She felt the pressure of his fingers as he gave her hand a gentle squeeze, then slid down off his mount. Unease crept in as he lifted his arms to her waist to help her down.

He never helped her dismount, there was no need. She was perfectly capable, and he was no gentleman.

"I suppose I could use a drink," she whispered.

His eyes held hers as she slid off the horse. He kept her close, her body sliding down tight against his chest, and if she had not been so scared she would have been lost in the sensation as he kept her shielded between him and the horse. She welcomed his touch, even knowing it was a ploy. His lips traced a path over her sun-scorched cheek to her ear where his words fell whispered in her hair as if only sweet endearments.

"We are being tracked. I think there are two men. One is behind us now. The other circles us."

She bit down over her lower lip as he pressed a kiss to that soft sensitive place near her collarbone.

"How long have you known?" she asked. His arm slipped down around her waist and he pulled her closer.

"Since we left the river."

"That was miles ago! You should have told me!" she hissed.

"There was no need for you to know!" he snapped back.

She ran her hands through his thick black hair, in part to continue the rouse, yet also to convey her frustration. He uttered a low growl in warning before he shoved her away. Stumbling backward a few paces before she regained her footing, she watched as Winn crouched into a defensive stance to face the two men who approached them.

The men were not strangers.

One stepped forward, knife raised.

"*Kweshkwesh.* You slither like a snake to follow us. Why?" Winn said, his words tempered with restraint. Maggie kept her eyes on them as they squared off, the two men circling as if bound in a creeping dance, each poised to strike.

Kweshkwesh glanced at her, his eyes dark orbs seared into the twisted mask of his face. She remembered him well, the sneaky warrior who had once stolen her from her husband. A scalp lock braid ran down the back of his neck, his skin a mesh of pox marked scars, and she could see him tremor as he confronted Winn.

As well he should. Her husband had spared his life on one occasion, and she was certain Winn would show no such mercy a second time.

She ran her thumb over the butt of the knife tucked in her waistband as she watched them, noticing the second man observing as well. She knew enough of the Powhatan ways to understand the test of honor before her. Kweshkwesh had been deeply shamed in front of the entire village when Winn refused to take his life nearly a year ago. It was a matter that would be settled now by blood.

"You know why. I will have the head of your Time Walker," Kweshkwesh said, his eyes shifting back to Winn.

Winn straightened from his crouch, extending the knife he held out toward Kweshkwesh, pointing it with precision at the other man's heart.

"I regret I spared your life once before. Come here, little warrior," Winn taunted him, waving to him as if in welcome. "I will end your suffering today."

They crashed together with a slew of slurred Powhatan curses, Winn taking the upper hand almost immediately. The muscles flexed across his broad back as he wrestled Kweshkwesh to the ground, and although Winn was built much thicker than his opponent, Kweshkwesh was still a formidable fighter and used his wiry strength to twist from Winn's grasp. Winn fell forward onto one knee and scrambled to rise.

Kweshkwesh lurched for Winn with his knife and the men crossed paths again. Maggie let out a cry as she watched the blade slice across Winn's chest and he kneeled down onto the sandy soil facing away from her. Back to back, both warriors paused, the sounds of their ragged breathing filling the dank humid air.

Kweshkwesh straightened upright in front of Maggie, his mouth contorted in a bizarre grin. He took a step toward her, then wavered, his gait unsteady, and raised a hand to his throat as his eyes widened. His words came forth garbled and wet, as were his hands, drenched in pulsing blood.

"*Elek?*" he choked.

He plummeted forward onto the ground with a sickening thud.

Winn turned toward her, rising up from his crouch, his chest smeared with crimson blood.

"Winn!" she cried.

He looked beyond her, his crystal blue eyes narrowed into slits, as if she neither stood there nor spoke to him, focused on something else to her left. She had no time to consider what he was looking at, too worried about the second warrior that now moved in to attack her husband.

"No!" she screamed.

Her skin prickled as she heard footsteps crush the forest debris near her flank, and before she could turn she felt a whoosh of air ripple her hair as something flew by from behind her ear. She choked on her own scream as the second man fell, taken down by a long-handled axe impaled in his sternum.

Winn reached her side, and she fell into his arms as they stared at the fallen warrior.

"Bloody Indians!"

They looked toward the brush as a man strode toward them. Of equal height to Winn and just as threatening in his demeanor, he parted a new path, stomping on the undergrowth and breaking through low growing branches as if they were twigs. Eyes of a berserker glared at them from a dense bearded face, the thick muscled arms flexed at the sides of a broad chest as his skin dappled with droplets of sweat.

He placed a foot on the body then closed his hands over the axe handle, jerking it away with one quick motion. Maggie could only watch, stunned as he sheathed the weapon on his back, and Winn pulled her to her feet.

"I can see nothing's changed. Ye still find trouble, no matter where you go, hmm, Maggie-mae?"

She flew into his arms.

"Marcus! How? Why? Oh!" she cried as he closed his arms around her. He lifted her off the ground, squeezing her so hard she laughed through the fresh burst of tears. She touched his face, covered with at least a few weeks worth of beard. "I didn't recognize you with this thing! You're here, you're really here!"

"Aye, lamb, s'all right now, don't cry," he said. "Ye were tricky to find, and worse to follow. Did ye know those men tracked you for miles?" he added, directing his question over her shoulder to her husband. She stepped away from Marcus and grabbed Winn's hand.

"Yes, I knew," Winn muttered.

"Winn, it's Marcus! I can't believe it, he's…he's…here." Winn was tense at her side, glaring at Marcus. Maggie felt as if she faded away at that moment, watching the two men locked in a silent battle as they stared each other down.

She squeezed Winn's hand. He nodded at Marcus.

"Time Walker," Winn said.

Marcus grunted some sort of acknowledgment.

"Winkeohkwet," Marcus replied.

Her eyes darted between the two men, her words jumbled as they poured forth amidst her rising confusion.

"Wait a second! You…you used a *Bloodstone*? Why? How? What are you doing here, Marcus?" she asked.

He shifted his stare to Maggie and sighed, running one hand through his thick black hair and then down to rub his beard. Maggie had never seen him with facial hair, the unkempt growth giving him a menacing demeanor despite her knowledge of his gentle nature. Standing before her with two wide leather straps crossing his chest and his muscles tensed in readiness to strike, she hardly recognized the man she had known her entire life.

"Aye, I have a lot to tell you, but most of it can wait for now. I've been to this place before, and God knows I never thought to see it again so soon. First off, I came for my son."

Winn's eyes narrowed.

"Benjamin returned to his time. That was more than two years ago," Winn answered.

"No, he's still here," Marcus insisted.

"But he went back. He used his Bloodstone, I saw him leave," Maggie replied.

Marcus shook his head. "He never made it. Last trail I could find of him was a record of his release from jail at Jamestown. Seems no witnesses survived the massacre, so there was no one to speak against him. Did he really murder two men, Maggie? Can ye tell me nothing else about it?"

She glanced back at Winn, who remained immobile. As much as revisiting the past pained them both, she could not stand in front of Marcus and withhold it from him. He deserved to know what happened to his son. By right of blood and sacrifice of his journey, she could give him nothing less. After all, Benjamin had once been her husband, and despite what he had done she still believed there was something redeemable in him.

"If he was held at Jamestown, then something went wrong with the Bloodstone. I last saw him at Martin's Hundred on the day of the Massacre…in the church," she placed her hand on his arm. "I have so much to tell you, too, Marcus, things I couldn't put in the letter. I think we should go home, and–and you'll come with us, won't you?"

He placed his hand over hers.

"I didn't hunt ye down through time for the hell of it, for sure. Of course I'll go with you. Can't leave ye alone with all these angry Indians about, can I?" he replied, raising a brow with a glance at Winn. Winn nodded in response but said nothing more.

"Marcus–"

"I'll get my horse."

Marcus went back the way he came, leaving her standing there with Winn. She watched Marcus go through the underbrush, afraid he would disappear like a wisp of a memory once he left her sight.

Winn led her pony close and gave her a leg up. He rested his hand on her thigh for a moment as she gathered her reins, and she looked down at him. The shallow wound on his chest was no more than a scratch, the bleeding crusted already across the flesh. Thankfully, it would need no stitches.

"What about–about them?" she asked, nodding toward the two fallen men. Bile burned in her throat as she glanced at the deceased and she turned away lest she vomit.

"Leave them. Let the scavengers feast."

She swallowed back against her dry mouth at his words, yet nodded in agreement all the same.

"And Marcus?"

"Let him return with us, if it pleases you, *ntehem*."

"I can't believe he's here. You're going to like him, you'll see," she promised. She could read the uncertainty etched into his face. It was a rare thing to see him rattled, yet she had a feeling it was not the last time the two men would rankle each other.

"Did you know he was a Time Walker?" he asked. She shook her head.

"My arrival here was an accident, I didn't know anything about how to use the Bloodstones. What difference does it make, anyway? I'm happy to see him no matter how he got here."

He gave her leg a gentle squeeze.

"He is right in one way, *ntehem*. Trouble follows you," he sighed. "It is good that I have two sharp eyes to watch you with. If I knew Blooded Ones would come for you, I would have dropped all the Bloodstones in the ocean so no other could use them."

"He won't be any trouble, I'm sure of it," she replied. Filled with the excitement of seeing Marcus, she had failed to consider how his arrival would affect her husband. As Winn stood looking up at her, she suddenly suspected what drove him to deny her happiness.

She twisted her fingers in her pony's mane and bent down, planting a firm kiss upon his tense mouth.

"I love you, warrior. My place is here with you, no matter what happens," she whispered. His hand slid up around the base of her neck and his fingers gripped her hair as he pressed his forehead to hers.

"I know," he replied.

Marcus rode into the clearing and they quickly separated. Winn nodded to the other man, then pointed the way toward home. Seeming pleased with the interlude, the horses set off at a brisk pace, and Maggie knew she would see her family soon. After seeing the way a simple trade visit to the Chosick village had turned out, she would be happy to see the day end.

They reached the settlement by nightfall, the glimmer of the sleepy sun fading as their temporary home came into view. A cottage marked the center of the settlement, made of rough hewn logs. It was flanked by the lean-to and peaked *yehakins* in a semi-circle around the water well. Winn issued a shrill greeting to announce them, and Maggie waved as his sister came into sight.

When Teyas entered the yard with the squirming toddler in her arms, Maggie urged her pony into a lope and left the men behind. It had only been one day, yet anytime away from her daughter left her uneasy. There were just too many things that could go wrong in the time they lived in.

Maggie's pony slid into a stop and she leapt off his back, covering the distance to her daughter in a few short strides. Winn's sister smiled as she handed the child over, her two black braids bouncing as she laughed.

"Take her, she's a pest!" Teyas teased, flicking her braids back over her shoulder. She squinted her brown eyes at Kwetii in mock disgust, and Maggie pecked the cheek of her sister-by-marriage as she pulled her daughter into her arms.

"Mama!" she child squealed, erupting into a fit of giggles when Maggie planted kisses over her face.

"A pest? Causing your Auntie trouble, hmm? Not my daughter!"

"Oh, no? She has not stopped howling since you left!" Teyas snorted. "Humph!"

"Is your Aunt a meany, Kwetii?" Maggie asked, holding the child up over her head. It seemed she recognized her name by the way she squealed, or it may have been the sight of her father walking toward her, yet whatever the reason Maggie was soon forgotten. The fickle child reached out to Winn and he swept her into his arms.

Marcus stood away a few paces away observing quietly with wide eyes, his arms crossed over his chest. Soon they would sit to talk, and all their questions would be answered. Even without Marcus admitting he had visited their time once before, she would have known it was so by the sheer level of comfort he displayed in his surroundings. Although he stood away from the family as they greeted each other, his behavior lent no lack of confidence. Apparently, he had arrived in her time well prepared and rapidly found a way to procure supplies like weapons and horses.

No, Marcus had not idly traveled to the past on a whim. He was apparently a powerful Blooded One, a full blown Time Walker, and furthermore, he had hid it from her during her entire life. As she watched him gazing patiently at her family, she dismissed the itch of betrayal she felt.

There must be some explanation. Once the baby was settled and there was food in their bellies, they would sit, and it would all be said.

"Marcus," she called, waving him over. "Come meet Kwetii."

"Pa-pa! Uppy, *uppy!*" Kwetii squealed. Maggie smiled as Winn tossed their daughter into the air and the child flailed, shrieking with laughter. The crop of dark waves on her head bounced against her caramel skin as she laughed, her chubby fingers gripping Winn's hands. So alike, yet so different, father and daughter were a pair that would not be separated. Maggie knew her daughter loved her, but when her father was present, everyone seemed to disappear. Maggie didn't mind so much. She was content to see the fierceness fade from her warrior as he looked down at their daughter with tenderness in his eyes.

"She's beautiful, Maggie," Marcus said softly.

"She is," Maggie agreed.

"Kwetii," Winn said, adjusting the toddler in his arms. "See this man? He is Marcus, friend to us."

Maggie did not miss the inflection in his tone with the words. She appreciated the effort he made to subdue his suspicion, yet she imagined he would have much more to say on the matter when they retired to their furs.

"Little one," Marcus said. "You look like yer mother, she was a pretty child as well," he murmured.

Maggie felt the trickle of unease flow stronger. He knew that *Kwetii* meant *little one* in Winn's language? She could see Winn picked up on it as well by the way his arms tensed around their daughter.

"Ooh, pretty, pretty!" Kwetii squealed, pointing at the sky with one chubby hand. Maggie raised her chin to see what her daughter fussed over.

Streaking across the night sky, leaving a crisscross of shimmering trails behind, bursts of light streamed overhead in a path toward the earth.

A meteor shower.

Winn handed Kwetii to her. Seeing the realization rise in his eyes, the way his jaw clamped shut and his skin flushed to the tips of his ears, she knew he remembered it too. She saw his hand shift to his side to rest on the butt of his knife as the words of an old prophecy rushed into her thoughts.

"A night when stars fall from the sky," the old woman said. *"That is when he will return."*

"Pale Feather?" she whispered, more to herself than the others.

Marcus frowned.

"It's been a long time since anyone called me that, but, aye. I was once called Pale Feather. This one comes from the Paspahegh, right?" Marcus said, nodding toward Winn. "I thought the English wiped them all out."

She thought Winn would explode. His voice finally surfaced as a growl through his clenched teeth.

"Not all of us, Time Walker. Go to the cabin, Maggie. Now."

Maggie could count the number of times she obeyed her husband without argument, and they were not numerous enough to take up the fingers of even one hand. Yet seeing Winn standing there with Marcus, the sky exploding overhead in a shower of falling meteors, she turned without hesitation and went into the house. Teyas followed close behind.

The men needed no further interruption. Winn and his father had much to talk about.

2

Maggie

There was a fire burning in the stone hearth, the scent of stew carried through the cottage by wisps of smoke. The small house was cozy yet afforded them enough space, serving their little family as the traditional community Long House would in the Paspahegh village. As an abandoned remnant from an English settler, it had not been difficult to procure the head rights to the property. Of the settlers who survived the Massacre of 1622, many had left their property and either moved close to Jamestown for protection or left the colony on the next ship back to England.

When Maggie and Winn expressed interest in the unoccupied piece of land, the Governor readily agreed. As long as Winn helped the English negotiate the return of prisoners, the English were content to allow their little family to live in peace. Winn thought it safest for them to live between two worlds, beholden entirely to neither the Indians nor the English. She agreed with him in that respect; although Opechancanough had given them the promise of safe passage, she was still a Time Walker, and there was still a price on her head.

"Did you cause so much trouble in your future life, sister?" Teyas asked.

Teyas handed her a sticky mug of steaming blackberry tea as Maggie sat down heavily on a bench. Kwetii climbed down from her lap and toddled off toward the hearth, where she plopped down to play with a discarded doll.

"He's Winn's father. Marcus, I mean. Marcus is Winn's father."

She spoke the words, yet still the meaning was impossible. Marcus, who had been kin to Maggie as long as she could remember, was the man who formed one cornerstone of the tiny family unit she grew up with–in the twenty-first century.

Maggie looked through the window at them. The image was blurred through the rough-hewn glass, but she could still see the two men standing together. Head to head, shoulder to shoulder, suddenly she could see the resemblance, and she wondered if she might have noticed it earlier had she not been so blind. She should have known her journey to the past was no isolated incident, that some greater power linked her and the people she loved to this time. Now she knew with a growing sense of unease that it was much more complicated than some simple episode of chance.

"So Finola spoke true. Pale Feather has returned," Teyas said. Maggie nodded. "Do you think they will harm each other?"

Maggie sighed. "I'm not sure. We'll have to stop them if they do. Where are Makedewa and Chetan?"

"They took Rebecca and Ahi Kekeleksu to the outpost for supplies. They should return soon."

"I hope so," she replied. Teyas joined her on the bench near the window to watch the men. Maggie could see them talking, or at least gesturing at each other, but she could not hear since they were too far off in the yard. She hoped Winn's brothers would arrive soon. They needed a distraction quickly, and the strength of the men would certainly come in handy.

"What of his brother?" Teyas asked.

"Hmm?" she murmured, intent on watching the men. "What of them? You said they'll be back soon, right?"

"No sister, I speak of his white brother. Benjamin. Is he truly here still, in our time?"

"Oh…Benjamin. His brother." It felt quite strange to make the connection aloud. "Marcus says he never returned to the future, that he found records of him in the past. I thought we'd be able to talk more about it, but I'm not sure we'll get the chance."

Teyas shrugged.

"It is no matter, we will all hear it soon. Get that bucket of water, sister. I think we have need of it."

Maggie flinched as the two men crashed together like a pair of titans, shoulder to shoulder, arms entwined. She grabbed the wooden pail and ran past Teyas into the yard.

3

Winn

Winn held his tongue until his wife and daughter entered the cabin. He surveyed his father silently during the interval. Yes, Marcus was everything Maggie had described him to be: an imposing Viking of a man with the face of a berserker, a man who could crush anyone who threatened him. Yet as Winn stood staring into the eyes that mirrored his own, he regarded him only as a coward. After all, the man had used his Bloodstone to abandon his pregnant wife, and with the way Marcus sniped about the Paspahegh, Winn wondered if the man had any regard for his mother at all.

"Pale Feather. I hear of you, yet you know nothing of me," Winn said once the cabin door closed.

His father's brows narrowed.

"I know enough," Marcus answered tersely. "And I know one lone Paspahegh is not enough to keep my kin safe. I won't let Maggie stay with you if this is how you protect her. Those men could have killed ye both today if I hadn't been there."

"You? You, of all, *you* question how I protect my wife? What of your wife? You left her like a coward, sneaking away with your Bloodstone!"

Winn saw a flicker in his eyes.

"*Chulensak Asuwak*? Ye don't know what you're talking about. I'm sure she's long gone with the rest of your people."

"My people? You speak of us like you were never Paspahegh!" Winn said, his voice rising with each syllable. How could his own sire behave in such a way? Or was Winn the biggest fool for expecting anything more?

"Paspahegh, Powhatan, they're all the same, and good riddance to the lot of them. Tell me what you think of them someday, when ye are hunted like a dog over a stupid old man's vision," Marcus replied, looking toward the house. "I'm here for one reason–to see my kin safe. If any of ye Indians get in my way, it will be the last thing ye ever do–no matter who ye are."

Marcus straightened up to his full height, which mirrored his own, and Winn tensed the muscles in his back as well.

"So why marry a Paspahegh, if you hate us so much?" Winn asked, unable to hold back the questions he held buried for so many years.

"What do ye know of that? Aye, it was arranged. It meant nothing other than keeping my head at the time, but she was a good woman, I am sorry to hear of her death."

Winn scowled at the causal manner in which his father dismissed his mother. He glanced back at the cabin. Maggie would be furious if he sent Marcus away. How could he ever explain it to her? Yet the urge to silence his father in a more permanent manner grew stronger with every moment in the man's presence.

"She lives. My mother lives," Winn said quietly. He expected a reaction from the man, but the result was nothing short of annoyance. Marcus scowled.

"Your mother, eh? So she finally got what she wanted. Pepamhu, was it? That Nansemond brave is your father? He was a good man. I have no quarrel with him."

The words barely left his lips before Winn lunged at his father.

They tumbled onto the ground, rolling in the dirt, neither willing to relent. Unbridled rage flowed from Winn like the surge of a dam held back, finally released by the harsh words from the man beneath him. Marcus would not be subdued easily, and Winn was taken aback by the fierceness with which he fought.

Relentless and calculated, every move meant to advance his dominance while sparing the bulk of his strength for his final assault. Marcus broke the hold Winn had on his neck and sent him sprawling with a sharp knee to his belly. Winn rolled to the side before his father's heel came crashing down in the dust where his head had just been, and as Marcus uttered a swear Winn grasped his heel and uprooted him with one swipe, knocking him flat on his back. They rolled and grabbed for each other at the same time.

The man fought like him. Or did Winn fight like his father?

"Stand down!" Marcus shouted as they each scrambled for control. Winn pinned him with one knee, one hand clutched around his throat. His chest heaved with the effort of catching a breath, his body unaccustomed to the effort it took to fight such a man.

"You coward! I'll kill you!" Winn yelled back.

"I'll take ye with me!"

As Winn closed his grip tighter on his father's neck he watched the man's face turn purple, with rage or lack of air he knew not. Marcus kept his blue eyes focused on Winn's as the breath left his lungs, and just as his lids began to droop, both men were doused in a stream of cold water.

They jumped apart, sputtering and gasping for air.

"No one is killing anyone today, *idiots*!" Maggie hollered.

Winn wiped his forearm over his drenched face and looked up at his wife. She held the bucket at her side, her green eyes blazing with irritation, her long auburn hair rippling behind her with the breeze. Her chapped cheeks were stained with remnants of dusty tears.

"Just stop it, okay?"

Winn shook his head, more to clear his thoughts than to refuse her.

"I'm sure Marcus will explain himself. And Marcus, you can hardly blame Winn for being angry–for Pete's sake, you're his father, and you just left with that stupid Bloodstone!"

Marcus recovered his bearings enough to stand up about the same time that Winn also rose from the ground. Winn watched his demeanor change from rank anger to something else, something confused and guarded.

"What are ye talking about?" Marcus asked, the words seeming caught in his throat.

"Winn, of course! Didn't he tell you? Well, then what on Earth are you two fighting about?" Maggie stammered.

Winn stared blankly at Marcus. He made a harsh grunting sound.

"There is nothing to talk about. This man dishonors my mother, he hates every Powhatan. I have no father."

"Winn, please –" Maggie pleaded.

Winn leveled his gaze on Marcus. "Speak your words to my wife. When I return I will show you the way back to town."

He did not look at any of them again as he walked away. He feared what he might do or say if he remained any longer. It would serve no purpose to frighten his wife with more fighting. Yet if he stayed in the presence of his father any longer, he knew they would come to blows again.

She would understand, he thought as he walked off toward the woods. Or at least she would have to put her objections aside until he returned.

4

Maggie

She did not move to stop him as he walked away. Maggie watched her husband take the trail toward the stream, and when she lost sight of his back through the trees in the moonlight, she turned to Marcus.

"Maggie–"

"He's your son. How could you leave him? And you lied to me–my entire life, you lied to me!" she accused.

"I dinna know about him, I swear it."

"Don't. Please don't tell me any more lies," she said softly.

He swiped at the dust on his face with one dirty hand and shrugged his shoulders, which loosened the leather straps crossing his chest. She looked at the long-handled axe lying on the ground apparently flung off during the fight, and wondered if her oldest friend might have used it on her husband if she had not intervened.

Marcus followed her gaze, and she heard him sigh.

"I never meant to keep it from ye so long. Yer grandda and I decided it was not time to tell ye yet, and then he got sick..." he said. She flinched and pulled back when he reached his hand toward her, the crushed look on his face smashing her resolve into shambles. He dropped his hands and then crossed them over his chest in an awkward motion, as if he knew not what to do with them.

"Go on," she said stiffly.

"Yer grandda and I–well, we lived here for a time. There were many of us then, the Indians called us Time Walkers. No name of our own doing, ye see, only what they knew us by." She saw his jaw tighten and his arms clench slightly as if the words pained him. "Opechancanough turned on us, and many were killed. Me and yer grandda, we were lucky to get away."

She thought the ground started to sway, but it was only the sensation of her blood draining to her feet. He stepped forward and firmly took hold of her upper arm, despite her trying to wave him off.

"My Granddad? You were both Time Walkers! You lied about that, too?" she whispered.

"Nay, we dinna lie. We planned to tell ye… you must understand, the Bloodstone magic is dangerous, it can kill ye as fast as it takes ye to another time. We could tell you nothing, less risk all our necks. Until ye were old enough, at least, to know where ye came from. It was my duty to protect my clan. I failed many, but I saved some by taking them to the future."

"I don't believe you. Why should I believe you now?" She wrenched her arm away and turned her back to him, unwilling to see the pain her words caused him. Never could she imagine she would be standing before him, this man she loved, spitting barbs at him as if there were no feeling left in her heart.

"Believe me or not, lamb, that's yer right. Ye know I came through time to fetch my son, ye see me standing here before ye. Have I ever failed you? Have I ever let anyone bring harm to ye? I know I deserve your anger now, but give me some credit. I'm still the man who raised ye."

She had no answer for that statement, trying her best to control the swell of tears that threatened to burst.

"My parents. They were Time Walkers, too?" she choked.

Maggie felt his presence beside her. She closed her eyes as he put his hands on her shoulders. He nodded.

"They are gone, like many of the others."

"What happened to Benjamin's mother then? Did she really leave you? Tell me all of it," she demanded.

"Young Helgrid. We were betrothed as children. She made it through to your time with us."

"Is she dead too?"

"She's gone. She left when Benjamin was a lad, I don't know where she ended up. She couldn't handle the future, not like the rest of us. But Benjamin–"

"Your son is a good man. Both sons. Both are good men," she murmured. She felt his fingers tighten on her arms.

"Will ye tell me of him? Of them?" he asked. "I didn't know about him–about Winn. His mother said nothing, you must believe that."

She sighed.

"Put away your weapons, and go up to the house. Teyas will let you in. I need to find Winn, he deserves to hear this."

"I'll go for the boy," Marcus quickly offered.

Maggie shook her head.

"No, I'll do it. He grabbed his bow before he left, I have no doubt he'd shoot your ass," she muttered. "And Marcus?" she added.

"Yes?"

"Don't call him 'boy.' I don't think he'd take that very well, coming from you."

She pointed to the cabin to shoo him away, and left to find her husband.

He was not difficult to locate. She found him sitting on a flat rock that jutted out over the edge of the shallow stream, a secluded spot they used for bathing. She felt his muscles tense and then relax when she put her arms around his shoulders and sat down behind him.

"Will you come home soon?" she asked. Her hands crossed over his chest, and he placed his hand on hers. When she pressed a gentle kiss to his neck, she could taste the bitterness of honeysuckle soap and salty sweat, the scent of the earth fresh upon his skin.

"Yes, I will," he said quietly.

"He says he didn't know about you."

"He speaks lies."

Winn caressed her hand with his thumb and then raised her hands to his lips to kiss her palms, one by one, hesitating for a moment over the faded silver scar knotted on her skin.

"Come home now, husband," she said softly, her voice lowering an octave.

"I would cause you pain, *ntehem*, when I send him away."

"Don't make him leave. At least talk to him first," she urged.

She felt his muscles stiffen beneath her fingers, his chest tensed as he passed slow shallow breaths.

"Please. I'm only asking you to talk to him. If you still want him to leave then, it's up to you."

He stood then and pulled her to her feet beside him.

"Come on. I will hear his words, and then send him away."

Maggie kept her relief hidden as they walked back to the yard. Her husband had already killed one man that day, and Marcus another. Perhaps they could yet avoid more bloodshed.

***

The threesome was sitting around the table when Maggie and Winn arrived, sharing the new batch of blackberry tea and passing around a basket of fresh bread. Kwetii sat happily on Marcus's lap, gumming a piece of crust, while Teyas tried to persuade the child to take a drink. Maggie was pleased to see Teyas had scrounged up a white trade shirt for Marcus, and he looked as if he had cleaned up a bit.

Kwetii squealed and held up her arms at the sight of her father. Maggie held her breath as Winn went to her. She could see it in his eyes as he glared at Marcus, the shadow of a strong little boy who grew up fighting for every scrap of respect he garnered. Sometimes loved, sometimes an outcast because of his heritage, Winn had lived as many lives as his Time Walker father, learning to adapt and survive no matter where his uncle sent him. Now as she watched her husband with his father, she wondered if there was any sliver of hope left for peace between them.

"Here, lamb, go to your da," Marcus said, urging the child to Winn. Kwetii climbed into her father's arms and smothered him with sloppy kisses.

"Hungry?" Teyas asked, breaking the silence. Maggie took a seat next to her.

"Starving," she murmured. Marcus and Winn did not acknowledge each other, but Winn sat down across from her and she was grateful he relented enough to join them. Kwetii babbled happily and picked at her father's food, trying to help him eat.

"Do you want me to take her?" she asked. Winn shook his head, barely raising his eyes in acknowledgement.

The silence was blessedly broken by the door swinging open. Winn's brothers returned fresh from a trip to the outpost, bags full of supplies slung over their shoulders. Rebecca and Ahi Kekeleksu followed close behind. Chetan halted at the sight of Marcus and put his hand on his young son's shoulder, stopping Ahi Kekeleksu from going near Marcus. The boy stared wordlessly at them, his eyes wide under his thick dark lashes as he waited for his father's command.

"*Chama Wingapo*," Chetan said slowly in welcome with a glance to Winn. Chetan stood motionless in survey of the stranger, his arms tensed at the sides of his thick-barreled chest. Maggie noticed the quick exchange between the brothers; a slightly raised brow, a twist in the corner of a lip, and an imperceptible nod. It took only a split second for Winn to convey his approval to his brothers. Chetan let go of Ahi Kekeleksu.

"*Wanishi*, friend," Marcus replied.

Maggie listened as the men exchanged cordial greetings in Paspahegh. She was by no means fluent in the language, but she had a conversational knowledge and understood a few of the words. She expected a show of surprise from Chetan when Marcus communicated as such, yet Chetan remained impassive. Always the calm one, Chetan regarded most situations in a peaceful manner, yet like his brothers, he was no man to tangle with. She had only seen him so provoked one time, and that had been immediately prior to the massacre when he helped save her from the English.

"What are they saying?" she whispered to Teyas. Teyas rolled her eyes.

"They act like wolves. They piss on their territory."

"Oh, Christ," Maggie replied. The men continued to speak rapidly amongst themselves. She noticed Ahi Kekeleksu standing aside, focused on the exchange as he tore off pieces of his ration of bread and stuffed them into his mouth.

Makedewa listened to the banter as well, adopting his usual disposition when matters annoyed him. The younger brother of the three, he was easily angered, full of rash temper and quick displays of aggression when provoked. He had become a bit less intimidating in the time she had known him, but Maggie still steered clear of him when he had a sour look on his face. Apparently he did not care for the tone of the discussion, his mouth clamped shut in a thin line and his arms folded over his wiry chest as he observed.

Winn said something loudly, causing the others to fall silent for a moment. She could see the way Marcus clenched his jaw through narrowed lips. He looked her way, his eyes meeting hers before he spoke.

"I told yer wife as I tell ye now, take my word or no. I knew naught of ye until this day. If I could change it I would, but I cannot, and I am sorry for it."

She bunched the edge of her cotton shift in her hand, waiting for Winn's response.

"Keep your words. You came for Benjamin. You may stay until you find him and no longer," Winn said. He would not look her way as he spoke, his gaze fixed instead on Marcus.

"I need yer help. That's why I tracked ye down. That, and to see Maggie safe." Marcus sighed. "I don't know how much Maggie has told ye of the future. They keep records then, more than you can imagine. After I found Maggie's letter, I found quite a lot of information on Benjamin...and on you and Maggie. You'd be surprised what people keep records of."

"About Winn and I? What records?" she interrupted. Marcus squinted and looked down at his drink, avoiding her gaze.

"Ah, land records, for one. That's how I knew where to find you. This head right of yours is unique. How did ye manage to convince the English to give ye a head right property, being a Paspahegh…and you, Maggie, now you're the same, according to the English, anyway."

"I serve as counsel to the English for my uncle. The English trust me for now," Winn answered.

"Do they trust ye enough to give ye information on Benjamin?" Marcus asked.

Winn nodded. "I know men who will talk. I will leave for Jamestown when the sun rises, if he was there, the English will tell me." Winn finally met her gaze before he spoke further. "You can ride there with me if you wish."

She saw Marcus relax his shoulders.

"Yes, I will. Thank ye," Marcus replied.

"Makedewa," Winn said, "you can tell me about this foolish coat you wear. Join me outside, brother, I need more hands to see to the horses."

Winn effectively ended the conversation, putting Kwetii on the ground. The toddler scurried to Rebecca and held up her hands, and the girl immediately picked her up.

Maggie watched Winn leave with his brother. Makedewa wore a scarlet coat studded with brass buttons, obviously obtained from one of the English soldiers.

"Do I want to know how he got that coat, Chetan?" she asked, expecting a straight answer from the more reliable of the two. Chetan grinned, a gesture that did not convey any reassurance to her.

"No Englishman died, Fire Heart. Makedewa is good at dice, especially when the soldiers drink rum. Mind your business, sister," he chuckled, using a phrase from her own repertoire. She jabbed him with her elbow and joined his laughter.

"Yeah, mind my business. Sure," she replied.

If only she could take such advice.

5

Maggie

Her laughter tapered off when Chetan followed his brothers outside. She would need to figure out a place for Marcus to sleep, preferably outside, but she was not sure where the best place would be. Of the two *yehakins,* she shared one with Winn, and his brothers shared the other with Chetan's son, Ahi Kekeleksu. Teyas and Rebecca slept in the cottage loft, leaving the small room in the rear of the cottage available, but she was reluctant to subject Rebecca to a stranger in the cottage. Although she was still angry at Marcus, it made little sense to see him sleep in the barn when there was a perfectly good cot available inside.

"I'll tend to my horse with the others," Marcus said.

"I'm sure the brothers will take care of it, it's no problem," Maggie replied. "Leave them be for now. Don't you think we should all just cool off? There's been a lot to take in today."

Marcus nodded.

"Yeah, I suppose you're right," he said quietly. "There sure has."

She heard the pause in his words as he looked out the window at the brothers. Suddenly she felt like a complete fool. Yes, Marcus had kept things from her, important things, but she was not so dense that she didn't understand why. As she watched her daughter playing, she could see exactly why Marcus and her grandfather kept the truth from her. She would do the same to protect her child from such dangerous magic.

She remembered the day when Benjamin disappeared as a boy and the pain it caused Marcus to lose his young son. Marcus had changed that day, from a man who laughed easily to one who rarely smiled. Though still loyal to fault and protective of his family, the loss of his child had changed him. Now as he stared out the window at the son he didn't know he had, she could see in him a fragment of the desolate bereaved parent he once was. Though he had traveled to the past to find one son, he now had two to consider, and she could hardly imagine how the man must be feeling.

"We shall take Kwetii to yer *yehakin*, if it pleases ye, Maggie," Rebecca said, breaking the silence. Kwetii grabbed the cap off Rebecca's head when the young woman lifted her up, causing her springy blond curls to fall loose.

"Thank you," Maggie replied. "I brought a bundle of garments back from trade with the Chosicks. You can take a look if you like."

Rebecca preferred the English manner of dress and continued to wear a heavy layered skirt over her shift with a jacket bodice fitted snugly over it, despite the constrictions it caused in the warm summer months. Maggie made the offer knowing Rebecca would likely refuse, but she was determined to keep trying to help her be more comfortable.

"Nay, I like my own just fine. G'night to ye."

Maggie gave Kwetii a kiss before she went off to bed. Rebecca adjusted the child on her hip and followed Teyas out the door, sneaking a glance at Marcus as she passed.

"Night," Maggie answered. "I'll be there soon, sweetheart."

When the door closed behind the women, she sat down heavily on the bench next to Marcus. She propped her elbows on the table and rested her head in her hands for a moment, the events of the day sinking in as she let out a sigh.

"Don't ye pass out. Yer husband will blame me for that as well," Marcus said.

"Yes, he would. He's a good man. He would give his life to protect his family, if it was necessary," she answered softly. "He's had a hard time of it, Marcus. He was shuttled around by his uncle to live wherever it suited him best–he lived with the Nansemond, the Paspahegh, and..." her words trailed off as she looked into his eyes. "With the English. He lived with Benjamin's family for two summers. They were like brothers."

"Like brothers," Marcus said, the corner of his lip dipping downward. "Aye, it must have been hard on the lad."

He ran his hands through his thick dark hair, the color of his skin flushed from neck to ears. He rose and thrust the wooden bench back with one quick shove, nearly causing her seat to topple as he arched his back and stared upward, as if begging the heavens for guidance.

"I never meant to cause this trouble. I thought to see you safe, find my son, and have words with yer husband…now this. My son? Benjamin is likely dead, and yer husband willna forgive me."

She shook her head.

"You're wrong on both counts. Benjamin is too damn stubborn to be dead. And Winn? Winn will come around. He just needs time. After a good night's rest, I think we'll all see things more clearly, right?"

She stuck her hand in the stitched pocket of her shift, which was belted over her short doeskin skirt. It took a moment to find it, but when she pulled out the raven figure his response was quick. His eyes softened and rimmed with moisture at the sight of it. He reached out for it, palm up, but then pulled his hand back.

"You had that all this time?" he choked.

"Yes. I think it sent me here. There's a reason for everything, Marcus, I'm more convinced of that than ever now."

He crossed his arms over chest, the thin white fabric of the trade shirt stretched to near tearing over his shoulders.

"When did ye turn into such an optimist? I hardly recognize ye!"

It felt good to smile, and hearing him joke opened the doorway to the playful banter they once shared.

"Optimist? That's about the only thing I haven't been accused of in this time," she laughed. She reached for his hand and squeezed it. "We have a lot to catch up on."

***

She waited as long as she could for Winn to retire to their *yehakin*, but as the night wore on the excitement of the day grew heavy and she succumbed to the fatigue to lie down without him. Should she search for him, or let him come home on his own? Perhaps the company of his brothers was what he needed, instead of his wife, who would ask him to forget the past and welcome his long-lost father.

What else could she do? Winn, the one who knew her best of all. He knew how much she loved Marcus, how the man had been family to her. Would he hold onto his anger, and follow through with the promise he made her long ago– the vow to kill his father should he ever meet him?

As much as she knew her husband, she admittedly knew little of the warrior he had been before they met. She could only guess upon it from the manner in which others regarded him. Even when his brothers voiced dissent, they still deferred to Winn's decisions on every matter despite the fact they no longer lived with the Paspahegh tribe and Winn was War Chief no more. Yet as she lay beside him at night and traced the winding tattoo upon his flat belly, she could recall the meaning of each mark as he conveyed it to her.

"This one, here," he said, "Is for the first man I killed. This part, here, is for the day I became a man. And this, this one shows I am different, that I am not true Paspahegh, that I carry the blood of the whites in my veins."

No, there were some things about him she might never truly understand. Nor did she need to. There was no reason for her to know how many he had killed, or when, or why. She did not ask it of him after the massacre, and she would not ask it now. It was his past, a part of him he could share if he chose, or hold onto if not.

Her eyes had just closed when he slipped into the *yehakin*. With his usual stealth he slid between the furs behind her, placing his arms around her to pull her against his chest. The heat of the day had skittered away and she snuggled into the warmth of his skin against her back. She smiled as his lips ran over her ear and he placed a soft kiss against her neck.

"Winn?" she said softly.

"Hmm?" he murmured.

Even as he rested his hand on her hip and pressed his lips into her hair, she could sense the pull of his unease. The gentle rise and fall of his chest against her cheek was soothing as she snuggled closer, aching to calm him as he did for her.

"You're going to town tomorrow?" she asked quietly.

His arms tightened around her.

"Yes," he said. "If Benjamin still lives, I will find what happened to him. Do not worry, I will return before the sun sleeps."

He rubbed her back absently, his blue eyes shadowed as he looked up at the moonlight through the smoke hole.

"I don't like you going into town. I'm afraid they'll turn on you. Look at how they burned the crops–they even attack the peaceful tribes. There's no sense to it."

"They have few men they trust to negotiate, and the new English soldiers have orders to keep peace. There will be no trouble for me, wife." He was right. The English crown had taken over control of the colony in the last few months after revoking the charter of the Virginia Company, and so far, the English had sought to calm relations between the settlers and the Indians. She hoped it would be enough to save her small crop of corn this season, as it had been burned by English scabs in the fall.

"You'll take your brothers, too, then?" she asked. "Makedewa and Chetan, I mean."

"If you would have it so, then yes," he replied.

She waited for him to acknowledge the unanswered question, giving him the chance to speak on it. After a few minutes his breathing slowed, and she knew if she did not broach the subject, it might never be said.

"Winn?" she whispered.

"Hmm?"

"What about your...brother?"

She traced the line of his tattoo from the point of his hip to the indent of his navel, the black ink design raised slightly from his skin. She felt him shudder and he grabbed her hand, bringing it to his lips for a kiss.

"Chetan had a wife, years ago, when we were young warriors. She was called *Sapalente*."

She opened her mouth to speak but thought better of it.

"English men visited the village to trade with us. We had little to share with them that year, enough for our people, but not enough for the English as well. They were angry, they thought our women hid the corn. So they took our women to the Long House, and bound them hand and foot. They put the women inside and set the Great *Yehakin* on fire."

His muscles grew tight beneath her hand. She could see the throbbing of the pulse in his neck, standing out like a cord. The flat Bloodstone pendant lay on his chest, betraying the quickening of his breath as he spoke.

"Many men were away hunting, as was Chetan. Makedewa and I stayed behind to meet with the Council. Men of the Council were old men, no warriors, and they were rounded up by the English as well. I killed the man who touched Sapalente first. And then Makedewa and I killed the others."

She swallowed hard.

"And the women? Sapalente? Did she live?" she asked.

"Yes. No women died that day."

"But what happened to her?"

"She birthed Ahi Kekeleksu and then died of the spotted fever. The English killed her after all." He frowned and looked down at her. "I tell you this to show you what a brother is. I would give my life for my brothers, as they would give for you. They need not ask it of me, they have it by honor of our bond. There was a time when Benjamin was brother to me, you know this," he said, his voice rising. Kwetii stirred and hiccupped across the *yehakin*.

"I understand, Winn, I do," she said, placing her hand on his cheek. She felt him tremble, the anger palatable under her fingertips.

"No, you do not. Chetan did not ask me to save his woman, he did not need to speak any words to show me the way. The day Benjamin took you from me, when I lay wounded with him at my side, I thought soon I might take my last breath. I asked it of Benjamin, to protect you, since I could not. Do you know what it means, to ask such a thing of a man?"

"Winn–"

"My English brother, the man I called friend? He stole you from me and left me for dead. He kept you with him by his lies. He sent you to hang as a witch–with my daughter in your belly! Do not ask it of me, wife. Do not ask me to call him brother. He is nothing to me but another Englishman."

"I won't ask it," she whispered. She bowed her head to his shoulder, tearing away from his searing blue eyes, unable to take in the intensity of his gaze. In the end, Benjamin had saved her, but that fact meant nothing to her husband. She could not fault him for his resolve, yet even as she held him and felt his tremors ease, she knew it was a matter long from settled.

"Stay out of the fields while I am gone tomorrow. Keep near the *yehakins* until we return," he mumbled, effectively ending the discussion with a demand. Although she did not voice her submission, she nodded in agreement.

He pulled her snugly against his chest and kissed her forehead. She felt his breathing grow shallow in the silence, and his heartbeat slowed beneath the touch of her ear pressed against his skin.

6

Winn

Chetan led the way, always the guide on any excursion they made. He was the best tracker of the three brothers, and Winn valued his skill above any other. Makedewa hung back in his usual position flanking the group from behind, keeping a careful watch for any danger that followed. Winn slowed his mount to ride with his younger brother, unwilling to ride alongside Marcus.

Pale Feather, the coward. Whoever the man was, he could ride alone.

"What do you think of the tempers in town?" Winn asked Makedewa. The other warrior shrugged and uttered a non-committal grunt.

"No different than usual. They speak with one face to you, another face to their King. For now we should have no trouble."

"I see you leave your pretty red coat behind. No need of it today?" Winn grinned, chiding him. Winn knew full well why Makedewa stopped wearing the English solider coat, and it had nothing to do with fearing the townsfolk. Makedewa won the coat fairly in a dice game, along with a small flask of gunpowder and a jug of sack. The three brothers had enjoyed the wine while tending to the horses the night before, and as they finished it Makedewa confessed he only wore it to impress Rebecca. Unfortunately, his attempt had backfired. The young Englishwoman thought it obscene and told the warrior as much.

"Ah, that coat reeks of *Tassantassas*. I will not wear it again," Makedewa grumbled.

"You worry too much of what that girl thinks. Wear it if you please."

Makedewa laughed aloud at Winn's words.

"Oh, yes, brother. I think too much of a woman? Maybe you do not see the sun through the clouds. If Maggie smiles, you smile. If she cries, you sulk. And help us, Creator, when she rages, for then you act a fool!" he laughed.

Winn shook his head in mock disgust, yet laughed with him.

"You will see, little brother."

"No, I will not," Makedewa said, as his laughter eased and his lips tightened. "She will never smile at me as Maggie smiles at you."

Winn cocked his head to the side as his pony plodded on. He looked up ahead to ensure the others did not listen, and once satisfied they paid no heed, he spoke quietly to his younger brother. He saw the change in Makedewa at his confession. Tall, lean, every ounce a powerful warrior, his brother had shown an unusual glimpse of kindness to the girl. It had been Makedewa who saved her during the Great Assault, slaying another warrior who meant to take her as captive. Since that fateful day more than two years past, Rebecca had remained living with them with no desire to return to the colony and Makedewa had mooned over her like a love struck buffoon. Whatever damage had been done to her, however, appeared lasting, and the young woman seemed to care for nothing more than friendship.

"Find a gift for her while we visit town today. Something to make her smile," he advised.

Makedewa shook his head.

"No. We have no time for such things."

"Says who? I say we do," Winn answered. He was willing to spare a few minutes in trade if it would make Makedewa happy. It would serve for the betterment of everyone to see some tension diminished between his brother and Rebecca, and if a simple trinket would make that happen, it was well worth the time lost.

"We shall find word of Benjamin and nothing more."

"Ah, *kemata tepahta!*" Winn cursed, rolling his eyes skyward with a snort. Makedewa continued to stare straight ahead, ignoring his outburst.

"He does not look so fierce," Makedewa commented, effectively changing the subject. Winn looked ahead to where Makedewa pointed.

Marcus rode beside Chetan, the two men seeming to speak in an easy rhythm as their ponies paced along. Winn wondered what they found in common to talk about, but then quickly purged the thought away. Why should he care for what the coward might speak of?

"Who says he is fierce?" Winn asked.

"Your wife said he killed Kweshkwesh with one blow of his axe," Makedewa replied, raising his brows.

"I killed Kweshkwesh. Marcus killed his son. And it is called a *bryntroll*, it is different from the weapon we have. So he says." Winn nodded to the small hand axe hanging from Makedewa's belt. "One large blade on a long handle, with symbols carved into the iron. I know not what meaning."

"It means Pale Feather is a fierce warrior," Makedewa muttered.

Maybe it means he is a coward and liar, Winn thought, although he kept it to himself. He would not let his brother bait him into an argument, which Makedewa seemed to enjoy doing.

"Is that what Norse-men look like?"

Winn shrugged the question off, his eyes now focused on his father's back. The stout *bryntroll* sat secured in the flat straps crossing his wide shoulders, over the white linen trade-shirt the women had given him. A heavy sword lay sheathed at his side, another weapon inlaid with intricate designs. Other than the shade of the tousled dark hair tied back with rawhide on his neck, Winn could see no resemblance between them. Perhaps they had similar height, and the breadth of their shoulders matched somewhat, but nothing more.

"He looks like only a man to me," Winn said.

"Are the weapons from his future time? Did you ask Fire Heart?"

"No."

"I will ask him."

"Go then. Ask if you must," Winn muttered.

Makedewa tapped his heels and urged the pony forward to meet the others. Chetan glanced back at Winn as Makedewa caught up, and Winn raised his chin a notch at the inquisition. They would reach town soon enough and all the foolishness would end.

The sooner they found the information Marcus needed, the sooner the man would be out of their lives. As Winn watched Marcus speak with his brothers, he thought perhaps Makedewa was right.

They had no time for such things.

***

Winn dropped down off his horse into the mud. Even with the dry summer air, the ground in James City remained sodden in places, especially in the heavily traveled areas like the town common. A straight sandy road cut the central market square in two, the narrow pathway through town littered with shallow ruts. A horse could be easily crippled if one did not pay close mind to the debris.

He grimaced at the stench as he tied his pony to a hitching post. It had been a month since he last visited the town, and he could see little had changed. The English still lived like pigs, growing their precious tobacco amidst hills of filth within their city palisades. He stepped out of the mud and went to join his companions.

In the two years since the Great Assault, the undressed log dwellings had been replaced by frame houses within the fort limits. The population had grown dense, with those who lived on the outskirts of the James City community drawing closer to town or moving within the palisades for protection. There was no doubt so many living in such close quarters contributed to the stench.

"Ye have a plan? Who to talk to?" Marcus asked. Winn glanced at his father while adjusting the knife at his waist. He wanted to take his musket as well, but thought better of it and left it behind, aware that the English soldiers always found a reason to confiscate such items from the Indians. Unlike some warriors, Winn would use whatever means necessary to fight the English, and if that meant using their weapons against them, then so be it.

"I know a man who will talk," Winn replied.

He noticed the way people stared when they entered town, and he was sure Marcus observed it as well. A group of men gathered in the square glared openly at them, growing silent as they left their horses and set off further into town. At the end of the row, standing like a statue against the clear morning sky was the church. Recently rebuilt with wide double wooden doors, it housed the English who huddled there seeking comfort in their singular God. As Winn and the others walked down the street, women clutched their hats and the crowds parted.

Winn could see Marcus tense. He shook his head when Marcus placed his hand on the butt of his sword.

"They mean no trouble, Pale Feather," Winn said.

His brothers looked up at his words. Marcus dropped his hand.

"Let's get where we're going, then," Marcus muttered.

It was a short walk to the gunsmith shop. A small dwelling made of coarse cut logs, it was one of the original structures to the settlement. Thick smoke rushed out through a shaft on the thatch roof, and the air inside was uncomfortably close.

Makedewa and Chetan kept watch at the door as Winn entered the building. He did not need to ask his brothers to keep track of the dispersing Englishmen as they conducted their business.

John Jackson looked up from his seat at his table and immediately rose to greet them, his eyes wide and hopeful. He was a slight man, standing a head shorter than even Chetan, uncharacteristically refined compared to most of the other Englishmen. His lithe stature was most likely a gift from his French mother; his long, thin face unfortunately came from his father.

"Winn! *Vous batard sournois! Que faites-vous ici!*"

Winn grinned at the oath riddled welcome. He had known John Jackson long enough to expect nothing less than to be called foul names in lieu of a proper greeting.

"*Oui, j'ai raté votre visage laid,*" he replied as they grasped forearms. Winn was unpracticed, but his French was still passable.

"Miss my ugly face, eh? Then fog off, ye bloody whoreson," John laughed. The gunsmith raised his chin in acknowledgement of Marcus, who stood behind Winn inside the cottage. "Who's ye friend? And why do ye darken my door today?"

Winn watched as John wiped his hands on his leather apron.

"Kin of my wife," Winn said quickly. He felt uneasy with the explanation, yet he could not describe Marcus in any other way. "I come to ask your help, friend. We look for Benjamin Dixon."

John stopped his ministrations abruptly. One eye squinted shut, the other focused on Marcus, he straightened up.

"Ye dinna bring yer wife here, did ye? Ye *puntain de batard–*"

"No, *salaud*!" Winn barked, his patience at an end with the jibes. The older Frenchman had a foul mouth and a loose tongue. "You know that would be foolish. We want no trouble."

"Ah, the townsfolk. They dinna forget the whole bloody mess, with her being accused of witchery and the like. There be no witness left to try her, but ye know folks remember."

"I know this. I ask for what you know of Dixon, nothing more."

The older man pursed his lips and turned his back on them. He opened a tall wooden cupboard stacked against the wall and fumbled with a drawer inside. After rifling through the contents for a moment, he produced a tiny satchel one might fit snugly into the palm of a large man.

"Governor Wyatt released him, oh, 'bout a months hence. On account there was no man for witness against him, like yer red-headed squaw."

Winn leaned over the table, his fingers gripping into the soft wood as he clenched his fists. He was nearing the end of his tolerance with the man's gibes. Acquaintance or friend, whatever the Frenchman was, he would be speaking through broken teeth if he kept up his banter.

"Why did they keep him so long, if they meant to release him?" Marcus interrupted. "Do ye know where he went, or where he might be now?"

"What meaning have ye? He only showed up a month hence, as I told ye. Right turned himself in, that one did, so folks thought him gone barmy. The minister at Martin's Hundred found him sleeping on the floor inside the church, daft as a loon. They took him here to stand trial, and that's when ye Governor set him loose."

Winn saw Marcus flex his grip over the handle of his sword. Winn gave him a quick shake of the head, relieved when Marcus lowered his hand.

"This helps us. Thank you," Winn said to the gunsmith. He noticed a movement beyond John by the entrance to the side room. It was a young boy of about six or seven, with a mop of blond hair and huge round eyes staring at them, peeking curiously around the corner.

"Who is the boy?" Winn asked.

"Don't ye know Old Morgan's boy? He has no kin, none to see him fed, in any case. He's a good lad. Pay him no heed." The child ducked away at the sound of his name.

John sat down across from Winn, his eyes shifting back and forth between the men. He dropped the tiny satchel on the table between them.

"Ye know what it's like to have yer kin stolen from ye. I want mine back, the same as ye. I'll tell ye where Dixon went, if ye send my sister back with the next batch." John pushed the bag toward Winn. "Ye still have that flintlock musket, I suppose? That's my best powder, ye know they can hang me fer giving it to ye. Take it, and whatever else ye want. Just give me yer word ye'll bring my sister home."

Winn bit back a retort as he looked into the man's pleading eyes. Yes, John was a sneaky fellow, but he had done no wrong to Winn and had helped him when he asked. Of course there was usually a price attached to his help, and Winn could not fault him for taking advantage in such circumstances. In this case, however, Winn would not be able to help him, and he was reluctant to disclose what he knew of John's sister.

"John, your sister is treated fairly in Pamukey. She has come to no harm, I can tell you that," Winn answered. He would not mention that John's sister was the wife of a Pamukey warrior, nor that in the two years since the Great Assault she had given birth to a son. It was assuredly more information than the Frenchman could tolerate.

"Then bring her back next. You've exchanged three women so far, why not my sister? If it's guns, or food, tell me what ye ask, and I will give it," John pleaded. Winn saw the rims of his eyes glisten as the man swiped the back of one hand over his face.

"It is not for me to choose. Governor Wyatt decides who we bargain for. You must speak to him for this. I am sorry," Winn said quietly.

John reached over and put the satchel in Winn's hand.

"Take it anyway. Just give me yer word she is safe, I see it as even exchange."

"I give you my word. And what of Dixon, what do you know of him?"

"He went looking for your kin, that Nansemond, Pepamhu. Said something about searching fer the woman Finola. I think he sought the Indian as a tracker. Lord knows, Dixon could ne'er track to save his skin."

Winn stood up. He dropped the gunpowder onto the table. As much as he needed it, he would not take it. He thanked the gunsmith for his trouble and left the cottage, Marcus trailing behind.

***

Marcus was quiet on the return home. Winn knew they did not find the answers he wanted, but he had enough to start the search so he considered it a day well spent. The sooner he could help Marcus find Benjamin, the sooner he would be out of their lives.

From the story John Jackson told, it seemed Benjamin was found lying senseless in the church at Martin's Hundred. It was the same place Maggie and Finola had given him the Bloodstone and sent him back to his future time on the day of the Great Assault, the day the English referred to as a massacre.

Winn knew little of how the stones worked, only that the magic was dangerous, so he was not shocked to hear that something had gone wrong with his brother's travel. Although his grandmother had tried to speak to him about the magic in his blood many times over the years, Winn had refused to hear her tales, denying any part of his white blood. He wondered exactly what part Finola played in all that had happened. She must have realized who Benjamin at some point, or perhaps she knew all along. Just looking at Marcus was like seeing an image of Benjamin, and Winn was certain his grandmother could not have mistaken it. Whatever secrets she held, she would account for them when he found her.

"The Pale Witch said you would return. She said on a night the stars fell from the sky, her son would come back to this time," Winn said. He did not turn his head toward his father as they rode.

"She was a *Seer*. Our people feared her magic," Marcus replied.

Winn nodded in agreement. "My uncle would not kill her, as he did the other Time Walkers. He feared her as well."

"She still lives? Do ye think Benjamin went searching for her?" Marcus asked.

"Yes. John Jackson said he searches for her. It makes sense that Benjamin would do so. He knows now he is a Time Walker, even if he is not very good at it," Winn said, a grin tugging at his lips despite his annoyance. "My grandmother finds her own way. She refused to come live with us. She lives with a family outside James City, working at the trading post."

"Ye don't look out for her?" Marcus shot back, his voice rising. Winn snorted under his breath, considering the fact that Marcus left her on her own when he fled to the future.

"When she has need, she makes it known. It has always been that way. She was banished when I was a boy, I did not truly know her until I lived with the English, and now…now she wishes to remain where she is. It is her decision."

"How far is it?"

"Too far for a visit today. I will show you the way on the day you leave."

Marcus said nothing, staring straight ahead as he rode. Winn wondered briefly if his father would search so faithfully for him, should the situation be reversed. He quickly dismissed the thought, his attention distracted as Chetan turned his horse in a tight circle and pointed ahead.

"*Winkeohkwet*! Look!" he shouted.

Over the tops of the evergreens, a cloud of black smoke wound up into the sky through the trees. It was coming from the same direction as their home.

They urged their horses into a gallop.

7

Maggie

Maggie pulled up the moonflower vine at the roots. Pretty, but damaging, the things grew rampant around the base of the corn stalks in a twist of blue and green buds. It was only a small garden plot, yet if it survived to maturity without being looted or burned, she would be grateful. One could only eat so much Tuckahoe.

She flicked her braid back over her shoulder with a quick flip of her chin and squinted up at the sky. It was another humid day in the Virginia sun, and she would be glad to see it end. Soon the men would be home, and they would enjoy a well-deserved meal together.

Rebecca sat cross legged on the ground between the rows, patiently showing Kwetii how to pull up weeds. Teyas worked alone nearby. Usually Winn's sister was the most productive of the group and today was no exception. Teyas was accustomed to such work, and although Rebecca made honest effort, the Englishwoman was simply not cut out for such things. As Maggie watched the blond-haired girl play with her daughter, she wondered if Rebecca would ever find such happiness of her own. Even two years past the massacre, she still seemed fragile, like a broken bird. Perhaps she would never recover from the trauma.

"Whoop! Whoop!" Ahi Kekeleksu waved his arms overhead, swatting at the black crows swooping in to pick at the corn. He raced down the aisle away from the women, taking his job as scarecrow most seriously. Kwetii giggled at his antics, and Maggie smiled.

The boy suddenly slid to a stop at the end of the aisle. The corn was not mature grown yet, and as Maggie stood to her feet she could easily see over the waving silk tassels to the direction the boy looked. Her breath hitched at the sight.

"Rebecca, take Kwetii to the house," Maggie ordered. Rebecca looked up from her game with a confused frown.

"Why? What's the matter?" she asked.

There were two riders with scarlet lined coats opened and flapping loose in the breeze as they galloped toward the settlement. Soldiers dressed in such disarray meant one thing: deserters. And deserters were even more dangerous than the law-abiding English.

"Teyas, take them and go. Hide in the house, you can all fit in the root cellar." Maggie took her sister's hand. "Please, take the children and Rebecca. I'll send them away," she insisted.

Maggie looked at Rebecca, standing wide eyed with Kwetii on her hip. She pressed her lips hard to her daughter's cheek and grabbed Rebecca by the chin.

"Do as I say. Go to the cellar and stay there until I come for you," Maggie demanded. Rebecca began to cry, but she nodded through her tears.

"I will stay with you," Teyas said.

"No, go! There's a better chance they'll listen to me then you, and you know it."

"Sister–"

"Damn it, Teyas, please! You can keep the others safe. I'll deal with the strangers. Ahi Kekeleksu! Take them! Go!"

Not yet a man, even Ahi Kekeleksu knew the danger they were in. The warriors had all left early that morning for town and would not arrive home until nightfall, and as the only man left among them he stepped up to protect them. He grabbed Rebecca's hand and barked a command at Teyas, and Maggie watched them hurry back toward the cottage.

The riders approached from the north, and she stood as if a barrier between them and those she loved. A mixed group of Indians and white women was an invitation for trouble. Rebecca was not strong enough to fight, neither in spirit nor body. Kwetii was completely vulnerable. Ahi Kekeleksu was full of heart with courage too big for his adolescent body. And Teyas, as strong as she was, she was the only one who had any hope of saving the others if Maggie could not send the soldiers away. She let out the breath she'd been holding once they reached the cottage and were safely inside.

She thought she felt the ground tremble beneath her feet, yet it might have been only the pounding of her pulse as she faced the deserters. Appearing even more unkempt as they came into close view, she held her ground and refused to flinch. They would expect some fading delicate flower and they would be sorely disappointed.

"This yer place, Miss?" the first one barked, none too politely. It appeared they would not waste time with pleasantries. He was a sallow faced man, his skin jaundiced over a scurvy twisted smile, the typical appearance of many of the English who were bereft of essential foods in their diets. She wondered if they deserted due to starvation, or if they were just disloyal dimwits who thought the grass was greener elsewhere.

"Yes, it is. I'm afraid you missed the path to town. It's back the way you came," she said. Her voice was loud and did not waver, even as the two men exchanged surly grins. The second man had the sleeves of his dull maroon coat rolled up to his elbows, the front hanging open like a slack jawed caricature. She noticed all the brass buttons were missing, likely sold or traded, marking them as men who had truly abandoned their honor. No loyal English solider would present himself in such a way.

"Aye. We know the way," the first man answered. They dismounted and the scurvy marked man walked toward her. She held her ground.

"Then take it. You have no business here."

The first man laughed. His teeth were brown nubs jutting from his gums.

"Ye have some new corn here, I think we might relieve ye of it. If that pleases ye, Mistress?" he smirked. He plucked a young ear from the stalk and broke it in two, sniffing it with his bulbous nose.

"Take it then and go. We have nothing else for you," she said. At her words the first man perked up. She bit the inside of her lower lip when he reached out to her, taking the end of her braid in his hand. He studied it, then directed his gaze down at her clothes, his muddy brown eyes lighting up as he considered her. She wore her cotton shift belted over a short buckskin skirt, typical to the Indians who traded with the English.

"Yer dressed like a squaw? Where's yer people now, squaw?" he taunted, pulling down hard on her braid. She jerked backward and he released her hair, but he snatched her arm before she could get further away. She saw the flash of a flame and the scent of thick smoke filled her nostrils as the corn was set on fire. It ignited quickly, so fast that she could feel the lick of the heat on her skin.

"Leave off 'er, Milt! We have no time fer this! I don't need any savages following us!" The other man snapped. Milt apparently had other intentions.

"Unhand me unless you want to lose those fingers," Maggie said, her words brave even as she felt hope of escaping trickle away. He raised one brow at her threat, and then struck her square in the cheek with his closed fist.

She crumpled to her knees as her head exploded in throbbing pain and her vision began to swirl. *Oh, Jesus*, she thought. *Please let the others be safe.*

The first man protested as his companion grabbed her by the hair, jerking her head backward until she cried out.

"Oh, a brave one, are ye? Brave little pretty thing."

She smelled his putrid scent before she realized he had unbound his trousers, causing bile to surge up in her throat. She tried to scramble backward but he shook her, his fingers tangled in her braid. Unwanted tears fell onto her cheeks as she choked back a sob, the skin of her knees rubbed raw in the stony earth. She fumbled for the butt of her knife and found it tucked in the strap at her waist.

When he tried to yank her to her feet she lunged with the knife, stabbing him in the right side of his groin. He screamed and bucked but she held on, twisting the knife deeper as blood began to squirt from the wound. *The femoral vein*, she thought. *It could kill him quickly.*

"She stabbed me! The whore sta–"

Milt's words were cut off and he suddenly slumped down over her, his limp body pinning hers to the ground in a shower of pulsing blood and rancid odor. She pushed furtively at him, scrambling under the weight of his body, her blood soaked fingers slipping uselessly with the effort.

She heard the sound of struggle yet could not see, familiar voices joining in with uttered threats and another sickening thud. The limp body was pushed off her and two firm hands pulled her up to a sitting position.

"Are you hurt?" Winn asked, shaking her by her shoulders when she did not answer. She stared blankly beyond him at the second man, felled by Chetan's blade stuck in his temple.

Too much. *It was all too much.*

Death, danger, something at every turn. She had done nothing but mind her own business tending to her crop, yet somehow she sat bathed in a stranger's blood and two men lay dead. Perhaps to Winn it was normal. To her, it was not.

"What are you doing out here? I told you to stay away from the fields!" he said through a clenched jaw. "Should I bind you when I leave, will that make you listen?"

She shoved away from her husband.

"I thought–"

"Let me see your wounds," he growled.

"No," she whispered. She pushed back with her heels and thrust away from him, away from the blood smeared over his chest, away from the gaping hole in the man's neck where Winn had sliced his jugular as if gutting a pig. She swallowed down a moan and shrunk away as he reached for her, even as she knew she caused him grief.

Winn sat back on one knee and dropped his hand. She could hear her pulse pounding in her head, or maybe it was the impact of the blow she suffered, she did not know. All she knew right then was that she needed to make it all stop. *She needed to get clean.*

"Maggie?"

She shook her head and scrambled over to the creek bed, needing to get away from the snap of the flames as her crop burned higher. She crawled into the shallow water and closed her eyes as the cold stream flowed over her. The frigid water numbed her skin, a blessed, consuming sensation to block out the horror of reality.

She heard Winn speak softly to his brother, and the sound of his footsteps as Chetan left them and took the path back to the cottage. She continued to let the water wash over her, sitting cross legged on the pebble flanked stream bed as she began to cry.

"My brave little Fire Heart," he said softly, kneeling down beside her in the stream. She stared at her open palms, now faded pink as the current cleansed her skin. He slowly reached out to take her hands and when she did not resist he began to rub them clean.

She watched her husband through her clouded vision. His fingers were gentle upon her flesh, washing away the evidence, his hands firm and familiar on her body.

"I'm not brave," she whispered.

He took her face into his hands, forcing her to look into his pained blue eyes. It was that which broke her, the dam of tears released by the strength of his touch, the certainty of his words a beacon to hold onto.

"*Pishi*, yes, you are," he said gently in return. She allowed him to embrace her, trembling as he pressed her to his chest, her body shuddering with the effort of holding back her tears. He let her rage, as he had once promised he would, no move to stop her when she clutched his chest and hit him with closed fists to vent her despair.

"Why would they do such a thing? What is *wrong* with men in this time?" she asked, expecting no answer. After all, Winn was a man of his era, unique in many ways, but still a seventeenth century male. Could he ever truly understand how it felt to grow up in another time, then live constrained by centuries old mentality? As much as he tried to sympathize, she suspected it was something one would have to experience to truly appreciate.

"They were cowards, not men."

She nodded and bent her head to his chest, relaxing her body into his. The pebbles beneath them in the streambed shifted with the weight of their joined bodies and their wet clothes stuck to their skin. They watched in silence as the fire consumed the last of the corn. It was a small crop and it would be finished burning soon.

"I'm ready. We can go now," she whispered.

They walked beside each other on the path to the cottage, close yet not touching, no further words spoken between them.

8

Makedewa

Makedewa urged his pony into a gallop toward the cottage, the thick smoke from the flaming corn field burning his eyes. He knew Winn and Chetan had found Maggie, yet he saw no sign of the others. Teyas, the children...or Rebecca.

Rebecca. He would give anything to see a flash of her bright yellow curls, even if she were running away from him as she usually did. In the two years since he had saved her from the Great Assault it was a dance they lived, tenuous friends, yet he knew she still regarded him with suspicion. He did not blame her for her fears as she was wary of all men, and he was, of course, only a man. As his eyes scanned the cottage for any sign of movement, he felt a pang in his chest when there was nothing. Where were they?

"I'll check the barn," Marcus called out.

"I'll see to the house," Makedewa agreed. He dismounted and left his pony ground-tied. At the door to the cottage he paused, his palm sweating as he placed it against the door. It was ajar.

Silence greeted him. The hearth was cool with not even a wisp of smoke in the ashes, and that meant they had been out in the fields most of the day. One of the shutters, blown loose from its latch, banged against the window with each pass of the faint breeze.

Next to the cold hearth was a red ribbon. As he bent slowly down to retrieve it his hand trembled. It belonged to Rebecca. He had given it to her when they moved to the head right property, a gift he had traded his own copper bands for. He clenched the ribbon in his fist and briefly closed his eyes. As he stood up his eye caught something out of place. The latch to the root cellar stood askew, the rusted ring perched outward instead of flush to the floor. He covered the space in one stride and wrenched the trapdoor open, jumping back when a barrage of screams greeted him.

"It is only me!" he hollered, his voice hoarse as he looked down at them. Teyas clutched Kwetii with a hand over the child's mouth, and Ahi Kekeleksu stood with his hands planted on his hips in front of Rebecca. The boy abandoned his warrior stance immediately at the sight of Makedewa, and they climbed out of the cellar as Kwetii burst into a fit of screams.

Teyas pecked his cheek with tearful thanks, but it was Rebecca who held his gaze. She was covered in dust from the cellar, her cheeks stained with tears, yet her pale eyes bespoke something he had never seen in her before. When she cleared the last step and threw herself into his arms, he held his hands wide, afraid to touch her. He could feel her heart pounding against his chest and the tremble of her body as she cried. Her fingers clutched his skin almost painfully and it was all he could do to soothe her as he slowly placed his hands around her back. He was not the sort of man to comfort a woman, and in truth he did not know how. Yet for her, he wanted to try.

"Is Maggie safe?" she asked, her face buried in his shoulder. He nodded, words slow to form as he struggled to speak. She was filthy, but the brush of her soft hair on his skin and the scent of her sweet soap caused him to tremble as well. The last time he had held her so close she had been wounded and he had carried her into the cave. In the time since then he had ached with longing to hold her again, never truly believing it would ever happen.

"Winn and Chetan see to her. She lives," he murmured, his voice strained.

"Did they hurt her?" she whispered. He suspected her meaning, and although he did not know the answer for certain, he shook his head.

"No. She's fine," he lied. *He would lie to the Great Creator himself before he would cause her any more distress.*

Kwetii wailed louder. Teyas bounced the child on her hip and pointed out the window.

"See? There they are, little one, it is fine now," Teyas said.

Marcus and Chetan walked toward the house, and they could see Winn and Maggie on the trail as well. Ahi Kekeleksu raced out to meet them, greeting their return with a string of uttered war cries. The intent of the boy's screams meant victory, a hollow utterance in the face of what might have happened.

Rebecca suddenly stiffened and looked up at him, then ducked her chin and backed away. He knew it might be a mistake but he took the chance, catching her fingertips in his hand as she tried to flee. He saw the panic there in her face, her sweet features creased with confusion, but she did not pull away. He opened his other hand where he clutched the red ribbon.

"Here," he said. He reached around her shoulders, taking care not to touch her further as he tied her hair back at the nape. How he wished to run his hands over her face, to feel her heart beat against his once more. He saw the pulse throbbing below her jaw and the way her eyes widened, and he dropped his hands.

"Go. See Maggie," he grunted.

She ran out of the cottage, her skirt flapping behind her as she followed Teyas to the others.

Part Two

9

Maggie

The sweet burning scent of pepper and fresh boiled meat made Maggie's stomach ache as she put a spoonful of broth to her lips. It tasted good and would feed them all well later that day. Although she used the last of their precious spice to enhance the flavor of the small amount of venison, it had to be used up. They simply would not have space to take everything with them on their journey south. At least if she used up their meager supply of luxuries, it would not feel so wasteful leaving them behind to scavengers.

The others left her alone most of the morning. Teyas knew her well, and knew when she needed time for reflection. Maggie was accustomed to handling events in stride. Killing, maiming, assault–just another part of living in the time she had chosen as her own. Yes, she had grown adept at dealing with it all, yet sometimes she still needed a bit of space for her own thoughts.

Winn obviously had no such compulsion. She looked up as he entered the cabin. Thankfully, he was alone.

"Is Kwetii with Teyas?" she asked. He dropped his knife onto the table, making a small pile of weapons when he added his bow.

"Yes. They help break down the *yehakins*."

"Oh," she answered.

She bit her lower lip, uncaring of the sting, needing the pinch of reality to bring her back to her senses. Winn had decided they were leaving and once he made his declaration there was no arguing with him.

He no longer held the title of War Chief, long lost since his village disbanded after the massacre, yet his every word was still viewed as law by his family. She would not presume to know everything of the ways of his world, but she could not sit silent without voicing her concerns.

"Can't we wait? At least until spring?"

He sat down on the bench and leaned back against the table. She handed him a pewter mug filled with cold water which he placed to his lips, watching her over the rim as she fidgeted. She crossed her arms over her chest, her foot tapping nervously on the floorboards.

"We must leave now to settle before winter. You know this," he replied. "I need to see you settled, so I can bring the Paspahegh to safety as well."

"You'll have them settle with us?" she asked. There were a dozen odd Paspahegh left that Winn worried about, struggling to remain independent of the conflicts with the settlers. The group had refused to settle with Maggie's family so close to the English, so leaving their home was meant to ease all their lives. Joining with a larger village would be beneficial to them all.

"If they will. Why do you worry on this?"

"I just wish we could stay in one place, that's all."

She pressed the flat of her palm to her aching belly. Her appetite had been erratic since weaning Kwetii, only recently returning over the last few weeks. Although she loved the thought of another child, the reality of enduring another birth when their lives were so uncertain made her afraid. Even if they tried, she was unsure if she were even capable. Her weight had dropped as their food supply dwindled and her menses only came sporadically. They were suffering nearly as much as the English when it came to food. Winn was right; they needed to move on if they were to survive.

He took her hand and pulled her to sit on his lap.

"I think you will like the Nansemond. I have many friends among their people."

She settled against his chest.

"Will you still help your uncle?"

He sighed.

"Yes."

She wanted to argue, but held her tongue. Winn believed remaining loyal to his uncle helped keep them safe. As emissary to the English, he served as a translator and negotiator when either side had need of such. Tensions were past breaking with the English, and she had to admit Winn knew what he was doing by remaining cordial with both sides. Winn tried to limit the dealings as much as possible yet the connection gave him standing in both communities and generally kept them safe from harm, at least most of the time. Incidents like the interaction with the deserters were something that could be neither predicted nor avoided.

"Will it take us long to get there?" she asked.

"If we leave with the sunrise, we should find them by nightfall on the third day. Perhaps more, if the women tire and we must stop." The corner of his lip turned up in a sly grin. "Your bladder is the size of a walnut, so you tell me."

She poked him in the ribs as she giggled.

"Only from having your daughter!"

His hand slipped down over her belly as he laughed, one eyebrow raised slightly in question. She shook her head.

"No, it was nothing," she said softly. She knew he questioned her diminished appetite and occasional bouts of nausea over the last week, but she was certain it was nothing more than weight loss and hunger pangs. Discussing such things as the arrival of her period was still a taboo subject for her, so she was glad when he took her word for it. There was no little Winn brewing in her womb.

"Oh. We must try harder, then, *ntehem*," he said. His voice was low and throaty, his breath against her neck sending a shiver down her back. He kissed her ear very softly, his hand caressing the base of her spine as he held her close. It was easy to forget everything when he touched her. His fingers pressed into her flesh, branding her with the magic of his touch, as his lips brushed along her jaw where her pulse beat madly. His heartbeat throbbed under the palm of her hand, steady and sure, her anchor to reality as it all seemed to explode around them.

She closed her eyes and groaned at the shock of pleasure as he ran his warm hand up her thigh. His blue eyes gleamed in the dim light.

"How you distract me, wife," he murmured. She smiled.

"I didn't do anything," she whispered.

"No?"

He pulled her slowly down across his lap so she straddled his hips, her skirt riding up to her waist. He kissed her as his palms gripped her bare buttocks.

"You're the one bothering me, warrior."

"Does this bother you?" he grinned.

"Yes," she choked as he took her hand and placed it on the swell of his breechcloth. She glanced at the door. It was still closed, but she could hear voices nearby.

He nodded toward the back room, and she eagerly followed him. The respite was not theirs to be had, however. Before they reached the privacy of closed quarters, the door swung open and Teyas entered, followed by Marcus and Rebecca. Kwetii squealed from where she sat perched on Rebecca's hip, launching into her own series of demands.

"Momma! Uppy! Uppy!"

Maggie took her daughter from Rebecca. She hid her flushed face against Kwetii and swung her around, causing the child to scream with laughter. Winn made a disjointed grunting sound, looking distinctly uncomfortable as he picked up his discarded weapons from the table and the others filed into the cottage. He kissed Kwetii on her head, and then his lips brushed Maggie's ear as they parted.

"Later, you are mine," he whispered. She smiled.

Teyas had a sharp eye and Maggie saw her nudge Winn as he passed.

"Interrupting something, brother?" Teyas asked.

"You have work to do," he grumbled. "We leave in the morning."

Maggie and Teyas exchanged grins as Winn left the cottage.

"He's right," Maggie agreed. "We all have a lot of work to do."

Teyas and Rebecca went up to the loft, talking of what to do with the furniture they had grown fond of. Growing up as a Paspahegh, Teyas was well accustomed to moving several times a year, even more if necessary. Yet Rebecca in particular was having a difficult time with the idea of moving. Maggie wondered if she had second thoughts about her decision to stay with them instead of returning to the English.

"You rascal, stop squirming!" Maggie said.

She adjusted her wiggling child and tried to keep her pinned on her hip, but when Kwetii decided she wanted down, she would not relent. Maggie juggled the wooden ladle while trying to subdue her daughter, surprised when Marcus took the child from her.

"Here, I'll watch her. She's a handful enough without ye tending the food," he said. He hefted Kwetii up against his shoulder and Maggie smiled when the toddler reached up and grabbed at his beard.

"She's never seen facial hair on a man. I'm sure she'll lose interest soon."

"Oh? I suppose she wouldna, living out here with ye."

Maggie turned back to the kettle, leaving them to their own devices. She heard Marcus clear his throat.

"We haven't had much time to talk, with the others always about."

She nodded, her back still turned to him. His voice betrayed his angst, his thick accent strained and his words stilted.

"I know ye married Benjamin, I found record of it. Will ye tell me, or leave me guessing what happened?"

"Things are different in this time," she said quietly.

"I know that very well."

"Winn was shot in front of my eyes, I thought he was dead. I didn't know what to do." She folded her hands and twisted her fingers together against her skirt as she turned to face him. "There was a man named Thomas Martin who claimed I was his niece, I suppose he did it for the bride price he would get when he settled a marriage contract. I had nowhere else to go."

"Surely the Paspahegh would have helped ye."

"I was carrying Kwetii. I thought they blamed me for Winn's death. I had no way to reach them, and no means to take care of myself. Benjamin offered his protection, and I took it. I didn't know who he was then. I didn't realize he was your son until the day—the day…" Her mouth suddenly dried and her throat felt tight at the memory of that day. *How could she possibly explain it all to him? Benjamin's jealous rage, how he turned her over to the English to be hanged as a witch? How she realized too late that he was the little boy she once played with? Then the massacre that followed? How Winn was alive and somehow, they found their way back to each other?* It was too much, the memories tearing her too deep, causing her defensiveness to rise up. "You have no idea what I've been through—what we've all been through. Go ahead and judge me if you must."

Kwetii reached for her, and Maggie pulled her into her arms. The toddler stuck her thumb in her mouth and rested her head on her shoulder. Maggie rocked slowly to soothe the child as Marcus gazed at her with a frown. She could see the crease across his forehead and the way his jaw tightened as he considered her words. She had only given him the bare bones of the story. What would he think of her if she told him all of it?

"There's no sin in such a thing, if that's what yer asking," he finally said. She swallowed hard.

"I didn't know who he was until the day we gave him the Bloodstone. I thought we sent him home…to you," she whispered, dipping her chin down into her daughter's hair. There was so much she wanted to say to him, this gentle hulk of a man who had always watched over her. Yet seeing his eyes glazed with emotion and knowing her own tears were ready to surge, she held back the bulk of the truth until her breathing slowed.

"So there's no hope for peace between Benjamin and Winn, then, is there?"

"You can't fault Winn for that. They were friends before this, like brothers…" she paused, the statement sounding quite foolish.

"Aye, maybe. But a woman has a way of changing things between friends. Even brothers."

Marcus turned to the window. She followed behind him, swaying gently to ease Kwetii to sleep. Through the glass, she could see the yard where Makedewa stood with Rebecca, engaged in some sort of awkward discussion. She leaned in next to Marcus to get a closer look.

"It seems like you hate the Paspahegh. Your son is part of them," she said quietly.

"Ye think I don't know that? No, I don't hate them. I hate the bloody foolish Weroance who caused all this grief. Without an old man's senseless vision, none of this would have happened. We would have stayed here in peace, living in our own way. We're the last of our people because of him, Maggie. We're what is left of the *Blooded Ones*."

"Finola used that term before. What does it mean?"

"It's from old magic. *Blooded Ones* are born with the power. It must be in yer blood, to use the stone. There were few of us even before Opechancanough wanted us all dead. He hunted them down, he ended our people. They're all gone, except for us."

"Us?" she asked.

"You, me. Benjamin and Winn. Your little one. There were others, but they are long dead now. That's why I took your mother to the future. It was my duty to protect the last of our most powerful blood, that which flows in yer veins. You know nothing of what magic lies in your blood."

"I think I know something of it," she murmured.

She held her hand out, palm side up. The scar had faded to a silver-white hue, but the knotted design was still as clear as the day the Bloodstone had burned it into her flesh as it thrust her back through time.

"I didn't have this until I came here. What really happened to my parents? Did you and Granddad lie about them, too?" she asked.

His mouth tensed tight at her question and his brows dipped down in a deep crease.

"They're gone like the rest." He said curtly, as if he meant to shield the flash of grief that briefly surfaced in his eyes. He reached inside his trade shirt and pulled out his Bloodstone. It was wrapped in tarnished copper, like Winn's, and hanging from a rawhide cord from his neck. "I didn't know if I could find ye and Benjamin, or if the Bloodstone would take my life when I traveled. It's been a long time since I worked the magic. But I had to try. Yer all that's left that matters to me."

His shoulders relaxed and he let out a sigh. He let the Bloodstone pendant drop back down against his chest.

"You have Winn now, as well," she said softly. "Will you stay here with us, once you find Benjamin?"

"It's a one-way ticket, lamb. I won't risk it again. Yes, I am here to stay."

He kissed Kwetii softly before he left to join the men, leaving her watching them from the window.

10

Makedewa

Makedewa threw an armful of sweet alfalfa grass to the ponies. He was restless, so he went to tend the horses and gather the livestock close to the houses. The animals now grazed loose inside the large barn, a remnant left over from the previous occupant of the farm. He did not care for the enclosed structure yet he had to admit it was a sensible method of keeping the horses ready at a quick notice. With the attack by the deserters, it was more important than ever to be ready for anything. As he watched the horses, he heard footsteps on the packed clay path and raised his head. Rebecca peered around the barn door. At the sight of her round flushed face and curious stare, he felt his throat constrict.

"Are ye occupied, Makedewa? I willna bother ye if so," she said softly.

Makedewa could utter nothing sensible, and all that came out was a half-snort, half-grunt as he shrugged.

"No, you are no bother to me," he said with a frown. Rebecca ducked her chin and looked at her own clenched hands at the callous response. "Stay if you wish."

"Are ye sure?"

"I said so, did I not?" he asked, his tone more irritated than he intended. "I meant–I–are you well, I mean?" he stammered.

She nodded and looked up at him, meeting his gaze for a fleeting moment, her corkscrew curls bouncing against her shoulders.

"I am well. It was only a fright for us hiding in the cellar. I worry for dear Maggie, though, she seems affected," she murmured.

"Maggie has the heart of a brave, ease your mind of that," Makedewa replied. Rebecca left the doorway and stepped into the barn, and he took an equal step backward. He did not wish to scare her off. In his haste to give her a wide berth, he knocked a pitchfork over and stumbled trying to catch it, and Rebecca leapt at it as well. They ended up each holding onto the tool, kneeling on the ground, laughing at each other.

"Makedewa?" she asked.

"Hmm?"

"Would ye teach me to–to shoot your bow? Or use thy knife? I think I should know more of such things, living among ye."

"If you wish," he muttered. "Tomorrow. I will teach you tomorrow."

She smiled, and they both stood up.

"Thank ye. If you wish, I will teach you to read. I–I used to teach the children…once."

Makedewa nodded without looking at her.

"A fair trade. You may teach me."

She turned quickly, giving him a brief smile and an awkward nod before she walked back to the cottage.

Makedewa watched her go. It had been a long two years waiting for her to smile on him, and he would do anything to see it again. He would not mention he was already quite fluent in reading English.

11

Rebecca

Rebecca decided it was time. For too long she had pushed his friendship away, yet still he persisted with silent patience. If there was ever a man she could trust, surely it was the quiet warrior who she shared a home with. She was tired of feeling like a burden to their mismatched family, the only woman among them who could not wield a weapon or contribute in a useful way. Yes, she cooked and cared for the children, but seeing the way Maggie and Winn interacted made her long for more. Her English life was long gone, and as Maggie had been telling her for months, there was much more to life than living in the past.

She lifted her skirts above her ankles as she made way through the tall grass. Makedewa was waiting in the field, where he had hung a hide against a wide tree trunk to take aim at. She watched him as she approached, noting with a flush of heat to her face how his skin glistened over his shoulders as he drew back the bow string, his arms flexed in readiness. He lowered the bow when he noticed her approach.

"The wind is quiet today. A good day to learn," he said, his eyes meeting hers. She glanced up at the bright sky.

"It's beautiful out today, surely," she agreed. She smiled but he scowled, and suddenly her brave intention flew away. Had she already done something to annoy him? Sometimes it seemed her very presence irritated him, and her hopes for the day dimmed.

"Turn around," he snapped. She did so without question, her breath a sharp intake when he untied the ribbon from her hair. He paused for a long moment, and then twisted her hair into a knot at her nape, securing it with a tug of the ribbon more toward her left shoulder.

"I'm sorry," she said softly. She turned to face him, perplexed at the way his eyes softened and his grimace lightened.

"For what?"

"I should have thought–my hair, I mean," she said.

"You know nothing of how to shoot. Be sorry for naught. It is only that I do not wish to see you hurt," he mumbled. "That is why my scalp is shaved here, so that the arrow does not get caught." He pointed to the swatch of crescent shaped skin over his right ear, the skin smooth of any offending hair. The rest of his black mane fell loose down his back, which was unusual for him since he most often wore it knotted or in a braid. She thought he looked softer somehow with it down, as if his body had relaxed with the easy motion. Even the corner of his mouth appeared to twitch as if he wanted to smile but held back.

He thrust a smaller bow into her hands, holding an arrow in his fist as he stepped away. He picked up his own larger bow and demonstrated how to pull back on the string.

"Try this first, before I give you the arrow. Make your arm straight. Pull your hand back to your nose."

She did so, plucking the string, which snapped back with a deep twang. She liked the feel of the curved wood in her hand and a smile spread over her lips as she glanced at Makedewa. He had dropped his bow and stood watching her, his arms crossed over his chest.

"Good. Here, now try this."

He leaned across her and placed the notched end of the arrow on the string, grunting his approval when she balanced it on top of her other outstretched fist. When he stepped away, she drew the string but the arrow faltered, dipping to the side. She made several attempts to steady the thing before he would assist her, stepping to her side again. As much as she wanted to shoot the blasted arrow, his presence beside her led to complete distraction. Like the day he pulled her from the root cellar and held her in his arms, she could smell the scent of sweat on his skin and feel the warmth of his breath on her neck. Her throat tightened when he placed his hand over hers to steady the arrow and he slowly circled her shoulders with his other arm.

"Hold tight, here. Looser, here," he said. She relaxed the fingers gripping the string and smiled when it worked. The arrow drifted back to meet the bow.

"Let go," he murmured. She released her fingers and the arrow took flight, striking the edge of the target flap to lodge into the bark. She squealed with delight.

"Did ye see that? I did it! I hit the tree!" she laughed, swirling around in her excitement. He was still very close with his hand resting on her waist, but she did not mind it. In fact, it felt quite nice, and he had the making of a grin on his lips. For a man who rarely smiled, when his deep dark eyes softened and he relaxed, he looked quite attractive.

"Good shot. Try again," he agreed. He bent abruptly to pick up his own bow, standing beside her to shoot at the target. They practiced like that until the target was full of holes and the tree bark was shredded beneath the hide. Makedewa gave her occasional instruction but otherwise just supervised as she found her own technique, and by the end of the afternoon, she was quite pleased to be hitting the hide on every shot.

Her fingers ached and there were blisters on her thumb when she finally sat down beside him where he had taken a break, lying on the soft moss beneath another tree. He offered her a drink from his flask, which she took, watching as he leaned back onto his elbows and stretched out.

"The bow I use is much smaller than yours. Should I try the one ye use?" she commented.

"Keep the small one. It fits your hand, as it should. I made it for you."

She smiled. It was strange to be alone with him, sitting in a field surrounded by nothingness. She thought briefly of her mother, and wondered what the woman would have thought of such a thing. Although she sometimes missed her parents, she did not miss the strict life they lived, with the constant threat of damnation forever held over her head. Learning to live with the Indians and accepting that she was no harlot for sharing the afternoon with a man? Well, those were things she still needed to resolve for herself.

His eyes closed to the sun overhead. As she looked down at him, sipping from his flask, she felt a tugging down deep in her belly. It was an unfamiliar sensation but it possessed her, and suddenly her hand moved as if directed by a devil and slid onto his chest. His body stiffened at her touch, the rise of his chest trapped in place, and he opened his eyes as he swallowed. He said nothing, his soft brown eyes fixed on hers as she slowly drew her hand away. He caught her fingers in his own and placed her hand flat against his heart.

"I–I'm sorry," she stammered.

"I am not," he replied, keeping her palm under his, his eyes still focused on hers. She felt the thud of his heart under her hand and saw the heat in his gaze pulling her closer. For once, she felt no panic. The only thing she knew was that she wanted to be closer to him, to explore something beyond their tenuous friendship. She had no experience with men, but she suspected he felt the same way underneath his angry facade.

"I never see ye smile, Makedewa," she whispered.

"I smile…at times," he said.

"Even now ye look angry. Do I anger ye?" she asked.

"It is not anger you see, I promise you."

She nearly drew away when his hand slid up to cup her face, but instead she turned her cheek into his hand and closed her eyes. He moved swiftly then, sitting up beside her and taking her into his arms. She kept her eyes tightly closed, the feel of his touch burning her skin with rivulets of anticipation. Then his soft lips were on hers, gently covering her trembling mouth, the scent of his leather and sweat sending her senses into a spiral. Searching yet restrained, holding her face so tenderly as if she might crumble, his kiss led her closer into his embrace. When he pulled away he placed his cheek against hers and she could feel he struggled to slow his breathing the same as she.

"Was that pleasing to ye?" she asked, at loss to say anything meaningful.

"You please me quite well," he replied, his voice low and measured. She felt the blush rise to her cheeks, and dipped her head to avoid his heated stare.

"I have never kissed a man," she said softly. She did not know why she felt the need to confess it to him, but suddenly she felt as if her heart was flayed open and she wished to share all the things she had kept buried for so long. He would not allow her to look away, taking her chin in his fingers and tilting it back upward.

"Then I thank you for that honor," he whispered. His hand caressed the small of her back as he captured her gaze. "I would be the only man to ever have that honor, if you would have me. I want you for my wife, Rebecca."

She did not realize she cried until he kissed her tears away, and when he covered her mouth again with his own she tasted the salt of her tears between them.

"Ye do not want me," she said quietly, as he tried to kiss away her protests. An urgent surge of need washed through her and she pressed closer into his lap, feeling the response of his body hard against her. She tried to stem the panic as their embrace became more heated, loving his gentle hands on her flesh, yet fighting the surge of buried memories all the same.

"I do. I have always wanted you," he murmured.

"How could ye, when ye know my shame?" she insisted. He held her face in his hands and stared into her eyes, his face etched as if in pain.

"You bear no shame for what was done to you," he whispered, his voice fierce and tense.

"But I am no maid," she protested.

"You are to me," he replied.

She placed her hand on his face and then kissed him softly.

"Why do ye act so fearful, when ye have such a kind heart?"

He sighed and made the agitated half growl, half snort the men often uttered.

"There is no kindness here, *chulentet*," he murmured. "Perhaps a bit for you, that is all, my little bird."

She smiled. They both looked up at the sound of voices. Ahi Kekeleksu had found them, calling them to the late day meal. It was an unwelcome distraction but they drew apart nonetheless. They gathered the bows and made their way back to the cottage, and for the first time in what seemed ages her heart soared with pleasure at the knowledge Makedewa watched her every move.

12

Maggie

Traveling with their party was by no means speedy, as Winn had predicted. After three longs days of being astride a horse she was ready to wash the sweat from her skin and catch a few hours of rest. When her feet finally hit the ground again her legs felt like jelly and she suspected she walked like an old cowboy, bowlegged and bedraggled to boot.

"The village is not far from here. We should reach it in the morning," Winn assured her when they stopped. As she helped Teyas start a fire while the men tended the horses, she took a look around. The forest was filled with dense growing cypress, the ancient trees more common the deeper they traveled inland. She had never been so far away from the banks of the streams they typically lived near, so although she expected the different terrain it still made her uneasy. The soil was less sandy than the lowlands, and the men were pleased to find small game more plentiful for hunting. Winn was right. Their lives would be better the further they lived from the English towns.

Makedewa resumed teaching Rebecca how to shoot the bow, and Maggie settled down by the fire to watch them. Exhausted from the travel, Kwetii slept curled into a ball on the furs beside her, with her tiny thumb pressed up against the roof of her gaping mouth as she gently snored. Maggie brushed the child's dark hair off her heart-shaped face with a smile.

Winn sat down beside her while the other men stood watching the lesson. He offered her a sip from his flask that she gladly took. It was the last of the sack Makedewa had won playing dice and it left a pleasant burning warmth in her belly as it settled.

"Is Rebecca well?" he asked. He sat resting his arm on one bent knee, watching his brother. Maggie raised an eyebrow.

"Why do you ask? She's fine, as far as I know." She noticed the subtle nuzzle Makedewa gave Rebecca when he leaned close in his instruction, and the way Rebecca leaned into him with a smile. Apparently, they were getting on quite fine.

"I thought she lost her sense. I never thought to see her use a weapon."

Maggie rolled her eyes.

"Oh, yeah, why not? She's as capable as anyone else is. She just needs a little confidence," Maggie replied. "Rebecca, strike quickly when you mean to kill a man! A warrior once told me that!" she called out. Winn chuckled.

"Leave them be, woman," he grinned.

"Us girls need to stick together."

"No doubt."

She snuck a sly glance at his profile. Sculpted and strong, with bright blue eyes set against thick brows, he still made her breath hitch when he looked at her. The way he cocked an eyebrow at her, or twisted the corner of his lip in that secret boyish grin, it was enough to render her senseless, even after all they had been through. Would it always be so between them?

She reached for his hand and he smiled, clasping it firmly in his own. He rubbed the base of her wrist with his thumb, a firm yet gentle pressure, sending a shock of goose bumps over her skin. She felt the warmth spread at the contact, and a flush rose to her cheeks.

Yes. It would never change. He would always be a flame in her darkness, searing her with his heat. As if he sensed her thoughts, he raised her hand to his lips and kissed the scar upon her palm.

"I'm sorry," she said softly.

"For what, *ntehem?*"

"For tending the fields that day. I didn't think any harm of it."

He squeezed her hand.

"You are no obedient wife. I know that well." He ran his fingers up the length of her arm and pressed a gentle kiss to her bared shoulder, where he rested his lips for a moment. "There are things I fear losing in this life now. Before you, I feared nothing."

His words were gentle, considering the circumstances. It was not the first time they had such conflict. Despite her desire to behave like a proper wife, it was an endless struggle to subdue what was left of the twenty-first century woman inside her. At times she feared the way their pasts pulled them apart, yet she knew it was their differences that also bound them together.

She stiffened and sat up as he pulled abruptly away. She saw them at the same time as he did, the strangers standing at the edge of the clearing. Two men, both tall, both fair skinned, with full beards and long, unruly hair.

Rebecca dropped the bow when Makedewa pushed her behind him, and Teyas grabbed her hand. Chetan crouched, hand on his knife, and Marcus unsheathed the axe on his back. The sound of metal sliding from the sheath screamed in the silence, followed by the clang of weapons revealed by the newcomers. Other than drawing weapons, the men remained still as they inspected each other.

Winn slowly stood, his eyes never wavering from them. Marcus stepped forward in front of the others, standing between all of them and the intruders.

"*Hvata bak, ofugr,*" one said, taking a step toward them. He was taller than the first but younger, nearly as broad as Marcus was through the shoulders. His hair was a russet gold hue, hanging thick down his back with a series of tiny braids edging his scalp. Crisscrossed over his chest he wore flat leather straps, which secured several weapons including a knife. The handle of a sword protruded over his shoulder from where it was secured to his back. She did not recognize the language he spoke, yet she suspected Marcus did by the way his eyes widened and his jaw dropped.

"Go back where you came from. You are not welcome here," the stranger said in stilted English.

There was a rustle from the woods beyond the clearing and suddenly a half-dozen more men came forward. All attired in a similar manner, every man appeared ready to fight.

"*Sa er tala?* Show me who commands ye," Marcus replied, his arms flexed with gripping the sword. Maggie gasped when Winn moved to stand beside Marcus. His knife was drawn, his muscles tensed, his body coiled like a spring as he shielded them from the intruders. Makedewa and Chetan flanked them.

An older man stepped forward. His russet hair was similar to the first, his beard longer and streaked with scattered grey. He put up his hand and motioned to the younger man, who immediately sheathed his weapon.

"*Dagr?*" the older man said. Marcus did not waver when he moved closer, his stark blue eyes widening. Marcus dropped his hand to his side.

"*Erich?*" Marcus replied.

The man called Erich suddenly reached out and clasped both hands around the one arm Marcus extended. They stared into each other's faces for a brief moment without words, and then the stranger dropped down on one knee before Marcus and Winn.

His deep voice was strangled yet loud when he spoke.

"Chief Dagr has finally returned to us! Thank the Gods for his safe passage! Long life to Chief Dagr!"

Maggie let out the breath she held as the strangers fell to their knees, the sounds of their reverence a growing murmur which rolled through them as a gathering roar.

"*Long life to Chief Dagr! Chief Dagr!*" they shouted. She saw Winn take a step back and look to his brothers, who were staring at the kneeling men in wonder.

She had never seen Marcus so unsettled. His back straightened and his eyes swept over the men before him. Biceps tensed, the veins standing out like a web over his skin, she watched him as he spoke.

"Rise. Stand up, ye needn't kneel to me," Marcus said, his voice strained and low. The man called Erich stood with a grin spreading across his face. The others remained bent in deference.

"Ach, no, ye never did wish to be Chief. But Chief ye are, and thank Odin you've returned to us. You've come back from Valhalla, yet you're no spirit."

"Nay, no spirit. Just a man," Marcus mumbled. "I thought you had taken the others and left for Vinland, Erich. Or worse—that you did not survive the attack."

"Then you are just in time. We never gave up on seeing you again as well, my friend."

Maggie watched as the men clasped arms again.

"This is Winkeohkwet. My son," Marcus said. Erich made a half bow, his head lowered in respect to Winn. "And his family. I–"

"By the Gods! *Esa?*" Erich whispered. The color drained from his face as he looked to Maggie. She stayed kneeling on the ground next her sleeping daughter, unwilling to risk waking the child in the midst of such confusion. She had no idea who the men were or what was going on, and until her husband made indication it was safe she would not leave the child. Erich started to approach her, and Winn immediately stepped between them with his knife drawn. Makedewa gripped his knife and Chetan moved closer to Maggie at Winn's motion.

"Please," Erich said. "I mean no harm." He slowly placed his sword on the ground and then held up both hands extended in a gesture of submission to Winn. Marcus put a hand on Winn's shoulder. After a terse exchange in Paspahegh between the brothers, they lowered their weapons.

"He willna harm them. He's kin to her," Marcus said. Maggie's head snapped up. Kin to her? She had no family, other than the loved ones she shared with Winn. The sting of realization of yet another betrayal by Marcus was only dampened by her curiosity. Who was the massive beast of a man staring at her?

"What is yer name, *astin min*?" he asked. He knelt beside her with his hand extended. She did not flinch when he gently touched her cheek with his calloused fingertips, too entranced by his deep jade eyes to move. It had been a long time since she had seen her own eyes in a mirror, yet she knew the ones staring at her mimicked her own.

"Maggie. Maggie McMillan," she said softly. His eyes widened and his lips parted.

"Maggie *MacMhaolian*. Aye, of course. And this wee miting by yer side, she be yer child?"

She nodded. "Winn's daughter and mine. Who are you?"

"I am Erich MacMhaolian. Thank ye, my lord," he said, bowing his head when Marcus placed a hand on his shoulder. "My greatest thanks for keeping her safe."

"Ye would do no less, in my stead," Marcus answered.

"Who are you?" she whispered.

"Yer uncle. Erich is brother to yer mother," Marcus said.

It was fortunate she chose to remain seated, for if not, she was certain she would have fallen on the ground.

"I thought my family was gone," she replied, glancing up at Marcus, who had the good sense to grimace at her accusation and bow his head.

"Aye, I was dead to ye, as far as a man in the past would be. We hoped to have ye returned to us one day, but it's been so long…one should never return to a time once lived, even with the magic of the Blooded Ones. I fear ye were lost to us, as were yer mother and my father."

"My mother?"

"And what of my sister, my lord?" Erich said to Marcus, although his eyes remained still fastened on her as if he feared she would disappear.

"I'm sorry. She's gone, and Malcolm as well. We honored our vow. Malcolm lived a long life. And Esa—Esa left her daughter in our keeping."

Erich's jaw tightened and he nodded his head. He slowly rose to his feet and extended a hand to Maggie.

"Come. We have much to celebrate."

***

At first glance, the Norse village could have been mistaken for Powhatan. A straight central path divided two rows of long-house style dwellings, taller and larger than the *yehakins* the Indians used, but similar in structure with thatched roofs and bark slat shingles. As they rode the path through the village, the sounds of crushed stone beneath the horse's hooves announced them. Wide-eyed women and children peered out from doorways as they passed, clad in homespun tunics with cord-wrapped waists, with long locks braided amongst red and golden hair. Maggie did not know if she felt sheltered or trapped as she rode surrounded by the Norse, her heart pounding against the toddler bound in her lap. As they came upon a massive Long House at the end of the path and dismounted, several young boys ran out to take the horses. She was stunned to see a copper-skinned youth among them, a boy with long black hair and eyes like coal pellets, dressed in breeches like the others. He was clearly part Indian, living among a colony of Norsemen.

The men walked clustered behind Marcus and Erich. They were an intimidating bunch, all brawn and steel weapons among bared chests and fur-covered shoulders. Most were brawny, like Marcus and Winn. Many were fair-haired like Erich, with reddish blond locks lying long down their backs. They carried decorated weapons, lavish appearing items that seemed out of place considering the simple way they lived.

Winn and Maggie were escorted to the end of a long plank table that sat centered in the *Noroanveror Skali*, the place they called the Northern Hall. End to end, it breached the span of the room, with enough spaces on the benches to hold more than the number of warriors that accompanied them. Other smaller tables lined one wall and a fire rose from a pit in the other corner. Women and children began filling in as well, and from the smell of thick venison in the air she imagined it was time for a meal. Teyas offered to take Kwetii and Maggie gladly complied.

"What is this place?" Maggie asked, craning her neck to see past the men. Winn studied the warriors in silence before he answered her.

"I have heard of *Tassantassas* that live near the Nansemond, but I have never been to this place. If my uncle knew of them, they would all be dead. What else Pale Feather lies about, I know not," Winn said tersely.

"I don't think he lied about this, Winn. He told me most of the other Time Walkers were gone. He seemed just as surprised as we were when they showed up. Maybe he didn't know."

He grunted his doubt.

"Believe what you must," he replied.

Maggie was shown a seat to the left of Marcus, who held position at the head of the table. She saw him attempt to refuse the chair but Erich insisted, and finally Marcus grabbed the tall chair and shoved it back, plunking down with a scowl on his face. She expected equal resistance from Winn, yet was surprised when he took the bench across from her at the immediate right hand of Marcus.

"I hope ye find our table suffices, my lady," Erich said as he sat down beside her. He stared at her for a moment with his full lips parted as if to speak, but then clamped his mouth shut while shaking his head.

"What is it?" she asked. She had no idea what to say to the stranger, nor how to address him. Growing accustomed to living in another time had been difficult enough, but now as she sat beside her newfound relative, the reality of it all felt like an elephant sitting on her chest. She held her breath, afraid to look too closely at him, lest he disappear. Was he truly her uncle, this massive brute of a man? And if so, why had he sent her mother, his sister, away with Marcus to the future?

"Ye have yer mother's look is all. I'm afraid ye might be a ghost sitting beside me, and if I look away for too long, ye'll be gone."

Erich looked sincere, but it was too much for her to tolerate much longer. Marcus, or *Dagr*, whatever name he was called by, sat perched at the head of the table like their long suffering King. Men came by, patting him on the shoulders with hearty welcome, then moved to Winn to welcome him. With the scowl on his face and the doubt in his eyes, she was perplexed to see him nod gracefully to each man who approached him. Makedewa and Chetan looked on, their faces reserved, while Ahi Kekeleksu made friends with the other youths running through the hall. The intensity of testosterone-induced semantics was rapidly rising to more than she could bear, so when Erich patted her hand in a soothing manner, she jerked away from him. She had known the man all of an afternoon. How dare he treat her as if he had claim to her, as if being a blood relative meant anything?

"You sent my mother away. Why? If you loved her so damn much, how could you do that?" she snapped, her voice rising a pitch. The murmurs in the hall silenced and heads turned their way. She stood up, knocking her bench over backward in the process, unflinching when it clattered to the ground.

"I can explain–" Erich said.

He reached for her hand and she shrunk back from him, stepping further away as a gasp came from the crowd.

"Don't touch me!" she said. In the next moment, Winn was at her side, catching her wrist before she slapped her uncle's perplexed face.

"Sit down, Fire Heart," he said. Erich drew away, and someone else righted her bench. Teyas and Rebecca made room for Winn to sit next to her.

She glared at Winn, every ounce of her frustration now bent on him, taking the last slice of her self-control to keep from screaming at him as well. She knew he could see it from the way she trembled, her finger nails digging into his arms.

"I sent yer mother with my lord to seek safety. I knew he would protect my sister with his life. Dagr is my Chief, and my most trusted friend," Erich said. Marcus watched the interaction, still seated, resting his elbows on the table in front on him. "I see ye know nothing of yer powerful blood. Have ye told her naught, my lord?" Erich said, directing his question to Marcus.

"She knows verra little. Her journey here was unexpected. I leave her teachings to ye now."

Eric grinned. He leaned up over the table, nearly upending his bench as he waved a younger man to his side.

"Harald! Up fer a tale, boy?" he shouted. "He fancies himself our *Skald*, ye know," Erich laughed, shooting a sly glance at Marcus.

The young man approached, eyeing them shyly from beneath thick dark lashes. His tousled brown hair was worn shoulder length, like some of the other men, with small sections wrapped in cord hanging about his narrow face.

"Yes, my Lord. A good one, fer our guests, then?" Harald said. Erich glanced in a questioning manner at Marcus, who waved him on with a flick of his wrist and resorted to downing the rest of his drink. When young Harald smiled, Maggie could not help but let out a giggle, which she muffled under her fist. He was missing the bottom half of one front tooth, which did not seem to bother him in the least as he started his story.

"Aye, but they are no guests. This man is son to our Chief. My lady is a blooded *MacMhaolian*. Make it yer best fer them, boy," Erich declared. Children gathered in a circle at his feet, shooed over by elders to enjoy the tale.

Harald made a sweeping bow to Marcus and then another to her, bringing a smile to her face. He was a gangly young man, eager to please, and she liked him immediately. He was a welcome contrast to the testosterone infused brawn and bulk that surrounded her, masquerading as newfound kinfolk.

"Once there was a man called Jarl Drustan. He was born at Brattahlid, in the land of Greenland, a most treacherous place, indeed," Harald jumped up onto the bench beside Maggie. He placed a hand across his brow, his knobby elbow sticking out, searching the room from end to end. "Jarl Drustan was a man of the sea. But he was a man of secrets as well, for it was his kin, and his alone that were bound by blood for a greater task!"

"What task? What task!" the children cried, their faces upturned in rapt anticipation.

"Oh, it is a great honor, that which he had! For Jarl Drustan protected the Blooded Ones, our very own blessed ones."

Maggie's heart skipped and her mouth felt suddenly dry.

"A finer man ye wouldna find in all the land, Our Lord Drustan. One fateful day our Lord Drustan was ordered to the sea, where he was to go a-Viking. He set out with his clan to search fer new lands, on a fine new Longship made fer such occasion."

"Where did he go?" A tow-headed boy called out. Maggie noticed Ahi Kekeleksu sitting with the boys, just as enthralled in the tale as the other children.

"He searched and searched, for many long days, and many long nights. He searched for land, but never found it. He searched until the last of the food was eaten, and the people began to suffer of hunger. There was no land to be found, and it seemed he had led his people to death." He crouched down in dramatic pause, on eye level with the children. "Aye, ye know this tale, do ye not?"

"Nay, nay, tell it again, again!" the children shouted.

"Well, our Lord and protector, he would not let his people die at sea fer his own fault. He knew the blood of a Chief could save them, and so he bid his lovely Finola goodbye. Before they could beg him off, he held his Bloodstone, and spilled his blood upon the vessel. He sent his people to a new place. They came safe to this time, aye, and now ye all sit before us, all ye little hens," he said, reaching out to pat the head of a blond haired girl. He tapped the heads of the children one by one as he murmured, "Each of ye have a bit of the *Blooded Ones* in ye, a sprinkle here, a tad bit there. Not enough fer such a grand journey, but enough in ye to be one of us."

"Why did he die? Could he not go with them?" the blond girl asked, her round face scrunched into a frown.

"Oh, nay, little one. It takes too much to send a whole Longship through time. It takes all the blood of a Chief to do such a great deed. The life of a Chief, or a blooded *MacMhaolian*, only one of them can make that magic work. Ye know the Bloodstone's a dangerous magic. That's why none of ye wear them round yer necks. None except our *MacMhaolian* lady, returned to us by our Great Chief Dagr."

All heads turned to Maggie as Harald knelt down beside her, taking her hand into his with a flourish. He made great sport of kissing it, and then bowed deep to both her and to Marcus. Maggie's pulse pounded in her throat as the hall full of onlookers focused on her.

Marcus lifted up his hand. In his fist was a long, tapered white horn, embellished with gold and silver filigree and studded with dozens of gemstones. The hall fell silent once again as he raised it in salute, then took a long drink.

"*Esa svá gott, sem gott kveþa,*

öl alda sunum,

þvít fæ'ra veit, es fleira drekkr,

síns til geþs gumi!"

The Long House erupted in chaos, men and women shouting and stomping, beating their fists on tables and screaming their approval. She looked slowly around the room. Erich had a grin on his lips, raising his tankard to Marcus in a silent gesture.

"What did he say?" she whispered, not directly addressing Erich, yet knowing he was the only one who might answer her.

"He shouts his thanks to be among his people once more, and bids us all many cups of mead."

Marcus left his perch, drinking horn held carefully out as he came to their side. He placed one hand on Winn's shoulder, and while he looked briefly at Winn, he offered the horn to Maggie.

"*Margret*, I have watched over ye since the day ye were born. There is much to tell you of how it came to pass, and tell ye, we will. But for now, drink. This is the vessel of my ancestors. Take of it, wife of my son, daughter of my heart. Drink and be happy."

She wanted nothing more than to pour it on his head, but when her husband took the horn and drank, she felt she had no choice. When both she and Winn had tasted, a roar of shouts emerged from the crowd once again. The ground beneath her feet seemed to rumble with the pounding of the drums, and the rowdy voices of men broke into song.

To her chagrin, Winn had the look of amusement about him. As those around them bent to the task of celebrating, he pulled her near and whispered in her ear.

"How is it?" he asked. She scrunched her brow.

"How is what?"

"Being the kin of a Norseman? Do they seem so brave to you now?"

"Not funny, Winn," she replied, kicking him lightly with the tip of her moccasin-clad toe. "Not funny at all."

13

Winn

Winn noticed the women gather the small children as they made ready to leave the Long House. Although he sat with Marcus and Erich, he waited for Maggie to look to him. Angry or no, she would not leave without some sort of acknowledgement. She wiped Kwetii's mouth with the edge of her shift and adjusted the sleepy child in her arms, and as she turned to say something to Teyas, her eyes met his across the room. She issued him a wry smile, and he nodded in return. It was a small gesture but a necessary one, and he was glad she had calmed her fire long enough to relax with her kin.

He stood up from his seat beside Marcus with intent to join his wife, but both Marcus and Erich protested. Other young men filled in the benches where the women had left, shouldering in to grab the next pass of the mead tankard. Winn had seen the Englishmen soused on ale many times, but it was nothing compared to how the Norse consumed. He lost track hours ago of how much he had taken, drank only because each warrior who greeted him insisted on filling his tankard after slapping him heartily on the back. Apparently, being the son of the leader held many perks among the Norse, and having a plentiful supply of mead was one of them.

"Stay. The women need us naught, let them tend the mitings," Marcus said, filling Winn's mug yet again. Winn eyed his father warily.

"You know little of my wife. She looks now to see there is no bloodshed." He felt her presence behind him before her fingers touched his shoulder, the scent of her musky skin stirring his blood. He clenched his jaw, wanting nothing more to bury his frustration into his wife's willing arms, but when he glanced at her he could see she was as agitated as he.

"I'll see you soon, husband?" she murmured, bending close to his ear. He nodded.

"Take your rest. I will join you soon."

He touched Kwetii's trailing heel before they left, and turned back to the men. He noticed Marcus and Erich watch her leave as well, and wondered how his wife would adapt with such change. Suddenly she had a family, when her entire life, she had only Marcus and her grandfather. He listened when she told him the stories of her childhood, often fascinated by the tales of the future she told, yet in one very deep-rooted way he could understand her anger. Suddenly thrust into a family where secrets and lies abounded? Yes, that was an anger he knew well.

"I know that woman as much as ye, and don't ye forget it. I'm surprised she hasn't split ye over the head yet, with the way ye order her about. She doesn't take so well to orders," Marcus grumbled, taking a swig of his mead. "They grow up different in the future. Where did ye find her, when the Bloodstone took her from me?"

"On a bluff overlooking the valley, near where I buried the Bloodstones you left."

Marcus sat back and crossed his arms over his chest.

"Why did ye bury them?"

"The Pale Witch said a Time Walker would come, a Blooded One that I would fail to kill. I meant to break the curse, to keep it from happening. I wanted no part of that magic, nor of any Time Walkers."

"That surely dinna work," Marcus replied with a half-choked snort. "Instead ye put them right in her path. The bluff over the valley? That's where we lived in the future. We had a farm on that same spot. It's the same place the Bloodstone took her from."

"You just leave Bloodstones lying around in your future?" Winn asked. Winn swallowed down another swig of mead, watching his father's face turn from amused to something else. The man lifted his head, looking out over the crowed room before he answered.

"No. Ye buried the stones. Whoever built the house dug them up and used them, not knowing what they were. It was pure chance that she stumbled upon them. Maybe ye meant to keep her away, but it's because of you she's here, all the same. She and I would both still be in the future if ye had not buried the bloody things."

"You would have left Benjamin here in the past?" Winn said, surprised at the confession Marcus spoke. His father's shoulders sagged and he uttered a deep sigh.

"I dinna know where he was, until I found the note from Maggie. Benjamin was just a lad when he disappeared. I thought his blasted mother took him, but I knew nothing fer sure. It could have been magic, or she could have just left with him. When Maggie was taken, I took a shovel to the barn floor. I found the stones, and the letter your wife left in a pewter flask. I realized Benjamin was here as well. That's when I knew I had to come find ye."

"That was near two years past. Why did you wait?"

"To prepare. To look for clues. I searched records and deeds, every church log I could find. It's different in the future, Winn. Some of us disappear from history, some remain. Marriage contracts, court logs. Birth records…death records. I found nothing of the Norse I left behind. There is no trace in history of any Norse who lived among the First People. I thought if any survived the attack by your uncle, they must have tried to flee to Vinland. Even so, I found enough clues to track ye down—you and Maggie."

Winn's chest tightened.

"You say there are records of us? Death records?" Winn said.

Marcus nodded, his lips tight in a thin line.

"There's much I know about how things will go," his father said quietly. "Best we leave it at that, don't ye think, lad? It's enough now to be here, with my kin once more. I thought they were all lost to me."

Winn remained silent. His thoughts scattered, lost in how it all happened. As an angry young man he had buried the cursed Bloodstones to prevent the Time Walker from using them. Instead, it was because of his actions that Maggie ended up in the past. He would not change it, even if he could, that selfish voice down deep in his blood making itself known. She belonged to him, to his time, and no other.

"She's a rare one, that Maggie is. Ye know I raised her as my own," Marcus said.

Winn eyed him, gazing square at blue eyes so like his own.

"I know this."

"Yer uncle waged war on us. All these men here," he said, waving one arm out to encompass the table. "I thought all these men dead, or gone into hiding. Opechancanough told me he had killed them and their women. Even my right hand, Erich, who sits here with us. I did what I must to protect the rest–Malcolm, Helgrid, and Maggie's young mother, Esa. It was my duty to protect Esa and her unborn babe. I knew nothing of ye, you must understand."

"Would it have mattered, even if you knew of me?"

Marcus hesitated before he spoke.

"Yes, it would have mattered. But still, I would have gone."

Winn clenched his tankard, and then made the effort to loosen his grip as he slowly released it. He waited for Marcus to explain himself further before he responded, staring into his cup as his father struggled to explain.

"Yer mother was a good woman, but she wanted Pepamhu, even then. Yer uncle and my mother arranged our marriage as a means to prevent more bloodshed, but it failed. Pepamhu helped us escape when it all went bad. I left knowing he would take her to wife. I regret that it pains ye, but that's the truth of it."

Winn let out the breath he held and let the tension recede from his flexed arms. After taking a swallow of the mead and feeling its warmth creep into his belly, he nodded.

"I thank ye for keeping her safe," Erich interrupted, reaching across Winn to smash his raised tankard to the horn Marcus held. Erich peered at Winn. "And fer ye, I'm verra pleased to have ye married to my niece. We always planned to see yer son wed to a *MacMhaolian*, did we not, Dagr?"

Winn saw the way his father's eyes narrowed and his brow creased. He suspected his father had a different son in mind, but being he was attempting to understand the man he let that suspicion lie.

"Aye, that we did," Marcus agreed. "Seems she chose just fine without us, and here we are."

Erich grinned, nodding along with Marcus.

"I dinna get the honor of making ye fight fer her. I think her cousin would have given ye good reason to treat her well, right Cormaic?" Erich hollered. The young warrior who had first greeted their party in the woods grinned from his seat at the end of the table, raising his arm amongst the crowd of men surrounding him.

"Aye, father! A good thrash I'd have given him, for the honor of my pretty cousin's hand!" Cormaic shouted. The men erupted in hoots and bellows around him. "It is not too late to show the Chief's son my hammer!"

"Ach, down with yer fookin *lucht* talk!" Erich laughed, waving a hand at them. "Save it fer the English whoresons, so ye can end them when we next meet."

"What of the English? Do they come to this place, like they do the other villages?" Winn interrupted. He had the uneasy feeling of not quite understanding their humor, with the thick accents they all spoke and the unfamiliar dialect. He could glean enough from their body language, however, so when the topic of Englishmen arose and the younger men stopped laughing, he suspected there was reason for it.

Marcus looked to Erich, who drained his cup and held it out for more. A younger man quickly refilled it, and Erich resumed drinking as he spoke, his brow furrowed and his eyes narrowed like emerald pebbles.

"They sent a man here a few days past, just one, and not much of a fighter, that be sure. The Englishman spoke naught of what he was sent fer, so we have no thought as to what they want. I sent a rider to the Nansemond to ask on it, he should return soon."

"This Englishman, he said nothing?" Marcus asked. Erich shrugged, lowering his head to his drink.

"Nay. He said nothing useful before I clouted the *lucht*."

The men roared with laughter, and although his cheeks flushed bright red, Erich grinned.

"Great. Ye've clouted the only man who could give us an answer. Nothing has changed, aye?" Marcus grumbled. "Ye hotheaded *MacMhaolian!*"

Winn grinned along with his wife's uncle, and finished the rest of his drink.

***

The plank door was ajar, and he pushed it further open so he might enter the structure. It was smaller than the Great Long House yet similar in build, with a tall peaked roof topped with a smoke hole. A fire pit along one wall of the single room warmed the space well, sheltering a pile of sleeping furs nearby that lay strewn across a low platform bed. Not that they needed much warmth on such a humid summer night, but he was pleased with the space they had been provided by the Norse.

Teyas stood with Kwetii on her hip, the child hanging limp with exhaustion. Maggie was shaking her head at Teyas in protest.

"She can stay here with us, really, Teyas! It's a strange place, what if she wakes up and needs me?"

"We are only over there. Take your rest, sister, I will tend her tonight."

He frowned. He placed one hand on Maggie's arm, and waved Teyas to go with the other, grunting a low command in Paspahegh. His sister answered him in kind, and with a respectful nod, took the sleeping child and left.

"I wanted her to stay here."

He paused before he spoke, unwilling to incite his combative wife any further. He could see she was on the edge of fury, her fists bunched at her sides, trembling under his touch. She simmered like a flame, but he knew her well enough to know it must be doused before she would listen to reason. He caressed the palm of her hand his thumb, making slow circles on her skin, watching her flashing green eyes waver at the connection.

"She is not far, and you know my sister cares for her well."

"I know that. I just wanted her here."

He took a chance and pulled her close, kissing her pursed lips until she softened and opened to him. She put one hand on his chest as if to push him away, but he knew her game and caught it instead to his chest, pressing it between their bodies.

"You want, you want, always what you want," he teased her. "I should have cut your tongue out long ago." He circled her neck with the fingers of one hand, pressing lightly as his lips moved downward. He smiled when she sighed. *Yes, finally, she would relent.*

"I know what you're doing," she whispered.

"And?"

"You can't distract me."

"We shall see."

He kneeled down in front of her, his hands following the curve of her back, slipping lower on her buttocks as she writhed away from his seeking lips. He slid one hand under her dress, caressing her softness with his calloused hands.

"Take it off," he ordered.

"Winn," she said, her voice hoarse.

"If you want to wear it again, take it off. Now." He struggled to keep his words low, feeling his own control slipping away at the sight of her sun-kissed skin. She was thinner than normal, but her hips were round and full, fitting perfectly in his grasp. He caught his breath when she lifted the dress slowly over her head, the doeskin catching on her nipples for a moment before she shed it.

"Come here," he said. She offered no resistance when he pulled her to her knees in front of him, only a little gasp when his mouth fell upon her skin. When a strangled moan left her lips his control vanished, and he pushed her down to the bedding platform. Slick flesh collided, heated skin upon skin. So many others suddenly laid claim to his woman, and he did not care for it one bit. Did he only want her, or did he need her, or was it the power of possession like a spoiled youth that drove him? He did not know.

He could only keep her close and hope it would be enough.

14

Makedewa

Makedewa sheathed the new sword on his back, sliding it into the harness Erich had given him. He enjoyed the company of the Norse more than he would admit to his brother, knowing it was a heated topic to broach with Winn. Winn's kinfolk knew how to make strong weapons, and although they did not possess the firepower that the English had, the strength of their fighting power seemed formidable. He wondered if his brother would wish to settle in the village, as his headstrong wife obviously desired. Only the Creator knew how that decision would play out between his brother and his wife.

The other men had gathered in the training field, and although he was eager to join them, he decided to check on Rebecca first. She still owed him a reading lesson, and as he thought of collecting on the bargain a smile formed on his lips. Perhaps he might thaw her tender heart a bit with a stolen moment alone. It had been days since he held her in his arms, more than a week, in fact, and the thought of continuing where they left off roared like a slow fire within. Since the day he rescued her from the massacre he had waited patiently to gain her trust. Now that he had tasted what it was like to have a piece of her heart, the only thing he could think of was to have it again.

She was alone when he found her in Winn's Long House, dousing the remnants of the fire. He reveled in watching the sweet curve of her backside as she bent to work, her hair strewn over her shoulders in a cascade of coils. Eager to have her in his arms, he closed the door softly and threw the latch with a click, the sound causing her to swing around with a panicked look on her face. Her anxiety eased when she realized it was him, and it sent a surge of heat through his blood to see her smile. He unsheathed his sword and left it propped against the wall.

"Ye startled me!" she laughed as he crossed the space. He gathered her into his arms, covering her soft mouth with his and stifling the remnants of her exclamation.

"It's only me," he murmured. He glanced toward the door. "You owe me a reading lesson. I've come to collect."

She let out a nervous laugh and backed away, and he let her go. He sat down on the edge of the bedding platform for want of anywhere else to sit, determined to put her at ease.

"I have no books to teach ye here. Perhaps we should just…talk?" she suggested shyly, her skin flushing pink. He grinned, watching her slow her breaths, knowing that she was just as affected by him as he was her. He took her hands and pulled her close. He kissed each of her clenched fists and looked up into her eyes.

"Talk? I would hear your answer. I want you as my wife, but you have yet to tell me yes." His chest clenched when he saw her round eyes fill with tears, and he pulled her onto his lap in a reflexive motion. He wanted to soothe her, to chase away her doubt, yet he was at loss how to show her his intention, especially when even being in the same space with her drove him to the point of madness. He had not lain with a woman since he became a man, which had not bothered him so much until he found Rebecca. The last two years spent watching her, cultivating her trust, and dreaming of her when he lay alone at night had felt like a slow torture, yet it was now a torrid burn that distracted his every thought.

"Oh, Makedewa," she said softly. He inched back onto the furs, his hands trembling as he pulled her with him. She lay lightly across his chest, looking down, her curls spilling over her shoulders onto his chest. He scarce drew breath as he watched her, thrilled at the weight of her body lying over his, yet afraid she would flee. With a slow measured touch he slipped his hand into her hair and drew her mouth to his, filling his blood with fire when she moaned and settled against him.

What would please her? What would make her agree to be his wife?

He moved his lips down her throat, his fingers working the tie of her shift, groaning when she arched up against his hand. Damn her English garments that he had no idea how to remove. Aching to feel her flesh, he ran his hands beneath her skirts up along her soft thighs to settle on her hips, pushing the heap of fabric upward until his breechcloth was the only barrier between them. He let out a strangled moan when she kissed him, and be it the failure of restraint as a man or the pain of wanting her so long, he flipped her deftly onto her back.

He expected some tension because of her past, but when she wrapped her arms around his neck he was sure it would be fleeting. Her bared breasts pressed against his chest, her fingers digging into his shoulders. He murmured sweet words of love as his lips caressed her skin and his knee parted her thighs.

"*Nouwami*," he whispered. He raised his head to kiss her again, and then the breath left his chest in a painful blow. Her eyes were clenched closed, her throat constricted so much he could see her pulse throbbing beneath her jaw. A tear slid down her cheek.

He rolled onto his side and pulled her into his arms, pressing his face into her soft hair as she trembled against his chest.

"I cannot be a good wife to ye," she whispered, her eyes buried away from him. He shifted and grasped her chin, gently turning it upward. Her eyes were puffy, her cheeks streaked with tears.

"Yes, you will. We can wait for this. I will wait for you," he insisted. He wanted to tell her that he had waited so long already without assurance she would want him, but now that he knew she cared he at least had that to hold. If only she would accept his pledge, he would give her as long as she needed.

"I wish ye to hold me like this, so much so it aches," she said. "But I fear I cannot be a wife to a man."

"If only I may hold you, that is enough for now," he replied, his voice strained. He had a sickly feeling of what she meant, and he did not want to hear the words.

"But if that is all I can give ye? Nay. I fear to see anger in your eyes when you look at me."

She stood up and gathered her shift to a semblance of decency. He could see her fingers tremble and his frustration rose. *Did she think so little of him?* Did she truly believe he only wished to share her bed, and that was all being a wife meant to him?

"You think I am angered now?" he asked. With her back to him he saw her shoulders sag, and she wrapped her arms around herself in a protective manner.

"I fear to look at ye," she admitted. "I can tell when ye are fierce. I see yer jaw is hard, and yer eyes are black as coals. I know the look of a man angered." Despite his agitation, he moved beside her, taking care not to touch her as they sat on the edge of the bedding platform.

"I am angered at the man who hurt you. I have no anger at you," he replied. "I would kill any man who harmed you," he added darkly. He reached for her hand, and sighed when she jerked it away.

"I am sorry," she whispered, her lip trembling. "Perhaps we should just…lay together. I will not stop ye. Then perhaps it will be easier."

Her suggestion tore through him like a blade and he jumped to his feet.

"No. Why do you say such a thing?" he said, his voice rising despite his effort to contain it. He ran his hands through his hair, then dropped to his knees before her. He laid his head down on her knees, wishing she would put hands on him to give him some semblance of hope, yet her fists remained closed at her sides. "I would never–I could not hurt you that way. When we lay together, it will be because you wish it, not to chase a ghost away."

"I fear the ghost of that man will always haunt me."

He clenched her skirts as her fingers slid over his head, holding him to her lap. Her scent was too close, too inviting, her skin too soft as he held her. Her tears no longer fell, her face now more a mask of certainty in her own failure than one hopeful of trudging through it. He needed to think, to figure out a way to mend things, but he could not do that when she looked at him with those haunted blue eyes, begging him to just take her no matter what the consequence.

"I am nothing like that man. He was of my people, but he was no warrior. Is it him you see, when you look at me?" he asked, raising his eyes to meet hers. Her throat tightened and she said nothing, looking down to avoid his stare. Her silence was far worse than what her words might have been.

He stood up away from her. He grabbed his new sword and sheathed it over his shoulder, then addressed her as calmly as he could muster with his back to her.

"Take your rest, *chulentet*. I must join the men, we can speak on this later," he muttered.

He felt like a swine for leaving her. Yet it was how he had dealt with painful emotion his entire life, and he knew no other way to journey.

15

Rebecca

"Oh, I thought Kwetii was with you."

Rebecca looked up at the sound of Maggie's voice. She wiped the back of her hand over her nose and then over her flyaway hair, acutely aware that she looked like a windblown mess. Except her appearance was not due to the wind, unless one counted the man who had just fled her side with the speed of a beach-swept breeze. She swallowed back a sob at the thought of his back to her and his cold words before he left her. Yes, she had angered him, even if he would not admit it so, and she feared there would never be a way to give him what he wanted.

"Nay, Teyas took her to play with other children. They have many little ones here," Rebecca answered. Maggie tilted her head a bit to the side, her mane of red hair falling across her face. With her lips pursed tight and her eyebrows raised, Rebecca knew that look. As much as she loved Maggie, the woman was tenacious when it came to knowing secrets, and if she suspected one held anything back she would be at it like a horsefly on sweating skin.

"What troubles you? Your eyes are red," Maggie asked. Rebecca shook her head in denial, knowing full well it would not be enough to placate Maggie.

"It is nothing to worry ye. Go on, be about yer tasks," she said. Instead of listening, Maggie plunked down on the bedding platform next to her. It was the space Makedewa had occupied only a few short moments ago, she thought with a pang in her belly. *What if Maggie had found them, doing what they were doing?* Her friend would surely think her nothing more than a harlot, as her poor dead mother would have.

"Come with me then. I'm going to watch the men train with Erich. I'd like you with me," Maggie offered. "Unless you'd rather tell me what makes you cry."

Rebecca sighed. It was no use keeping anything from her.

"Makedewa asked me to be his wife," she murmured, her voice cracking somewhat. She jumped when Maggie let out a squeal and threw her arms around her, hugging her and jumping up and down.

"That's wonderful! Oh, that's perfect! We'll have a beautiful wedding here–I'm sure Marcus will help, and–"

"There will be no wedding," Rebecca interrupted, putting an abrupt stop to Maggie's excited tirade.

"Why? What happened?"

"I willna be a good wife for any man, Maggie. Especially one such as he."

Maggie drew back, her brows squinted down over her bright jade eyes as she shook her head in a motherly manner.

"You'd be a fine wife to him, sweetheart," she said. "I'm sure he'd treat you kindly. He loves you so, it's plain to see."

Rebecca felt the tears escape at Maggie's declaration, and she let the other woman hold her then. Yes, she loved him as well, if she was bent on making confessions. It only made it that much more difficult to hear that Makedewa loved her the same way.

"Does it always feel so…so frightful…when a man lays with a woman?" she asked shyly, her voice barely audible. She knew her cheeks flamed when she spoke, but Maggie was the only one she trusted enough who could give her any hope.

Maggie rocked her gently as she would have done with Kwetii.

"No, lamb, it's not. It's a beautiful thing. I'm sure you would find it was very special with Makedewa. He would never hurt you," Maggie replied, her voice comforting, even as Rebecca heard the nervous falter in her tone. She swallowed back her pride, determined to ask the questions on her mind.

"But I've heard ye sometimes at night. It sounds like Winn's killing ye."

It was Maggie's turn to blush, and her skin flushed from her ears to her chest. Her breathing came a bit faster as she struggled to answer, and Rebecca waited patiently. If anyone would tell her the truth, it would be Maggie.

"No, no. I know it must sound–it sounds strange. It's only because we both enjoy it. It's normal to–to make sounds," Maggie stammered. "Because it feels...nice."

Rebecca buried her face in her hands. She understood what Maggie was getting at, and she certainly knew the pleasure of Makedewa's touch on her body. It was what came after kissing that she was afraid she could never do. Worse yet, she feared disappointing him. She was no idiot; she witnessed the raw passion between Maggie and Winn on a daily basis. Yet Maggie never seemed angered or upset after their episodes, in fact, she seemed placated. He made her happy, no matter what he was doing to her in their marriage bed. She identified with the happy aspect, as she had been the happiest of her life since the day Makedewa confessed his feelings for her. Yet along with the pleasure of exploring touches and stolen kisses, fear of the natural course of things began to smother her thoughts. Until that very afternoon, she thought she could push it aside.

"Will ye send me back to the English if I do not marry him?" she whispered. Maggie pulled her into a hug.

"Of course not. You're family, no matter what. You will always have a place with us," Maggie insisted.

They clung together for a long time in silence, with Maggie rocking her as if they were born blood sisters.

16

Maggie

Maggie walked beside Erich to the training field. She could see the men gathered in a semi-circle, watching a pair of combatants as they sparred. Winn stood with his brothers among the Norsemen, his legs banked shoulder-width apart, his hands folded across his bare chest as he watched. It was strange to see him amongst the others, these men whose bloodlines he shared. She was surprised to see Makedewa wearing a fur lined harness, similar to what Marcus wore, with a shiny new steel sword strapped to his back. Makedewa was the flamboyant one compared to his brothers, and seeing him attired like the Norseman was something to behold.

"Why are they training? Do you expect trouble?" she asked.

Erich showed her to a rough hewn wooden bench and sat down beside her, his eyes on the men. She wondered why he did not join them.

"We must always be ready. Trouble comes when ye least expect," he replied. He tilted his head to her and pointed to the two men fighting. "See that lad? The one who first found yer family in the woods? That man is yer cousin, Young Cormaic, my son."

He was the tall young man who had spoken with Marcus before Erich intervened. Metal clashed and squealed as they struck, the sounds of hollow thuds spiking the silence from the blows upon their shields. Cormaic was the aggressor in the pair, pushing his opponent back until the man knelt down in defeat. Erich grinned.

"My son has never been defeated since he reached manhood."

"He looks tough," she mumbled. He raised an eyebrow.

"What meaning is that?"

"Strong. Tough means strong." She looked down at her hands, folding them together in her lap. "Your wife. Is she here?"

He nodded. "I will take you to her. She would have come sooner to see ye, but she tends a sick man."

"All right."

"We can take yer wean as well. Yer aunt will be happy to meet ye both."

She heard the way his voice cracked, and stole a curious glance at him out of the corner of her eye. His almond shaped eyes were squinted nearly shut as he watched the men, his back stiff and straight beside her. He cleared his throat with a cough and kept his eyes averted.

"Dagr has been my friend since we were children. He's done well in protecting ye. I'm proud to see ye grown, so much like yer mother. It is something I never thought to see with mine own eyes, so I thank ye for it."

"You don't have to thank me. Just please…try to understand how strange this is. I grew up with only Marcus and my Grandfather. You can't expect me to–to know how to act."

He smiled a bit, and his eyes softened.

"Ye staying here is enough. We have plenty of time now."

"I don't know how long we will stay, Erich–uh, uncle–I don't even know what to call you!"

"Ye can call me Erich if ye like," he said quietly. She bit her lower lip, keeping her gaze on the warriors.

"All right. Erich then. But my husband wants us to go live with the Nansemond, I'm sure we won't be here much longer."

"I spoke to him on it. He says he will leave ye here for a time, whilst he rides to do his tribe's bidding. I tried to have him leave off of it but he would not be swayed. He's a hard man, yer Indian husband."

"He's not leaving me anywhere. He wouldn't just leave us here," she snapped, agitated at the revelation that Erich knew more of her husband's plans than she did. It was unlike Winn to make such a decision without at least telling her of it, and she was not ready to believe he would leave her among strangers. Family, yes, but they were still strangers, no matter if one was her uncle and one was Winn's long-lost father.

Erich laughed, a hearty guffaw that brought a flush to her cheeks.

"What is so funny?"

"Ye think ye can turn that man's vow once he's made it? He's a bull-headed lad if ever I met one, not likely ye have any say in it!"

"Humph," she snorted. She turned to him, lips pursed. "You have a lot to learn about women from the future, *uncle*."

"Aye, surely I do!" he laughed. She smiled along with him despite her annoyance.

Her grin diminished when she saw the next warrior enter the circle. It was Winn, and he held a long sword. Sunlight shimmered off the polished metal as he turned it in his hands, as if he tested its weight. Makedewa and Chetan looked on from the sidelines, and several other Norsemen pounded him on the back as he adjusted his grip on the weapon. Cormaic stood a few paces away, stretching his arms above his head.

"What is he doing?" she asked, more to herself than to Erich.

"Fighting, fer sure," he grinned. She stood up and made to move past him, but he caught her by the upper arm and deposited her back in her seat.

"He's never used a sword!" Maggie said.

"He's doing just fine. Keep yerself here, are ye daft thinking ye might stop them?" She blew out her air in a snort and crossed her arms over her chest.

"This is ridiculous!" she hissed. "I'm going down there!"

"No, my lady, ye are not!"

He leaned down, so close she could see the crease across his forehead and the tiny flecks of gold within his green eyes. He placed a hand on either side of her on the bench.

"If ye want to shame him before the men, then go down there. If not, I bid ye to keep yer arse on the bench and pay heed as yer man fights."

"I don't want to shame him," she said softly.

"Then pay him honor by watching. Do they teach ye no manners in the time ye came from? I swear ye act right barmy!"

She ducked her head as the unwanted grin crossed her lips.

"You sound like Granddad. He used to say I had rocks in my brain."

"Well, Da was a sharp man. Might been some truth to that," he replied. He stood back and opened his arms, waving a hand at the warriors. "So ye'll sit then, like I bid ye?"

"If you're asking, then, yes," she agreed.

She flinched at the clash of metal upon metal, her attention captivated by the fight before them. Winn was not quite as tall as Cormaic, yet he was equal in musculature. Wearing only a breechcloth and leggings, Winn seemed less encumbered than his opponent, his gait swift and precise as he tested the limits of the weapon. Cormaic was more brawn than speed, yet he was no opponent to be dismissed as even she could see. Each blow connected with a squeal and thud of the weapons, and she saw his muscles standing out as tense sinews when Winn deflected each assault.

Winn stepped back as he blocked an overhead blow, shaking his head as Cormaic advanced. He adjusted the sword in his hands, twirling it before he gripped it more securely. Cormaic's skin was drenched with sweat as he approached, his chest heaving as he prepared his sword for another strike. When he struck high again, Winn went down onto one knee.

Erich put a hand on her shoulder when she gasped and started to rise, and she sat back down with an audible thump.

"Sit!" he warned. She gritted her jaw.

Cormaic stepped back and Winn rose slowly to his feet. He adjusted the sword again, his face a blank mask as he considered it. Giving him no more quarter, Cormaic closed in, striking low as the men around them roared their approval. She felt numb and heavy all over as she watched, bound to the bench even without Erich's hand keeping her there.

Winn blocked the blow and threw Cormaic back with one powerful twist of the sword. Cormaic stumbled, recovered, and a perplexed look crossed his face as he looked down at his hands. Fresh blood stained his wrist where Winn had marked him.

She put her hands over her eyes as the two men crashed together in a spray of metal and straining flesh. The sounds of the battle were worse than the vision, so it was not long before she parted her fingers to peer out between them.

Suddenly, Winn had Cormaic in retreat, stumbling backward as Winn advanced with a series of heavy blows. Low to the side, low to the other, and then high overhead.

Cormaic fell onto his backside with the point of Winn's sword nicking his neck. She could see Cormaic's throat as he swallowed and a trickle of blood ran down his skin where the sword pierced him, his chest heaving as he lay immobile in the dirt. There was no sound or movement from the men as they all watched.

Winn looked down on Cormaic for a long moment. Finally, he drew the sword away and extended a hand. A wide grin crossed Cormaic's face, and he clasped Winn's arm to get to his feet.

"Well done, lad. Well done," Erich said. "Son of a Chief, no doubt."

Maggie rolled her eyes. The gesture was entirely lost on her uncle, but it made her feel better, in any case.

***

Erich's wife was a buxom woman, her smile a rash of round flushed cheeks and a sweet heart-shaped face. When Erich made a short explanation of who Maggie was, Gwen flew across the room and tackled her head-on, nearly knocking her off her feet as she cried.

"Oh, child!" was all she said, repeating it as if it were the only thing she knew to say. "Oh, sweet Odin, child!" Although she struggled with feeling any connection to the strangers she now called kin, as the older woman embraced her and sobbed, Maggie felt tears rim her own eyes. She had never felt the embrace of a mother, nor anything close, and to feel the arms around her as she had often held her own child brought a sting of emotion she could not deny. Warm, soft, welcoming–the embrace of one who loved unconditionally–it was enough to thaw the ice in her heart.

"What do they call ye? Margret, ye say?" she woman asked, looking toward Erich for confirmation.

"Maggie they named 'er. It's like yon Margret, I suppose. But Esa's daughter she is. My niece, all the same. Our own Blooded *MacMhaolian*, returned to us."

Maggie glanced back at Erich, who leaned against the doorframe, watching them. He smiled, but she could see the pain in his eyes when he spoke her mother's name. She wanted to ask of her, but she feared the barrier it might bring to the blossoming relationship they had formed. After all, she had waited a lifetime to know her kin, a few more days would not be so long before she could demand answers.

"Ye used the Bloodstone to come here? Dinna Dagr tell ye how dangerous it is? Even if he meant to see ye married to his son, he risks too much!" Gwen suddenly squealed, pushing Maggie back to glare at Erich. Erich shrugged, apparently expecting the question.

"Dagr dinna send her back. It was an accident, ye know how it can happen, woman," he answered, his words clipped. "And she is married to his son. His *Indian* son. It happened with no help from him or I, so bide yer venom." She scowled. Maggie noticed the inflection in Erich's tone, and the warning glance he shot his wife.

"Well, good thing ye have yer aunt here, child. It seems like ye need a good dose of help if you'll be using that blasted magic!" she grumbled.

"None of that, Gwen. She'll not be using any more of it, not while I take breath. I'll not have ye foolin' with it. Ye know the laws as well as I."

"What laws?" Maggie asked. Gwen and Erich fell silent. "Well, are you going to tell me, or do I have to ask Marcus? And what is this nonsense about marrying a son of Marcus?"

Erich uttered a groan and waved his hand at them in dismissal.

"Yer mother was the last Blooded *MacMhaolian*, the most powerful ones among us. We meant to protect her, and ye, by sending ye forward in time. But using a Bloodstone to return to the past like ye did is forbidden. No one will question Chief Dagr, but ye must know it's not permitted among our people. Best ye forget about the Bloodstone. Leave off with it, aye?"

"So Marcus can do whatever he wants. Must be nice to be the Chief," Maggie muttered.

"He followed ye back to see ye safe, child. He's a good Chief, and a fine man. Ye'd do well to be wed to any son of his," Gwen murmured. Erich shot her a seething stare.

Gwen put an arm around Maggie's shoulders and shuffled her away as she muttered under her breath. Maggie could not help smiling. Her aunt seemed like a right fine woman.

"Here, take ye some mead, it's from the old stock, but still fine," she said to Erich, pushing a pewter tankard across the table toward him. He grunted in acknowledgement and sat down on the bench, his sword clattering against the wood and catching on the edge of the table.

"Take ye sword off, ye bloody fookin idiot!" Gwen screeched. Maggie covered her mouth with her hand to hide her smile, pretending she needed to cough, while she watched Erich's eyes open wide as he scrambled to right himself. Clearly he respected the woman, and she was certainly the kind of woman Maggie could see being friends with.

"I should clapper yer tongue, ye know that, woman?" he snarled, taking a swig of the mead once he was settled. He raised an eyebrow at her, his mouth twisted in a half-grin.

"Aye, and yer arse needs a good washin', ye bletherin' fool, but ye no hear me makin' sass about it, do ye?"

"Ah!" Erich growled.

"Right then!" Gwen retorted, as she glowered at him. "Here, keep the girl company whilst I tend to the *lucht*."

"What does *lucht* mean?" Maggie whispered. Erich grinned.

"It's not fit fer yer ears," he replied with a chuckle.

The older woman swung one thick blond braid over her shoulder then grabbed a pitcher and a stack of linen. Erich shrugged and waved her off, so she followed Gwen into the back of the house where she ducked behind a curtain hanging across the thatched roof.

Lying on a narrow cot was a sleeping, or unconscious man. He was too tall for the bed, his feet hanging off at the ankles, and his shoulders resting a good two inches off each side so much it appeared he might topple over. A thick dark beard covered his face, and as Gwen knelt down next to him and put a sponge to his forehead, Maggie sucked in a sharp breath.

"What's wrong with him?" she whispered.

"He took a blow to the head. He's been like this for past a sennight. Why does it trouble you, girl?" Gwen asked as she wiped his sweating brow.

Maggie sank down beside her and took the man's hand.

"It's Benjamin. We've been looking for him."

***

Maggie watched as Marcus sat in silence beside him, unmoving as he stared down at his lost son. Finally, he bowed his head, his thick curling hair falling gently forward to shield the sadness on his face, and he placed one large hand over Benjamin's. Clasped together and folded on his chest, Benjamin looked like a body prepared for burial, not a man who might yet live. There were no outward signs of severe injury, yet his skin held a grey pallor and the right side of his forehead had a slight swelling accompanied by a bluish-yellow bruise. To her it did not appear serious, yet evidently, it was the injury that put him down.

When she confided to Gwen who Benjamin was, both her aunt and uncle were shocked. Erich confessed his culpability in Benjamin's current condition. About a week prior, the English stranger came into the village asking questions about Bloodstones and Time Walkers, and then became violent when they told him to leave. It was Erich who clouted him in the head, intending to give him a chance to cool off. Instead the blow rendered him unconscious, and he had been unresponsive ever since.

When she heard Marcus sigh, she could no longer let him suffer alone. Although she knew Erich did not want her to intervene with their newly restored Chief, he knew nothing of her relationship with Marcus. Yes, things between them had changed irrevocably, yet he was the same man who had raised her. She would give him no less than the comfort he had always shown her.

"I'm so sorry," she said softly, placing her hand on his shoulder from behind. His throat contracted as he swallowed.

"The last time I saw him, he was only a lad. Look at him now, a man full grown," he said quietly. "We canna take care of him here. Not like this," he said.

She held her tongue. What he alluded to was clearly forbidden, as both Erich and Gwen had proclaimed. Yet Marcus was their leader, a man they called Chief. Would he challenge them all by using the Bloodstone magic again? She had little doubt. If she knew anything about Marcus, it was that he would do whatever it took to keep his family safe. If he thought returning Benjamin to the future would save him, then he would do it, and God help any man who would stand in his way.

"He could wake up anytime. There's no wound, just some swelling," she said.

"It's been more than a week, Maggie. Ye and I both know enough of modern medicine to see it's serious. They canna care for him here, not like doctors do where we came from."

"You wouldn't do that. You can't leave," she replied.

"Says who? I'll do as I need, as I always have."

"You'd leave me? And your son? For Christ's sake, if you do that, I will never forgive you!" she snapped, trying to keep her voice level, yet failing miserably.

"He's my son. He needs a hospital, and I don't see one here for three hundred years!" he bellowed back. "I'll do what I must to see my son healed!"

"There are *laws* on using the magic, aren't there?" she shouted. "You can't just jump around through time however you please!"

"I can if I see fit, it's my right!" he bellowed.

"Benjamin is not the only son you have, *Chief Dagr*!" she shot back. She felt a hand on her upper arm and shook it angrily off. "No, leave me be! If you leave, I will never forgive you! Do you hear me, Marcus Neilsson? Never."

She swung around on her heel, and crashed into her husband, who had been standing behind her. Her heart sank as she realized he must have heard the entire exchange. She shrugged past him and left the cottage, back to her own temporary space.

***

The drying line was too high for her to reach, so she searched the room for something to stand on. Makedewa had hung it for her earlier in the day, stringing a thin piece of braided rawhide across two rafters on the roof so that she could dry clothes more effectively by the fire. As she jumped and tried to toss a damp swaddling cloth across the improvised clothesline, she heard a chuckle behind her.

"You do it, then," she said, handing the nappy to her husband. He laid it carefully over the line, adjusted the adjacent garment, and gave her a smirk.

"Have you always been so small, wife?"

She smiled in return, but she knew it did not reach her eyes. She ducked her gaze and grabbed a pile of clothes, sorting through them to keep busy. His breath on her skin was warm, his unique scent sending goose bumps down the back of her neck. The smell of damp earth from training and a touch of evergreen, mixed with the sweat of his work, it was his smell, and she closed her eyes to it for a moment. He put his hands on her shoulders, and kissed her ear very softly.

"Will you tell me?" he asked.

"Tell you what?" she murmured.

"What troubles you."

She turned to face him, wringing her hands in the damp shift she held.

"I'm just shocked, that's all."

He nodded.

"As am I. Do you think he will live?"

"Does it matter?" she said, regretting the words the moment they left her lips.

He dropped his hands from her shoulders and stepped back. She watched as he silently removed his weapons and placed them on the table, first his knife, then the new sword at his side. It was heavy, a broad steel blade, the handle encrusted with colorful stones. Along one edge near the hilt were symbols she could not decipher, but she suspected they were runes. She had seen rune symbols carved into nearly everything in the village.

"A sword?" she asked.

"From Erich. He said it belonged to Drustan Neilsson, father to Pale Feather. It is still quite sharp." Winn traced his finger along the length of the blade, looking up to meet her stare. "I will leave today to fetch the English prisoner from the Nansemond. Then I will bring Finola here. Chetan will ride with me. We will not be gone long."

"But I don't want you to go," she said.

"Makedewa will stay here."

"I don't want your brother, I want you," she insisted. She saw his jaw flex and his brows dart down. Could she put her foot in her mouth any further?

"I meant–" she added quickly, but he cut her off.

"I know what you meant. It changes nothing. You will stay here. I will return soon. Prepare to leave when I return, we will join the Nansemond."

"But–"

"Enough!" he snapped, snatching the linens from her hand. "I say where we live, not you. I will hear no more on this, woman!" He looked at the clothes for a moment, then bunched them up and tossed them into a basket on the floor. He threw his hands up and made an agitated grunting sound, cursing in Paspahegh from what she could gather.

"Fine. Do what you want. I'll just sit here and twiddle my thumbs while you're gone, like a good little wife!" she shouted. She grabbed the linen basket off the floor and moved to stalk past him. When she reached the door she paused, her chest heaving with shallow breaths and her heart racing. What on earth were they fighting about? Was it Benjamin's presence bringing so much strife between them? She heard him let out a long sigh and then felt his presence at her side.

"Here. Let me help you," he said, his voice strained.

"All right," she agreed. She handed him the basket. He tucked it under one arm, and cupped her face with his free hand.

"A good little wife, hmm?"

She smiled despite her annoyance. When he kissed her, relief flooded through her. They would not part angry at each other.

"As always," she murmured.

17

Winn

It had been nearly two years since the Great Assault. Although his uncle, the Weroance Opechancanough had envisioned it would drive the English back across the sea, the coordinated effort served only to worsen conditions for both the Indians and the English. As Winn and Chetan rode through the lands of *Tsenacommacah* to the village of Mattanock, he felt a growing sense of dread. Perhaps it was his imagination, or only his own bitterness, but he could swear the songs of the birds had deserted the Powhatan lands, and the very earth they rode on wept for a time long destroyed. He knew Chetan noticed it as well, as the hollow tap of hooves on packed clay emitted the only sound in the forest.

The village looked worse than before. The Nansemond were a peaceful people, but nevertheless they had supported Opechancanough in his war and they had paid the price. As they rode through the fields, he could see the crops were minimal, hardly enough to sustain a family such as Winn's, let alone a village of hungry people. What food they managed to grow without being burned by the English he did not know, but if the sight of the soot-blackened fields was an indication, he suspected it was not much. Winn could still smell the smoke from the most recent burning.

He saw Chetan bow his head as they passed through the fields, his brother's stout body nodding with the rhythm of his pony. It was brisk again at night as fall descended and Chetan wore a fur-lined cloak Cormaic had gifted to him. It was decorated with the strange rune marks the Norse used on everything, and knew Chetan would wear it proudly among the Indians. No one would dare question Chetan.

A group of children rang out welcome when they arrived, and as he listened to the joyful cries and laughter Winn felt an ache in his chest. He had lived in Mattanock with the Nansemond for a time, and although to some he had never been truly accepted, he had been treated fairly. For a fleeting moment he recalled how Pepamhu had branded part of the tattoo on his torso, and his hand reached down to cover it as if by reflex. It no longer ached, but it marked him.

Pepamhu came forth to greet them, flanked by his mother. She looked older than he remembered, her face thinner than he recalled and her clothes fitting loose about her body. Pepamhu, however, retained his lean disposition, appearing younger than his years. His physique still reflected a man who trained daily with his warriors, always prepared to face the next threat to his people. After the children took the ponies, Winn and Chetan bowed in respectful greeting to the brave. Winn was glad to see the man Maggie called his 'step-father' and he knew Chetan was happy to visit as well.

"It has been too long, my sons," Pepamhu said, clapping his hand down on Chetan's shoulder as he glanced at Winn. "I hope your journey was peaceful."

"It was," Winn agreed. His mother stood quietly at Pepamhu's side and Winn gave her a tiny smile. She would wait to be spoken to. He wondered briefly if his wife would ever behave as his mother did, but shook the thought from his mind. No, Maggie did not have a submissive bone in her body, and he would want it no other way. Despite their differences, he loved her spirit and would not wish it dampened.

When Pepamhu motioned for them to follow, his mother reached out and touched his arm as he passed, dipping her head down. He gave her hand a gentle squeeze and continued inside the Great Yehakin with her husband. Winn would find her after speaking with Pepamhu. Women were not permitted inside when the men gathered, but he knew he would see her after they spoke.

A handful elder tribesmen were gathered inside when they sat down. There was a high platform in the corner which remained empty, reserved for the times the Weroance visited the village. Pepamhu was a leader by his skill in negotiation; he spoke several languages as well as Winn did, and he had a talent for securing peace between enemies when all else had failed. Mattanock had lost its minor Weroance not long after the Great Assault, as many of the tribes had, and they had not recovered the strength of their numbers. Winn noticed a few *Tassantassas* among the villagers, which was not unheard of, especially since the Nansemond had claimed several English prisoners on the day of the Great Assault. Winn wondered which woman was the one to be returned to the English in trade.

"*Hupotam*," Pepamhu said, holding out a pipe in offering. Winn nodded briefly as he received it, taking a long, slow inhale of the sweet smoke before he passed it to Chetan. It had been months since he enjoyed such things, and although it never crossed his mind to miss it, his spirit lifted as the tingle settled through his blood. As he exhaled, his limbs felt heavy and he relaxed forward to rest his arms on his upraised knees.

"You come for the English woman. She is not happy to leave, but she will go with you. Governor Wyatt has given much in exchange, so we will honor the trade," Pepamhu said. The others in the circle continued to pass the pipe, the tangy smoke a cloud around their heads as they murmured in agreement.

"Good. We will leave when the sun rises. I wish to return to my family without delay," Winn answered.

"How is your Red Woman? And your daughter?"

The pipe made rounds back to him and he gladly took it. It was a powerful blend, causing a ripple of numbness to creep over his skin.

"They are well. We stay with Pale Feather's people for now. I know not when we will leave them."

The murmurs abruptly ceased, and all heads turned toward Winn. Pepamhu made a coarse grunting command at the elder tribesmen and they resumed speaking amongst themselves, but Winn felt the unease among them. Yes, his wife was safe, according to the order of Opechancanough, but the Powhatans had hunted the Time Walkers for too long to forget. Although the Nansemond elders knew of the Norse village, speaking of it aloud was another matter entirely.

Winn straightened his back. He would not cower to them over the *Tassantassas* blood he bore, as he once had. He was no longer that young brave who sought such approval.

"So Pale Feather has returned, and you join them in their village."

"For now."

Chetan leaned in toward them, his voice low.

"His father is Chief of the Norsemen, and a good fighter. They call Winn *Jarl* now. Jarl Winn, Jarl Winn," Chetan chuckled. Winn scowled at his brother as Pepamhu grinned.

"Pale Feather was a great warrior, for a *Tassantassas*," Pepamhu agreed. "I see you still have two arms, and two legs. Was your father a worthy fighter?"

Winn's eyes narrowed. His mother's husband had been the closest thing Winn ever knew to a father, and Pepamhu was well aware of the anger Winn held toward the man who sired him. To see Chetan and Pepamhu make light of it caused his arms to clench and his back to stiffen once more.

"He fights well, but I am better," Winn muttered through gritted teeth. "Perhaps I should show you, Chetan."

Chetan rolled his eyes and plucked the pipe from Winn's hands.

"Now, or later, brother? I think you forget the strength of my fist," Chetan smirked. Pepamhu laughed aloud, jabbing Winn in the ribs with a bony elbow.

"Ah, enough, the two of you!" he said. "There is much to speak of tonight. Your sister, she is well?"

Winn nodded.

"She seems so," Winn replied, eager to change the topic of the discussion.

"It is time to see her back to her mother. The warrior Osawas has given many gifts for her hand, so she must return here to marry him," Pepamhu said.

Winn's head jerked up.

"Osawas of Weanock?" Winn asked. "To Teyas? She is to be married?"

"She is too long without a husband. Would you have her stay with your family, with no hope for a husband of her own? It will make her mother happy to see this match. It will please me as well," Pepamhu answered.

Chetan passed Winn the pipe, but he waved his brother off. He had no idea if Teyas wished to marry or not, but he had learned something of the ways of women after watching his wife and sister over the last two years. They had a strong bond, one which would pain them terribly to break. Yet if Teyas left to live with the Weanock, she must leave alone. It was at least five days ride to Weanock, and that meant it would be a very long time between visits. How he would break such news to his sister and his wife he did not know.

"I know she must have a husband. But she has grown attached to my wife, and I fear they will not wish to part."

Pepamhu raised a brow.

"Then you must show them the way," he said. "Return here with Teyas after you exchange the English prisoner. Osawas will arrive with his family, and I want my daughter here to welcome them."

Winn opened his mouth for a moment and then closed it. Chetan uttered a low cough, clearing his throat and exhaling a long breath of smoke. Chetan leaned forward, pushing Winn aside.

"We will see our sister home, father. Do not worry. It is a great match," Chetan murmured, casting a sideways glance at Winn.

Pepamhu nodded, and they resumed sharing the pipe in silence.

***

Winn spotted his mother walking toward him as he made way to the Great Fire. He shook his head a bit to clear the remnants of the smoke, feeling his stomach rumble as the scent of fresh cooked meat filled his nostrils. At least he would enjoy a good meal before he returned to the Norse, and perhaps have a few words with his mother. He did not wish to upset her, but he thought she would want to know that Pale Feather returned.

"My son," she said softly, bowing her head down before him. He placed both hands on her shoulders and pulled her gently upward, shaking his head.

"No, mother, please rise," he insisted. She smiled as he kissed her cheek.

"It has been too long. How is Kwetii? Does she have a new name yet? And Ahi Kekeleksu? I miss the children."

"They grow fast, like weeds in a swamp. Kwetii has the look of her mother, and a temper to match," he grinned. Chulensak Asuwak laughed, her weathered face creased in a grin over her small white teeth.

"What color grows her hair?" she asked.

"Still black as a raven. At least she has that much of me."

They walked side by side to the Great Fire, where the entire village was gathered for the meal. He noticed Chetan sitting with Pepamhu, deep in conversation. The warrior had always favored Chetan, and although Pepamhu claimed Winn as a son, Winn had known he was different. Chetan looked much like Pepamhu. Short, stout, with a squared stubborn jaw and almond-shaped brown eyes, the men shared many traits. For a moment, Winn was reminded of how Benjamin resembled Marcus.

Perhaps someday he would have a son with Maggie, one who might share his features in the same way. With all the future talk and bleak predictions, it seemed a simple thing to hope for, yet it comforted him to think of such base desires for their lives.

"And Pale Feather? He has returned to you?" Chulensak Asuwak murmured.

Winn nodded.

"I know not why you married him, mother. He is nothing like us."

She smiled, casting her soft brown eyes downward, her face holding a secret amusement he wondered if she would share.

"Your father was kind to me, and a good husband. Would you hear now why we were married, my stubborn son?"

"No," he muttered.

She stopped walking and grabbed his wrist, her fingers wrapped in a surprisingly tight grip.

"Pepamhu was always the man of my heart. Your uncle forbid us to marry, and he arranged Pepamhu's marriage to another woman. Opechancanough thought he must control everything, even the heart of his sister. You should know no man can sway a woman's heart once it has set."

"Stop, mother, I do not wish to hear this."

"You will hear it!" she hissed, stomping her foot so that even her long braid shook. "I disobeyed your uncle, and I met with Pepamhu. Even though he was married, and it was wrong, I met with him. One day, a warrior found me leaving Pepamhu, and he told Opechancanough. I was to be shamed before the village for meeting with a married man...and my brother wished to see Pepamhu dead for my shame."

"You make no sense. Then why Pale Feather? Why did you wed him?" Winn snapped, listening to her tirade despite his agitation.

"Pale Feather went to Opechancanough, in front of the entire village. Your father claimed it was him that I met in the woods that day, not Pepamhu. My brother accepted his claim, and he arranged our marriage that day. Pepamhu was saved from death, and my shame was spared. Pale Feather is a good man, no matter what you think of his absence. I would have remained his loyal wife, if he had stayed here in this time."

"But you say you wanted Pepamhu."

"Yes, I did. He has always held my heart. When my brother ordered the death of the Time Walkers, we helped them in secret. Some were able to get away, they are the ones that you stay with now. Pale Feather was trapped here, with me, and a few others he wished to protect. Pepamhu helped him hide until he could use his Bloodstone magic to leave. Your father gave Pepamhu all the wealth he owned before he left, so that Pepamhu could take me as a second wife."

Winn fell silent. Never could he have imagined Marcus was such a selfless man. All his life he had thought of his father as a deserter, a coward, no better than any English scum. Yet if what his mother said was true, it seemed the man had sacrificed much more than many a man could bear.

"Are you so different from your father?" she asked quietly. He raised his eyes to hers, chagrined by the twinkle of mischief he noted there when the matter between them was so serious.

"We are nothing alike," he answered.

"Humph," she smiled. "You shall see. So you will stay with the Norsemen. I hear Pale Feather is a brave leader to them, he will be proud to have you by his side."

"I have made no such decision. My future lies where it is safe for my family, and I am not certain the village is that place."

"Winkeohkwet," she said, squeezing his hand. "You belong to more than one place, and there is no shame in that. I only see shame in a man who will not embrace his true path. Do not let your anger stray your journey. I fear you will regret it if you do. Please think on that before you decide."

"Fine. I will think on it. Go join the women," he mumbled.

He kissed his mother on her upraised cheek, and then left her to join the men.

***

Winn and Chetan escorted the English captive back to Jamestown without incident, and then rode up on the isolated farm where Finola lived and worked. It was far enough away from the city that it appeared clean and tidy, unlike the squalor those inside the palisades seemed to enjoy living in. It was a working farm, with a large barn housing a small trading post, one they visited often. It was the safest place for outsiders like Winn to obtain the few items they needed, and whenever they visited they could see that Finola was faring well. This time, however, she did not run out to greet them, and when only a servant boy stood in the yard, he felt a twinge of unease.

"Where is the healer today, boy?" Winn asked.

The tow-headed youth scowled at him and snatched the reins with grubby hands. His threadbare breeches were torn at both knees, and his shirt, which may have been white at one time, was tattered at the cuffs and hemline. Winn wondered if the English had any care at all for the well-being of their servants. At least the Indians saw their captives fed and clothed properly.

"She's taken ill. Aren't ye her blood kin? My master will be glad to see ye."

"Ill? How so? Why did he not send for us?" Winn replied, his ire rising. If his grandmother had been ill, the blasted English should have sent word. He should not be surprised at their incompetence, but still it angered him.

"She won't move or eat. Maybe an apoplexy. She just stares at ye, sometime she speaks in tongues. Might be the devil himself."

Chetan handed his reins to the boy and then followed Winn to the house. James Dobson, Finola's employer, met them at the door.

"Master Dobson," Chetan said with a nod when the Englishman admitted them inside. Dobson was a stout man, all portly curves squeezed into an ill-fitting vest, with a dark grey cap stretched tight over his brown hair. He glared crossly at them as he waved them toward the back room.

"Thank our Lord ye've come fer her! She's done nothing but stare fer weeks now, and I've had to tend the shop myself. She's no use to me like this!"

Winn knelt down by her side. Finola sat upright in a chair by the window, her body still and unyielding even as he took her hand. Her pale hair was streaked with more grey than he recalled, strewn down her back with rows of twisted knots. Her blue eyes, once so lively and bright, were empty chasms glazed with a milky white color as she stared out the window into the still yard. She must have seen them arrive, yet even as he clenched her hand, she continued to stare blankly, as if nothing touched her at all.

He leaned closer to peer into her face, noting the stench of her sweat-laden skin and her soiled English dress.

"She speaks to no one. Take her. I had to take on her share of work myself. But ye'll pay me fer her, she's cost me much in food and board as she sits there, like a blasted barmy witch!"

Winn dropped Finola's hand and turned on Master Dobson in a fury. He snatched him by the neck and drove him straight back into the mantle, knocking the man's head into the wood with a distinct crack.

"You let her suffer like this, sitting in her own filth? And you say I should pay you for your care?" Winn growled. He felt Chetan's hand on his shoulder and shook it off. Winn released his hold on Dobson, who fell to the ground in a heap. The man's face swelled up like a ripe melon as he choked and sputtered his indignation.

Chetan gently lifted Finola from the chair, and although his brother remained silent, he could see his nose wrinkle at the stench.

"Ye can't just come here and take my property, she's indentured to me!" Dobson shouted.

Winn snatched the knife from his belt and pressed it to the man's throat.

"Consider her debt paid," he said, the tip of his knife drawing a bead of blood next to Dobson's quivering pulse. Dobson wisely kept his mouth shut when Winn dropped his hand.

Chetan carried Finola out of the dwelling. Winn took a quick glance around the room, noting that there was nothing she owned worth taking with them. It would be enough of a journey just to return with her to the village.

His grandmother still held a blank stare as they rode away. She had journeyed to another place, one no man could follow her to. Winn had seen those who entered the spirit world before. For some reason she had passed through to that place, and he knew it would be up to her to return or remain. He noticed she held onto Chetan, but other than that slight protective gesture, she did not stir. What had been done to her, he had no notion, but he hoped she would wake from her journey and tell him.

If only she would give him a word, Winn would be glad to return to Master Dobson and repay his English kindness.

18

Maggie

While Winn and Chetan were away from the village, she kept as busy as she could. She did not like when they were separated, even for a few days. It seemed like no matter how careful they were, or how much they used her knowledge of the future, they still ran into trouble. She did not regret the decision to remain in the past with Winn, but at times she wondered if was possible to live a peaceful life in the time they had chosen.

She looked at Kwetii as her daughter played with Gwen, and she was certain she did not regret any of it. She was a striking child, with dark wavy hair and a heart-shaped face. Her skin was lighter than her father's, appearing slightly suntanned against her startling blue eyes, a unique combination no matter what time they lived in. The child spoke words in both Paspahegh and English, and Maggie noticed in the few days they spent with the Norse, she learned the Norse word for *no* as well.

"*Nei! Nei,* Da!" Kwetii had cried, begging Winn not to leave. Winn had held the child and whispered into her ear, but Maggie had noticed he was surprised by her use of the Norse language. Kwetii was a clever child who took everything in.

Maggie tended to Benjamin while Gwen prepared a salve. The older woman hoped slathering his head with the thick gooey substance would help his mind heal and let him wake. Maggie was not too hopeful, but she figured it was worth a shot. She was still angry at Marcus for the ease at which he spoke of leaving, so if they could just get Benjamin to wake up, at least that issue would be resolved.

As she filled a pitcher with water by the hearth, she noticed a row of neatly carved figurines on the stone mantle. They were similar in size to her raven, but they looked quite new, with a fresh sheen to the grey metal and few pock-marks like her trinket had. She patted the fold of her skirt where the raven was tucked, relieved to feel it still in her possession. It was a tiny thing, but it mattered to her, being the last remnant of a future life she hoped to share with her daughter someday.

"Where do these things come from, Gwen?" she called. The other woman looked up from her mixing.

"Oh, the charms?" she said. "Erich makes them. He taught yer cousin Cormaic to make them, but the lad's not interested in such little things."

"So did Erich make this?" Maggie asked, taking the raven from her pocket. At the sight of the figurine, Gwen stopped mixing and her eyes grew wider.

"Aye, he made this. He gave it to yer mother when she found she was carrying ye. Erich is a Seer as well, ye know, but he will no admit it to ye. He makes these when he has a vision, and only then. I suppose he's had more visions of late, he's made more since ye returned than he has in years."

"What vision did he have for the raven?" she asked, curious to learn all she could of the mysterious magic in her blood. It was rare to get Gwen to open up about it, so if her aunt would continue to answer questions, Maggie would press on.

"Ye know, lamb. A raven, a great black bird, it would protect ye someday. He gave it to Esa, for ye. We all wish to see ye safe, no matter what those blasted men make ye wonder," she muttered.

"What's so special about my blood? Aren't you all Blooded Ones, just like me?" she asked.

"Aye, some of us more than others. But ye have the blood from both yer parents, and that is a very rare thing to us now. Those of us left here have a sprinkling, here and there, but you? Well, you have more power in a drop of yer blood than all of us combined. That is, except fer yer wee miting over there. I suppose she takes that honor now, for want of the Chief's blood in her veins."

"But power for *what?* I can't *do* anything!" she sighed, snapping her hands out in front of her in demonstration. She waved her hands, pointed her fingers, and then wiggled her nose like she'd seen a witch on television do once. "See? Nothing. I think you're all just mixed up."

Gwen chuckled, bending back to her mixing.

"Do ye know how much power it takes, to send a Longship full of people through time?" Gwen whispered, as if to herself. "Most of us can only travel with a Bloodstone, and then we take only ourselves. You, my dear, ye could take a village with ye, if you meant to. Aye, ye have the power. Yer the one who's addled." Maggie opened her mouth, then snapped it shut, not sure exactly what she wanted to say to that revelation. In a reflexive motion, she pressed her hand to the Bloodstone that lay nestled beneath her shift. Gwen shook her head, muttering in Norse.

"Go tend to young Benjamin. Here, take this," Gwen said, thrusting the bowl of salve at her. Maggie followed her command, her thoughts scattered as Gwen abruptly stopped talking and dismissed her. With her mind distracted due to the tidbits of information, she went to tend Benjamin.

Sitting down beside him, she put her hand on his arm. She looked away to search for a towel, and suddenly felt fingers close around her wrist. She slowly turned to him.

He was awake.

His blue eyes were tinged pink around the edges, his brow creased, and his jaw hung slightly open. His lips looked so parched and dry, she could think of nothing else to do but help him drink. She grabbed a cup, filled it with water, and leaned over to press it to his lips.

He remained silent, his eyes locked on hers as he pushed to a sitting position. She saw him grimace and waver, so she reached out to steady him back to the pillows. He took a few swallows of the cold water, and then ran his tongue over his dry lips.

"Yer verra beautiful today, wife," he finally said, his voice cracked in a hoarse whisper. She felt her stomach drop at his words and made to pull back, but he caught her hand, surprisingly strong, and held her there.

"Let go of me!" she whispered, yanking away from him. The cup overturned and splashed his bared chest, but he seemed not to notice. She sat back, pulling against his grip and staring into his frantic eyes as if it might jog his delusional memory. He had been asleep too long, however, and after his initial burst of strength, his grip loosened and he dropped her hand.

"I'm not your wife anymore," she said. He cocked his head slightly to one side.

"Are ye a ghost, then?" he asked.

"No, I'm flesh and blood. I haven't seen you since Finola and I gave you the Bloodstone," she whispered. Suddenly his face fell.

"Oh, aye. I remember that."

He closed his eyes and laid his head back on the pillows.

"Here, drink this," she stammered, refilling the fallen cup and holding it out to him. He squinted through one partly opened eye and sighed.

"Why are you here?" he asked. She put the cup to his lips and he raised his hand to take it, but when his finger touched her knuckles, he pulled back.

"Your father has been searching for you. He came looking when you never made it to the future," she said, her words slow and careful. She was uncertain as to how to speak to the man who had once been her husband.

"Was he expecting me?" Benjamin asked.

"Yes. I wrote him a letter. He found it and figured out where, or rather *when*, we were at. He's here now, I'm sure he would like to see you awake. You have a lot to catch up on."

"Is this hell? I've gone to hell for using that evil magic, haven't I?" he whispered.

She subdued the urge to tell him that yes, it *was* hell, and that he had gone there for his deceitful ways. After all, she had forgiven him, hadn't she?

"No. It's not hell. Don't you remember your father? Or the farm we lived on?" she asked. Yes, he had been a child when the Bloodstone first took him, but he was old enough to recall a few details. Finola once told her Benjamin had arrived half-naked, starving, and mute, but eventually he told Finola fantastical tales about his future time.

"I remember. All of it," he said softly. "Ye were the last one I saw that day, when I picked up that stone as a boy. And ye were the last one I touched before it took me again, as a man. Aye, I remember."

His eyes met hers, soft and knowing.

"Ye say yer no longer my wife. Ye found him, then?"

She nodded. She knew who he referred to.

"Be off with ye, Maggie. I need to piss, and it willna be fit fer ye to see," he mumbled. She tried to contain her smile at the absurdity of his words, seeing how serious he was about the matter, but she failed in her attempt and let out a muffled laugh. After all, they had been married once, and she had seen much more than that.

"Really? Come on now, if you try to sit up by yourself, you'll fall on your stubborn head! Here, I'll help you, then I'll leave you to it," she laughed. His pale cheeks filled with color, yet his lip turned up in a grin.

Benjamin let her help him sit up and put his feet on the floor. His legs were thin, and he had lost weight all over, but it was his face that was most changed. Covered by a full, black beard, even through the mass of hair she could see the sharp lines of his cheeks and the way his blue eyes seemed hollow in his head. Eyes so much like his brother.

"Oh, damn!" she murmured.

"What?"

"I'm going to fetch your father. Don't fall over, you'll split your head. Again," she said. She left him sitting on the edge of the bed, pulling the curtain behind her as she went. She kicked a piss pot under the curtain, sending it sliding across the floor until it stopped with a thump.

"Thank ye," he called.

"You're welcome," she mumbled.

Maggie updated Gwen on Benjamin's awakening, and the older woman ran off to find Marcus.

Benjamin took the news surprisingly well. After Marcus entered the cottage to speak with his awakened son, Maggie and Gwen played with Kwetii to keep occupied while the men talked. With a few glances between them, Maggie and Gwen made a silent pact to remain in the adjacent room. Maggie stayed out of curiosity, and she figured Gwen stayed from loyalty to her Chief. The voices started out low, but as the conversation wore on it became louder, and at one point there was a dull thud against the floor.

As Gwen fiddled with some kindling by the fire, Marcus parted the curtain. He stood wide legged, arms flexed, and Maggie could see he shook as if cold. He eyed them up, his face a mixture of confusion and joy.

"Will ye help him? I'll send Cormaic and Erich to bring him to the hall, but he's a bit weak still yet," he said.

"Of course we'll help him, but do you really think it's a good idea to get him up so soon? He's been unconscious for a week," she answered, crossing her arms over her chest.

She heard Gwen gasp, but ignored her. Maggie knew she was expected to defer to the Chief's every whim, but for Pete's sake, he was still the same old Marcus. Marcus ruffled Kwetii on her head as he met Maggie's questioning gaze.

"The lad wants to meet his kin. It's about time he takes his place among his people."

***

The Northern Hall was louder than it had been the night they arrived, if that was possible. She counted the numbers but rapidly lost track. There were over thirty people joining the celebration, and she knew that was not the whole of them. The crowd was a mash up of cultures, with Indians and Norse living together, and Maggie suspected she heard the inkling of other languages among a few of the men and women. She listened intently to tidbits of conversations around her, and in the days they spent in the company of the Norse she came to realize they had a close relationship with the Nansemond who lived nearby. She imagined it was that alliance that helped keep them hidden in the mountains, essentially undisturbed by the encroaching English settlers. Unless the Norse chose to interact, the village was unlikely to be of interest to the English. It seemed they ventured into town very rarely, trading on occasion with the Indians more than they did with the English. Gwen told her they had settled in the area prior to the arrival of the English, and since they kept to themselves high up away from the James River, they had very little trouble.

Without Winn there, she did not feel up for celebrating, but when both Teyas and Rebecca were excited to go, she decided to join them. Ahi Kekeleksu made friends with a group of boys his age, among them the Indian youth she noticed earlier, and they raced around the Northern Hall screeching and play-fighting. Maggie noticed Makedewa hanging back in the shadows, his eyes following Rebecca, yet he stayed away with the other men while Rebecca carried Kwetii. Cormaic was speaking with Rebecca and fussing over the child as much as a big lug could, and they both laughed as they spoke. Maggie took her tankard and made her way to where Makedewa stood.

"Fire Heart," he mumbled gruffly with a nod when she approached. His arms were crossed over his lean chest as he watched Rebecca eat with the women. He wore a new vest over his bare torso, made from the thick hide of a brown bear and edged with a knot work of intricate silver thread, a gift from Erich to welcome him to the village.

"You could go sit with her," she commented. He made a shallow grunting sound.

"I can stand here, just as well," he replied.

"You're as stubborn as your brother," she teased, taking a sip of her drink. He tilted his head a bit and raised an eyebrow at her.

"Hmm. Who is more stubborn, my brother, or his wife? He is much changed from the brother I know."

"What is that supposed to mean?"

He shrugged, turning back to watch the crowd.

"My brother forgets his people for you. Yet still you cannot be happy. What would you have of him? To live here? With his white brother, whose bed you once shared?"

She froze at his hateful words, her response caught in her dry throat.

"I'm happy as long as I'm with Winn," she finally whispered.

"My brother is the strongest brave I know. But even he could not bear what you want of him."

"I'll go wherever he wants."

Makedewa sighed as he shook his head.

"No. You will stay here, and Winn will let you. He forgets who he is, for you. With each sunrise I see less of my brother, and more of a *Tassantassas* in his skin." Makedewa drained his mug. "If that is what being bound to a woman makes a man, I will stay away. Let her find a *Tassantassas* to make her happy."

Her mouth dropped open when he abruptly turned and walked away. His hateful words stung, the truth of it mixed in with his conflicted feelings for Rebecca. She shook her head to clear the rush of tears that threatened, trying to convince herself he did not mean what he said. Yet on some level, she knew he did, and the guilt nipped at her heart.

She took a long gulp of mead and made her way back to the table to join the women, where perhaps the conversation would be more welcoming. She took a seat on the bench next to her aunt.

"Who is that boy?" she asked Gwen, as the Indian youth began to wrestle with Ahi Kekeleksu in the crowd. Gwen was fussing with her kirtle strings which had fallen loose, and she stopped for a moment at Maggie's question.

"Iain? He's son to Ellie-dear, by a Chesapeake brave. Some of them stayed here for a bit when the Powhatans attacked. We've taken in quite a few stragglers. We're not the only people who've lost their kin," she said. Maggie raised her eyebrows in surprise.

"Why did he go after the Chesapeake?"

"We heard it was a prophecy. It was the old Chief Powhatan back then, he and his brother Opechancanough were much alike in that way," Gwen said with a shrug of her shoulders. "A priest said the Chesapeake would rise up against the Powhatan Empire, so he attacked them. We sheltered some of the Chesapeake for a time. Most of them moved on with the Nansemond, but Ellie and Iain stayed with us."

"Is Ellie-dear here?" Maggie asked.

"Oh, aye. She's the blond one, sitting near yer sister. Her boy's an Indian, like yer husband," Gwen replied, nodding toward the end of the table where Teyas sat.

Maggie did not know how to respond to that as she looked over at her husband's sister. Cultural tolerance aside, she was well aware that the Norse were uncharacteristically welcoming to the Indians. Perhaps it was their shared history that bound them, or the need to have allies to survive. Whatever the reason, she was glad for it.

She spotted Ellie-dear sitting beside Teyas, engaged in a discussion. Ellie had long, straight blond hair, pulled demurely back with a single tie at the base of her neck. Her features were delicate, like Rebecca's, and although Ellie was older, she was clearly English.

"What a pretty lady," Maggie murmured. Gwen chuckled as Maggie took a bite of bread.

"That Chesapeake brave thought so, too. He took her to wife from that group of Roonok settlers, and she's lucky to be alive. I think all her kin are dead."

The bread caught in a dense lump in her throat and Maggie gasped into a choking fit. Gwen thumped her on the back with a closed fist until Maggie was able to suck the air back into her lungs and catch her breath.

"Shoo, slow ye down! Can't have ye choke yerself into the grave!" her Aunt chastised. Maggie took a swig of the proffered wine, coughed up more bread, and took another sip.

"Elli's from *Roanoke*?" she sputtered.

"Nay, I said *Roonok*. The English left a few of their people on the Island early on, and they right starved to death until the Chesapeake took them in. Elli-dear's one of them. Her ma died when she was still a wee thing, so they called her by her ma's name. Eleanor," Gwen mused, "Eleanor died early on. Terrible time, that was."

"Eleanor Dare," she whispered. The lost colonists, starved and desolate, had sought shelter with the local Indians, just as historians had suggested. She recalled no one knew for sure what happened to them. Some surmised they went to the Chesapeake, others believed they went to the Croatoan. There were various rumors of blue-eyed, fair-haired people living amongst the Indians, but the reports were unreliable and impossible to verify. Knowing firsthand how those early years of English settlement played out, Maggie was not shocked to hear of whites living among the Indians. Yet the village of Time Walkers had apparently escaped documentation in written history, just the same as the fate of the Roanoke Colony.

With a sinking desperation in her belly, Maggie realized her safety and that of her family was just as tenuous. She could hardly believe she was sharing a meal with Virginia Dare, as the woman's half-Indian son ran amok in a breechcloth amongst a group of Viking children. The Roanoke Colony had met a gruesome end no matter how history reported it, as evidenced by the lone survivor sitting across the table. Would her family fare any better?

She braced her elbows on the table and rested her forehead in her hands for a moment. Gwen patted her shoulder.

"Ye sick, dear?" Gwen asked. "Ye look like ye've had a fright?"

"I'm fine," Maggie murmured.

Marcus raised his drinking horn to start the celebration, and the crowd responded with a roar. Pounding fists rocked the tables, and a lyre wailed a joyful tune. Her mouth watered as the scent of thick spicy venison rippled through the air, a smoky cloud lingering over the still-smoldering meat laid out on the long table.

Maggie waited to raise her own cup, knowing it was the proper way to behave toward the esteemed chief. She often felt frustrated with the cultural constraints of the time, and becoming acclimated to the Norse way of life was no easy task. The more time she spent in the village, the more she felt she belonged, even when she was expected to defer her opinions to the men around her. As Maggie stared down the table at her kin, she wondered what her life would be like if they settled with the Nansemond. Would she raise a strong, proud, daughter? Or a subservient woman waiting for the next order from a warrior? It was a question only Winn could answer, and she would have to abide by it.

A raucous thud of fists upon the dry wood table roused her thoughts, and she looked up toward the men.

Benjamin sat to the right hand of Marcus, and she could not help noticing it was the place of honor Winn had occupied the day prior. Although Winn was resistant to forging a relationship with Marcus, she was pleased they stopped trying to kill each other. At least that was progress.

Yet as she watched Benjamin sit beside Marcus, reveling in the attention like the long-lost Prince, she wondered how it would affect her husband. He spoke little of his feelings for his father, but Winn had gradually involved himself in the Norse activities within the village and seemed to fit in. She hoped when he returned matters would continue in the same vein.

"May the Gods bless the return of my son. Thank ye, Odin, for waking him from his rest!" Marcus shouted. He raised the horn higher, and then took a long gulp. The men shouted in agreement and the pounding of fists resumed. Erich stood, raising his tankard as well, and although heads turned to listen, there was still a rowdy murmur among the crowd.

"Bless his hard head, yet it might be made of rock! It is good to have ye back, Young Neilsson!"

A roar of laughter ensued, and both Marcus and Benjamin grinned.

"Why, thank ye, Erich, I hear I owe ye a clouting for this lump on my skull," Benjamin said.

"Aye, ye'll get your chance, lad. I expect to see ye training as soon as ye get yer fancy arse outta Gwen's sickbed. Unless ye prefer the women helping ye piss, I'd say it's time to find another place fer ye to sleep."

"There's space among the men, it will suit him fine," Marcus said.

Maggie suspected they spoke of one of the larger long-houses where the single men slept. Their sleeping accommodations were similar to the Indians in that respect. Marcus, the Chief, slept in his own house, which had previously been occupied by the men. On the day of their arrival, Erich had insisted on giving it to Marcus, and although they argued about it, Erich prevailed. The single men moved to another Long House, and it looked like Benjamin would join them. It seemed the only other way to procure a private space was by being married or by having several children.

Maggie's emotions toward Benjamin ran the gamut between relief and frustration. Of course, she was glad to see he lived after wondering if the magic of the Bloodstone had taken his life. Although he had lied to keep her as his wife, she vowed to put her anger aside. No good would come of holding onto the past.

Then there was Marcus and Winn to consider as well. She cared enough about Marcus to want his son returned to him, yet it was a confusing desire to see reconciled. Benjamin had been taken from Marcus as a child, and Winn had never known a father. She hoped her old friend wanted to make a relationship with both of the men who were his sons.

After glancing down the table at Kwetii, who was sitting happily with the other women, Maggie left her seat to refill her tankard. As she dipped it in the large oval serving kettle, a familiar shadow fell over her shoulder.

"They have good drink here, at least," Benjamin said.

She nodded, without turning toward him.

"Vikings know how to make merry," she agreed. She raised her full tankard to her lips and drank down the brimming rim.

"Would you walk with me for a spot, Maggie? It's quite loud in here, I canna hear much at all. Mayhap it's the ringing in my ears, or the mead, I do not know. But I would like to speak with you."

She wrapped both hand around the tankard and squeezed it as she raised it to her mouth, turning to stare at him. She drained half of it before she spoke.

"No, I will not. I'm glad you're not dead, but that's it. I have nothing else to say to you."

"You need say nothing. I only ask ye to listen."

She shook her head.

"None of it matters now, just let it go, Benjamin. You have a new life, take it and be happy. Leave me be."

"I woke up today in a strange place. All these strangers," he said, his voice strained with emotion as he waved toward the crowd, "they say it was two years past. But for what I know, you were my wife only a sennight ago."

"If that is what you recall, then you must remember sending me to hang as well!" she whispered.

"I set ye free, didn't I? I sent ye back to him!"

He took hold of her wrist, and she looked slowly down at it in awe. How dare he put his hands on her!

"Take your hand off me," she warned him. His throat tensed as he swallowed, and he ran his other hand through his thick black hair.

"Must ye hate me so? I willna harm ye, I only want to talk!"

She shook her hand away, and he released her wrist without further issue.

"My wife says she does not wish to speak to you, Englishman."

Maggie froze at the sound of Winn's voice. Winn placed a hand on her shoulder as he joined her, standing by her side to face Benjamin. She tried to edge back to push him away and give them distance, but Winn would have none of it and remained firmly rooted in place. She could only hear the three of them, as if a fog descended around them, and it seemed the other Norse continued their celebration without interruption. Perhaps she could get Winn away before something terrible happened.

"Let's go, Winn," she whispered, trying to pull her husband back. Her attempt was unsuccessful, and she felt the muscles of his arm tense beneath her hand. She saw Chetan standing a few feet away and cast him a pleading look, hoping he would intervene before there was bloodshed.

"She can speak with me if she wishes, *brother*," Benjamin replied tersely. "By English law, she is still my wife."

Maggie put herself between the men, but it was too late.

19

Winn

Winn meant to walk away.

Yet somehow he found his hands around Benjamin's throat. He slammed the Englishman up against the table, jostling the mead bucket so that a considerable amount of it splashed their feet. The confrontation passed by as a blur, his vision clouded by fury at the sight of his brother near his wife. Benjamin gripped his wrists with more strength than Winn expected, and although his white face paled as Winn squeezed his neck, his brother held a look of quiet anger hooded in his blue eyes.

"Is this how ye treat her, ye bloody savage?" Benjamin groaned through his narrowed airway. Winn frowned and glanced to his side, where he expected Maggie to be. She was a few feet away beside an overturned chair, and Chetan helped her to her feet. Her bright red hair fell about her shoulders in a tangled wave, and she brushed her hand over a scrape on her forearm. He felt a rising heat in the pit of his stomach as he realized he must have shoved her. Winn dropped his hands from Benjamin's throat and stepped back.

"I'm fine!" she hissed at Chetan, slapping her hands against her skirt to brush off the dust. He wanted nothing more than to finish what he started with his deceitful brother, but seeing what he had done to his wife took the wind from his lungs.

With the last semblance of control he could muster, Winn turned away from Benjamin without answer to his taunt. He swallowed hard when Maggie slipped her hand into his. He could feel her tremble, with anger or fear, he knew not. He only knew Benjamin would not yet face justice for what he had done.

Marcus stood up as Winn took Maggie by the arm and led her away. The Chief observed without intervention as they parted. Winn felt his father's eyes upon him, but he owed the man nothing and would not acknowledge his silent question. The altercation had occurred in the corner away from prying ears, the music and celebration continuing on as if no disturbance had occurred. Marcus watched quietly as Winn left the Northern Hall.

"Winn?" she asked softly. "Kwetii is with Teyas–"

He swung around and barked a command to Chetan, who grunted a curse at him in reply, yet returned to stay with Kwetii nonetheless. Chetan would watch over the women and children and see them safely to their Long House when they finished the meal. For all his bluster, Winn knew Chetan could see how angry he was, and he was grateful to have the kinship of his true brother.

His blood brother, his family. Chetan and Makedewa, they were the ones he knew would never betray him, who would stand at his side no matter what the cost. The sniveling Englishman inside? Well, he knew nothing of true brotherhood. The fact that they shared a father was of no consequence.

"Leave her with my sister. Chetan and Makedewa will see to them," he snapped. He saw Maggie flinch, her mouth falling open at his tone.

"Fine," she said. Her voice wavered, and she made a point of walking faster so that she reached the Long House before he did. He tried to slow his breathing as he followed her, making the effort to calm his irritation so that they might speak. It caused nothing but grief when they railed at each other in anger, and he needed to speak with her on other matters. Benjamin was a complication, one which Winn saw as temporary.

"What are you doing?" he asked, his fists clenched at his sides. Once they entered the dark Long House, she began to rifle through a basket of linens. She pulled out a long drying cloth and a cake of soap Gwen had given her, and then produced a bone-handled comb.

"If Teyas is babysitting, I'm going to take a bath. It's not like I get much time to myself," she said. "It's call de-stressing. I need to think." He frowned.

"You can't go to the river alone."

"I'm not. Gwen showed me the bath house, I'm going to try it out."

He raised an eyebrow, his curiosity peaked. Bathing inside a house? Perhaps he would escort her.

"I will see you there," he snapped, his voice sharper than he intended. She shrugged. Gathering her bundle in her arms, she left the Long House and he followed her. "I need to speak with you first. I have news from Pepamhu," he said.

"Then come on. I'll let you scrub my back while you talk," she chirped, casting a sly look over her shoulder. She trudged on toward the edge of the settlement, and soon he could see a miniature Long House nestled into a crop of boulders. The house appeared built on top of the rocks, the roof extending across an overhang and dipping into a crevice, topped by a round smoke hole. When he followed her inside, he was pleased to feel a warm mist heating the space, rising up from a bubbling hot spring inside a nest of boulders.

"Wow. Gwen was right, this is nice. It looks like a whirlpool!" she laughed.

Her attention was on the shallow bath, but his attention was on her. Her laughter was a ringing of bells as she shed her clothes. She lifted her chemise over her head and tossed it on the ground, then shimmied out of her doeskin skirt and dropped it at her feet. His breath caught in his throat as moonlight illuminated her lithe body and she bent to place one tentative toe into the water. She squealed with joy and stepped into the pool, immediately submerging herself. By the time she surfaced, he had already shed his breechcloth and leggings and was stepping down to join her.

It was good to see her laugh. Despite the upheaval in their lives she managed to trudge on, doing her best to care for their daughter and keep their family together, yet he knew it wore on her in ways she would not admit. Her stubborn streak was her greatest strength, and also her weakness, her refusal to give in to despair that which drove her on. As he watched her dip her long red hair back into the water, he wished he could shield her from it all. The last thing he wished to do was tell her about Teyas, and about Finola's condition. And even worse to think on was his anger at Benjamin—and how his brother's presence might affect them.

"This is amazing!" she said. He stood waist deep in the pool next to her, and as she reached up to squeeze the dampness from her hair he could bear it no longer. He needed his wife in his arms.

"Yes, amazing," he murmured, pulling her against his chest. She let out a squeak and he smiled, running his lips gently over hers. He felt her relax as his fingers caressed her back and moved lower to her buttocks, slick, yet firm, beneath the water.

"You're not going to wash my hair, are you?" she whispered.

"If you wish it so, I will wash it now," he replied. He slid his knee between her willing thighs, covering her mouth with his when she moaned.

"Later. Wash it later," she agreed. She let out a gasp when he moved inside her, her hands encircling his neck as he pushed her back. He held her close, pinned against the smooth rock, their flesh making a soft sucking sound as they moved beneath the water.

The ache rose within, that monstrous demon held deep in his blood. It rose up to consume them, wrapping them in steely tendons as thoughts of losing her nipped at his mind. He could bury himself in her softness, feel his soul merge into hers, through hers, as if nothing could part them, yet he drove himself further to push past the truth.

If only he could make time weep, as he made her cry out with pleasure, make it stand still and obey him as he tried to make her obey. Neither would be conquered, however, and as she cried his name against his ear, he knew it was the closest he could come to being master of either.

He gently kissed her cheeks, tasting the salt of her tears on his lips. He could feel the welts her nails left upon his skin and the sting of his wounds from the warm water, but he held her close all the same.

"*Ntehem,*" he murmured. "*Nouwami.*"

"I love you, too," she whispered.

They gently bathed each other, taking care with the fragile silence between them. He recalled she once explained what a chauvinist pig was, and he wondered sometimes if she still thought that of him after all the time they spent together. Yet if his actions angered her, he suspected she would tell him so. At least he had been sure of that a few short weeks past. Since they had arrived in the Norse village, the bond they shared seemed strained, a tenuous thread that might break loose at any moment. Winn hesitated to share the news of Finola…and he had no idea how he would discuss the marriage of his sister.

"Finola is here. We took her from her English master," he finally admitted as they walked back toward their Long House after their bath.

"She's here? Can I see her?"

Winn was afraid she would ask, and he would not deny her.

"She is not well, *ntehem*. Perhaps wait until tomorrow to see her. Gwen cares for her now, I am sure she is sleeping."

"I just want to say hello, we won't stay long. Come on," she insisted, taking his hand firmly as she broke into a faster pace toward Gwen's house.

"And what do you mean, you took her from the English?" she muttered. Maggie thrust the door open unannounced, obviously expecting a different sight than what greeted her. Instead, he watched, unable to soothe her, as her face crumpled. Finola looked worse than before. There was no way to hide it.

"What happened to her?" Maggie whispered. Winn stood helplessly by as she went to Finola. Gwen muttered something low under her breath in what sounded like her Norse language, shaking her head. The older woman looked strained, her face weary as she watched them.

"She's had a fright, I think," Gwen answered.

Finola stared forward, even as Maggie squeezed her hand. At least Gwen had bathed her, so in that respect her care had improved. He wondered if anything could be done to help her.

"What is wrong with her eyes?" Maggie asked. Winn had noticed it earlier. Finola's eyes, once a clear blue like his own, now clouded near white in color with only a hint of their former luster.

"I've only seen it once before, when a *Seer* left this earth on a journey. When a *Seer* knows too much, it can haunt her. Sometimes the visions can take her away, and she cannot return."

"So she'll wake up soon, then?" Maggie asked.

"It was a man I saw it happen to, and nay, he did not wake. I am sorry, lamb," Gwen spoke. "Can ye imagine, knowing what will happen to those you love, yet having no power to stop it? She must have seen something dreadful. Aye, I think she is on her own journey for now. Pray Odin will not welcome her at his table just yet."

Winn took his wife by the shoulders and gently urged her away. For once, she let him guide her.

"You will tell us if she wakes?" Winn said to Gwen.

"Aye, ye and my Chief. Without delay."

***

Later, when they returned to the Long House, they lay nestled together under the furs with Kwetii sleeping peacefully nearby. His wife was silent, which was unusual for her, and although he knew the events of the day wore heavy on her, he did not expect her silence. She laid her head in the bend of his arm and pressed her lips against his chest, her breathing shallow as if she were near sleep.

"We should leave within a sennight," he said. He felt her breathing catch, and her hand resting on his belly slowly clenched into a fist.

"Finola can't travel," she quickly answered.

"She will stay here with my father."

"You're *important* to these people. We can stay here among them," she replied.

"My father has his true son returned to him. It is time we go."

His muscles tightened and he felt his ire rise at her words. Did she truly wish to remain with the Norse? As if he had not shown enough restraint yet, did she ask more of him?

"These are your people, too. And mine," she added.

His mouth felt dry. Of course, she would want to stay with her kin, as well as Marcus. He could not fault her for that, but it still angered him. There was nothing for him among the Norse, except to stay as the ill-favored son of a Time Walker Chieftain. For a time he thought perhaps they could make a life with the Norse, since even Chetan and Makedewa fit in well with the warriors, but having Benjamin there changed things entirely. Winn heard the words his father spoke, and although he understood the reasoning, he could not forgive him the intent. He thought of the words often, since that day.

"Would it have mattered, even if you knew of me?" Winn asked.

Marcus hesitated before he spoke.

"Yes, it would have mattered. But still, I would have gone."

Such things should not trouble a man full-grown, yet it still stung him. Winn would never leave his daughter, nor his wife, not even if the hands of the Great Creator tried to take him from them.

"You seem to like it here. It's safe, there are plenty of men to defend the village. We could stay here, and never see the English again, or your uncle, either," she said. He shook his head.

"No."

"I'm tired of fighting with the English. Is that it? Do you like all the killing, all the fighting?" she asked, suddenly sitting up, her voice rising a pitch. She clutched a fur to her breasts as she confronted him.

"Yes, I have killed many *Tassantassas*! What of it?" he countered, rising up next to her. He pulled her back to him, wanting her warmth and softness instead of her anger. "Does that make me less of a man to you, that I would spill blood? I tell you now, I would do it again. I would burn down their houses, I would steal from them. I would squeeze the life from their tiny white necks. If needed of me, I would do it. I would do it to keep you. I would take the life of my brother, for you."

He could see her teeth biting into her bottom lip as he stared into her flashing green eyes. She trembled in his hands.

"I belong to you. Nothing will change that, no matter where we live," she whispered. His stomach curled and dropped, and he slowly loosened his grip on her.

"Then lay down your fists, and rest your head. When you wake in the morning, you will see your kin. That is all I can promise you."

He felt her breath leave her body in a sigh as she sank back down into his arms beneath the furs. As she submitted to sleep, he continued to hold her, his eyes focused on the moon above through the smoke hole.

Yes, he would do anything to keep her. Yet what she asked of him was more than he could give. How he would end it, he did not know.

20

Makedewa

Makedewa glanced up above at the grassy hillside as he walked with his brothers toward the training field. He could see Rebecca's skirts whipping in the breeze as she chased after the devious Kwetii, who squealed with laughter at the game. He had not spoken with her since that day in Winn's Long House, and as the time wore on, he became more convinced it was for the best. She seemed to settle in amongst the Norse as if she belonged, and he would not disturb her newfound comfort. Although he ached with jealousy whenever he saw Cormaic or the other men speak to her, he was also proud of her for overcoming her fears. Perhaps as she became stronger in herself, she would grow to trust him as well. It was the only hope he could muster at their situation.

"And you, Makedewa?" Winn called. Makedewa followed a few paces behind Winn and Chetan, lost in his own thoughts as they walked. He jogged to catch up with them when Winn called his name.

"Hmm?" Makedewa asked.

"Will you ride with us to take Teyas to Mattanock? We would leave in a few days," Winn said as he adjusted the new sword strapped across his back. Makedewa admired Winn's elaborate weapon, layered with intricate carved rune symbols and inlaid with gemstones along the hilt. It was the weapon of a leader, as his brother should have, being the son of the Norse Chief Pale Feather.

"I will go. Which of us will stay here?" Makedewa answered.

"Marcus will watch over Maggie and Rebecca. I do not wish to take them to Mattanock while the Weanock warriors are there. I fear for trouble if we do so," Winn said. Chetan nodded in agreement, shrugging his fur clad shoulders.

"I think your wife will not like that," Makedewa sniped. Winn frowned, squinting a brow downward at him.

"She will do as I ask," Winn replied.

Chetan and Makedewa both burst into laughter, bringing a flush to Winn's face with an outraged scowl.

"Humph, Fire Heart will do as you ask? Not likely!" Chetan said with a grin.

Makedewa shoved Winn with the point of his elbow, which his older brother shrugged off with a grunt. Winn appeared angered at the taunt, but Makedewa could see the corner of his mouth twitching as if he wished to laugh.

"Just wait, brother. Wait until you marry Rebecca. You shall see," Winn mumbled.

"I think that will never happen, so no, I will not see."

"No reading lessons then?" Chetan asked, his voice alight with a teasing melody.

Makedewa sighed, kicking at a stone on the path. The training field was ahead, filled with the Norse warriors, and the last thing he wanted was to have them hear of his troubles with Rebecca.

"I offered her marriage. She refused me. There is nothing more to it," Makedewa said evenly.

Winn and Chetan both stopped and turned to him, the joking immediately ceased between them. Makedewa was not a man to speak of personal feelings, and he knew that admitting as much would grab their attention. However, he wished to be out with it so he could cast it aside, before his brothers heard of it from the women. He rushed forward with an explanation before they could formulate any assumptions.

"It is better this way. I was a fool to think on it. She says she does not wish to be a wife to any man."

"Ah, that's not true. It is clear she is fond of you," Chetan said. Makedewa shook his head, his single braid bouncing down his back.

"Maybe. But not enough to be a wife."

"Perhaps if Maggie speaks with her–" Winn said.

"No. Speak no more of it. It is finished," he muttered, shaking off the hand that Winn put on his shoulder. Winn closed his fingers into a fist, and with one powerful thrust struck Makedewa a blow in the chest, knocking the breath from his lungs. Winn grabbed Makedewa by both shoulders and shook him hard.

"Then go fight, warrior," his older brother intoned. Makedewa glared into his face, his brother's steel blue eyes betraying not even an inch of sorrow for him. He admired that about Winn. His brother was always ready to channel his anger into more meaningful tasks.

He just needed to get the foolish thoughts of Rebecca out of his head. Then he would be back on the path to being the warrior he was meant to be.

Makedewa shoved Winn's fist away as he gasped for air, and took off into a jog down to the field.

Part Three

21

Maggie

Winn kept his promise. They remained in the Norse village, and though Maggie knew it was temporary, she hoped his heart would soften toward his kinsmen. He was a man who rarely showed what lay in his thoughts, but to her it was evident he wished for some compromise to their problem. He did not speak of leaving again. It hung between them, spearing the distance further the more time they remained in the village. She wished the problem would simply evaporate, but since the issue was a living, breathing, human, there was no hope for that.

Benjamin celebrated in his new role as the Chieftain's son, and by every facet of his behavior, it appeared he planned on staying. Maggie knew the time to leave was approaching fast, but she could not bury that part of herself that wished to stay.

She immersed herself in learning the Norse ways, and was pleased to see Teyas and Rebecca seemed to like the village as well. Of course, it would be that much more difficult when it was time to leave, but at least for the time being they could focus on something other than running from the next threat. They spent time with her aunt Gwen and the other Norse women, and Finola kept her silent vigil sitting by the hearth most days with rarely a word spoken.

It was evident that the village was a blending of cultures, not only by the appearance of the people, but by their habits. Elli-dear's son was not the only half-brave in the village, and there were a few Norse men married to Indian women. She imagined their lifestyle was a combination of the different worlds. One, from the displaced Chesapeake tribe, and the other from the Old Norse.

Gwen gave bits and pieces of their history, but Maggie had the feeling she held much of it back. Whether it was from loyalty or fear, she did not know, and she would not push the issue. Although Maggie had much to learn of the Norse ways, she already was quite clear on a few things: One did not challenge the newly restored Chief, and one did not mess with magic. In fact, one was much better off forgetting magic existed altogether.

The women spent the day gathering wool on the hills surrounding the training field. As summer drew to a close the weather became less humid, and the manual labor was much easier to accomplish. They broke up in groups to attend to daily chores, some women staying behind in the Northern Hall to start the evening meal while other smaller groups spread out to undertake tasks such as woolgathering and tending the beehives.

The village was larger than she thought when she first arrived. Everything centered on the Northern Hall, with many Long Houses clumped around it. A deep water well stood in front of the Northern Hall, convenient to a small blacksmith's cottage and several storage houses. Gwen carried the role of healer, Maggie was not sure if it was due to her magical blood or her domineering attitude, but it gave her greater status in the community and as thus, she shared a larger Long House with her husband. The bathhouse was nearly always in use, Maggie recalled with a pleasant flush over her skin. She and Winn had been fortunate to steal a few moments alone there.

Kwetii ran down the hillside, squealing after Rebecca. The child asked often for Ahi Kekeleksu, but since they arrived in the village he spent all his time cavorting with the other youths, his young female cousin momentarily forgotten. Maggie saw Kwetii point toward the training field. The girl had spotted her cousin, who stood watching the men fight.

"He's busy, Kwetii," Maggie called.

"Play with Keke!" the girl replied, pointing again with a pout on her round face. Rebecca held an armful of wool above her head, and then dropped it over the toddler. Kwetii laughed as it rained down over her face like soft fuzzy snowflakes. Sufficiently distracted, the child followed Rebecca and helped her return the wool to her burlap sack.

"If ye would like to learn to weave, I can send ye to Sigrun Olafsson. She's the finest we have," Gwen called out. Maggie plucked a handful of loose wool from a low lying tree branch and shoved it in her sack.

"That would be nice, I'd like that," she replied. She did not have the heart to admit to her Aunt that their stay would likely end soon. Maggie looked downhill to the training field, where Winn was in the midst of a fight with Cormaic. The other men stood watching in usual formation, egging them on with whoops and howls. Since the day Winn had beaten her cousin, they had fought each other daily, and last she heard the score was dead even. Both men were formidable warriors, and neither were willing to be the last defeated.

Winn seemed to enjoy sparring with the men, and Maggie wondered how difficult it would be for him to leave them. She knew he still felt the pull of responsibility to the few remaining Paspahegh, and that he still wished to live near the Nansemond village. As much as she wanted to stay with the Norse, she could not ask her husband to abandon the last remnant tying him to the tribe. Yet she wished, someday, he might think of the Norse as his people in the same way. To her, it was the only way to stay clear of the danger to come, especially after learning the fate of the Roanoke Colony. Although she often answered Winn's questions about the future, he still insisted on making his own way for their family. It was certainly no democracy in their household; Winn would decide where they would settle, and that was the end of it.

"He's a fine man," Gwen commented. Caught staring at her husband, Maggie blushed. Sun-darkened skin gleaming, tensed over the striated muscles in his chest and arms, he certainly looked the part of royalty as he raised the heavy sword over his head and sent it crashing down onto Cormaic's wooden shield. She was surprised to see him wear a pair of wool braies like the other men, long, slim pants tied at the waist with a cord that fit him quite fine. Very fine, in fact.

"Yes, he is," she murmured. Gwen broke into hearty laughter.

"Aye, I meant my Erich, but yer husband is fetching, too, dear!" the woman giggled. Maggie laughed along with her.

Kwetii let out another shrill cry, and at first Maggie did not recognize it as anything other than playful chatter. When Rebecca picked up the toddler and Kwetii continued to wail, however, she dropped her gathering bag and ran over to meet them.

"What happened?" Maggie asked. Kwetii's face was screwed up like one round red apple as she cried, tears coursing down her cheeks. Maggie took her from Rebecca's arms, which quieted her tears a bit, but did not serve to make her much less miserable.

"I think it was a bee. Look, there on her neck," Rebecca said.

Maggie pushed the child's gunna aside to reveal the skin of her throat. Near the base of her neck, where she should have a tiny hollow, was instead an angry welt the size of a ripe cherry.

"It's just a bee sting, sweetling, you'll be okay," Maggie soothed her. Kwetii half-sobbed, half-hiccupped.

"Hurts, mama!" Kwetii cried. Maggie was startled to hear the child's voice come out coarse instead of high-pitched. When Kwetii took in a breath, it made a whistling sound.

"Gwen–do you have something to make this go down? It's swelling up fast," Maggie asked, her unease steadily rising. The welt seemed to be growing by the second, and each time Kwetii inhaled or exhaled, she made a peculiar strangled sound.

When Gwen took a look at the swelling and her face lost color, Maggie swallowed back her own panic.

Kwetii had never been stung before. What should have been a simple childhood boo-boo was rapidly turning into an emergency. It seemed her child was allergic to bees, and they had no way to help her as her throat closed off.

"Take her back to the village," Gwen said.

"Mama?" Kwetii wheezed.

"Hush, sweetheart, hush," she whispered, pressing a kiss to her daughter's forehead. Kwetii was a solid toddler and carrying her was no easy task, but Maggie cradled her close the best she could as they hurried back to the village.

***

Kwetii continued to wheeze with every breath as the day wore into night. They tucked her into the cot in Gwen's Long House where they could best keep watch over her. Finola kept her silence, staring into the fire as she swayed idly in a rocker next to the hearth. It unnerved Maggie to see her in such a state. She would give anything to see the woman break free from her torment and join them again. Even when Gwen bent down and looked into Finola's eyes, asking her to help Kwetii, Finola still did not stir.

Maggie worried Kwetii would fuss and cause the swelling to worsen, but as the hours passed the sting seemed to take a toll on her little body, and she drifted in and out of sleep. Gwen smeared a thick clay poultice over the sting to ease the swelling, which seemed to help, but the child continued to struggle with every breath despite the efforts. It was all they could do to keep her resting until the swelling subsided.

Epi-pens, she thought. *They had epi-pens to fix it in the future.* Perhaps she was no better than Marcus. If she could take Kwetii to the future and know it would save her life, would she do it?

Winn placed his hand over hers where it rested at Kwetii's side.

"Lay down your head," he said softly.

"I can't," she replied. She would not admit to him that she feared the child would stop breathing, and although she remained silent, she knew he could see the tears on her cheeks. The thought of sitting by helplessly as her child died from a simple bee sting was beyond her comprehension.

Her husband uttered a sigh as he rose to his feet, pulling her with him. As she opened her mouth to protest, he touched her lips gently with his thumb and shook his head.

"Stay here. I will return."

She nodded mutely and watched him leave. She sat back down at the bedside and took Kwetii's hand. The child uttered a whistling sigh as the breath struggled past her tiny constricted air way, but otherwise did not stir.

When Maggie felt a hand on her shoulder she assumed it was her husband, but she was shocked to discover her assumption was wrong. Although her blue eyes were still glazed a milky white, Finola stood beside her, looking down at Kwetii.

"Fret no longer, dearest. This will pass. The child will live," the old woman said, her words a harsh utterance through her cracked lips.

"You–you don't know that," Maggie stammered. She was torn between terror at seeing Finola standing like a ghost beside her and relief to see her slumber interrupted. Yet the woman she had known was somehow different now, a darker, guarded version of the healer she loved. "Gwen!" Maggie called out.

No matter what the reason for her semi-recovery, the woman was too frail to remain at Kwetii's bedside. When Gwen entered the room her face paled at the sight.

"Oh, my, sweet Odin! How did she get in here? Fer sure, Finola, come away! It's no place fer ye here!" Gwen admonished her. Gwen put her arm around Finola's shoulders and tried to steer her to the door, but the old healer would not budge.

Finola reached out with a thin, wrinkled hand and placed it on Maggie's arm.

"Kwetii will play with her brother when spring comes. Ye shall see. He will have the eyes of his father, and the spirit of his mother, like this one, here," Finola murmured, looking down on Kwetii. She touched the child's cheek with one finger, and then let it drop to her side as Gwen led her back to her chair.

Gwen joined Maggie a few moments later, her skin a fretful pallor as she trembled.

"She looks a fright. I've never seen one return from a journey, but perhaps she still has some fight left. It's the bad visions that send her away from us. Maybe the good visions will steer her back," Gwen nodded, as if to herself, then patted Maggie softly on her shoulder. "Aye, if she says yer breeding a son, then it is truth. Did ye already know?" Gwen asked.

"No. I–I didn't know for sure," Maggie replied quietly.

"Well, now ye know. And ye know yer daughter will be fine soon," Gwen assured her.

Maggie's hand slipped down over her belly. She had suspected, but ignored the signs, too wrapped up in the discord of their lives to acknowledge what her body was telling her. Although it gave her comfort to hear the prediction of a healthy son, the glimmer of hope that Kwetii might yet survive was what she focused on.

Winn returned later with a sack in his hands. She glanced up at him through tear-swollen eyes.

"Finola woke and she spoke to me. She said Kwetii will be fine," she whispered. She did not mention the rest of Finola's predictions, keeping the news close to her heart for the moment. There would be plenty of time to share it with Winn after Kwetii was healed.

"Gwen told me. Finola is a wise *Seer*, I am sure she speaks the truth."

He sank down beside her and took something from the sack. His eyes were hollow beneath his thick brows, creased at the edges as if speaking aloud pained him.

"I bought this for you when we were in town. I meant to give it to you when I returned."

He handed her a small, leather bound book. It was worn around the edges, but the stitching was intact and it still smelled of tanned hide when she flipped through the pages. It was handmade, with shimmering golden flecks pressed into the paper, and a flat jade colored stone embedded in the cover beneath the etching of a rainbow.

"It's beautiful," she said.

"John Jackson said it belonged to an English Princess. How he came to have it, I do not know, but he parted with it, no less. I thought it might make you smile when you read it to our daughter," he said softly.

He brushed the tears from her cheek and placed a gentle kiss on her forehead.

"Thank you," she whispered.

"You read. We will listen," he said.

Winn placed the open book on the bed next to Kwetii and thumbed to the first page.

She rested her shoulder against his and started to read. Although she squinted at the scrolled Old English words, she had little difficulty reading the familiar first lines.

"Once upon a time, there was a beautiful princess. She lived in a grand castle..."

***

Maggie woke to the sound of a gentle snore. Tiny fingers were twisted in her hair, gently pulling in rhythm with the rise and fall of Kwetii's chest. It was a purring snore, one she made often when sleeping. The strained whistling sound was gone.

Winn stirred when Maggie moved and she placed two fingers to her lips to silence him as he opened his mouth to speak, his blue eyes wide and hopeful. There would be time later to tell him her news, but for now it would wait as they enjoyed the peaceful slumber of the little girl between them.

"It is time to give her a new name," he whispered. "She has earned one of her own."

"I like her name," Maggie said softly. Winn smiled.

"As do I, but we cannot call her *little one* forever. She will not like that when she is grown."

"Do you have another name?" she asked. The question had never occurred to her, even though she knew it was common for the Paspahegh people to have several names throughout their lifetimes.

"*Opinkwe*," he said, his voice low. "The boy with a white face," he added, more as an afterthought to himself rather than to her unasked question. "That is what *Opinkwe* means. It is my secret name, one I tell no man, lest he take my spirit by calling my true name."

Her throat tightened at the sadness in his tone. She leaned into his chest and settled back against him, pulling his warm arms around her.

"You, *ntehem*," he said as his lips pressed into her hair, "You have no need to call my true name. My spirit is already yours to command."

She smiled.

"I will hold you to that, warrior," she answered.

22

Winn

Winn watched the dancers as the music pounded around them. It was like the Paspahegh dances he was accustomed to in some ways, with a crowd gathered in a circle around those who knew the steps. The rumble of a deep hollow drum pounded out the beat, and the singing of the women along with the squeal of a lyre rounded out the melee. Maggie danced with the other women, swirling past him in her long flowing gunna, her arms locked at the elbows with Teyas as they laughed. The long dress reminded him of the time she spent with the English, and although he knew it was not the same, it still caused a stir of annoyance down deep.

"Erich says you plan to leave. Is there naught I can say to keep ye here?"

Winn eyed his father. He stopped calling him Pale Feather, a title which he could see clearly irritated the man, yet Winn still struggled with how to speak to him. Marcus took a sip from his drinking horn as Winn considered his response.

"Chief Dagr. Marcus Neilsson. What should I call you, father?" Winn asked as he continued to stare into the crowd. Marcus cleared his throat.

"Dagr Markús Neilsson is the name borne to me. Chief is by right of blood, as was my father. Dagr Markús was the name given to me by my father to honor his father. And Neilsson marks me as get of my sire. Call me what ye will."

"I have only known you as Pale Feather," Winn replied. He left the rest unspoken.

"Well, the Paspahegh called me that. Use it if ye must, it is only a name." Marcus drained the last of the mead from his drinking horn and held it out to Winn. "There's more to these people than ye know. Take this horn. It belonged to my father, and his sire before him. I give it now to you, my eldest son, so that you will know your place here among your people."

Marcus placed the horn into his hand before Winn could dismiss him. It felt heavy in his grip, warmed by his father's fist, and he looked down at it in his curiosity. It was the vessel of a king, and Marcus had placed it in his hand.

"I think you hand this to the wrong son," Winn said, turning it over in his hands before he handed it back to Marcus. Marcus flexed his jaw. They both glanced over to the long table, where Benjamin sat at the head, surrounded by the other men. His brother, nearly a replica of Marcus, laughed along with Erich and Cormaic, as the younger men hung on his every word. Yes, Benjamin had always been a charismatic one. Winn once admired that about him. Winn had also once believed his brother was an honest man, beyond reproach.

"Nay. Keep it. Think on this before you leave. You belong with these people, just as much as ye once belonged to the Paspahegh. Think of yer wife, as well, lad. She has kin here, the same as ye. It willna be an easy life if ye return to the tribe." Marcus paused, looking toward Maggie as she danced. "Has she told ye much of the future? Of what happens to the tribes?"

"Yes. I know we will be driven from our lands. I know the English will never stop, that they will keep coming from across the sea."

Winn felt his ire rise, and felt his muscles quiver as he gripped the drinking horn. Marcus waved a hand toward the men at the table.

"Nothing is truly gone. These men you see, their sons will live on, as will their sons. My sons will live on. Someday, your daughter will have daughters, who will survive as we always have. It is about surviving, here, in this place where ye are now, and making a life for yer weans.

We stay here, away from the cities, and someday our children will venture into that world. But not yet, not until the time is right. If I have learned naught from time-travel, I have at least learned that."

"So running and hiding is how you wish to survive," Winn said evenly. Over the last few weeks, his father had gained his grudging respect, but perhaps it was misplaced.

"We fight when we must. Yes, we have killed plenty of English. Erich tells me for the most part they stay clear of us here. What issue is there with knowing the future, and using it to keep yer kin safe? It canna be such a bad thing, if we can use it that way."

"I can keep my kin safe without your magic," Winn said. He spotted Maggie making her way through the crowd toward them, and Marcus straightened up when he noticed her as well.

"Aye, that ye can, Winn *Neilsson*. That ye can." Marcus placed a hand on his shoulder. "Maggie will never be safe amongst the Powhatan, no matter what yer uncle has promised ye. Think on it before you make yer choice."

Winn covered his scowl when Maggie launched herself into his arms. She laughed as he swirled her around, burying his face in her soft auburn hair to inhale her sweet honeysuckle scent. Her cheeks were flushed and her eyes bright with mischief as she glanced back and forth between him and Marcus.

"Why aren't you dancing? Does the brooding Viking have you stuck in some dull conversation?" she asked him, wrapping her arms around his waist. He shrugged out of her grasp as Marcus chuckled.

"You dance, I will watch," he said.

"And ye haven't seen brooding yet, my lady, if ye think that was it!" Marcus laughed. "I'll take a turn with ye, if ye insist. I still have moves."

"Right. Your moves? I know you can't dance, you old fart. But we can give it a whirl if you want," she giggled, taking Marcus by the arm. "Oh, wait, let me check on Kwetii first. I'll be right back. Gwen put her to sleep and I need to say goodnight."

Maggie dropped a quick kiss on Winn's cheek and then punched Marcus in the arm before she jaunted off out of the Northern Hall.

"What did she just say?" Winn asked. "And why did she hit you?" The only meaning he gleaned from her utterance was that she was going to check on their daughter. Marcus shrugged as he rubbed his bicep.

"Future talk. I took my oath as protector seriously. Nary a lad put a hand on that hellion if I could help it," he sighed. "She still has a mean right hook."

Winn grunted in reply. Marcus clapped him on the shoulder and left him standing there with the drinking horn in his hand. He noticed Chetan dancing with Rebecca in the middle of the crowd, and was not surprised to see Makedewa glaring at them from the corner. When the song paused, Cormaic switched places with Chetan, and suddenly Makedewa went from indifferent annoyance to full-blown fury. Winn saw Makedewa's eyes narrow at the dancing pair as they flew by. He also noticed the way Cormaic pulled Rebecca a bit closer when they swirled near the men.

He wanted to laugh at his brother, but after seeing how disturbed the younger man was, he decided to join him. Perhaps they would share mead from the exotic drinking horn that now belonged to him.

When Winn reached his brother's side, Cormaic swung Rebecca so close that her skirts flared out and brushed his knee. He dimmed the grin from his face as Makedewa made a rough snorting sound and proceeded to gulp his drink.

"You should dance with her," Winn advised his brother.

"Warriors do not dance like that," Makedewa barked.

"I see many warriors here dancing. One with your woman," Winn replied, his brow raised slightly.

"She is not my woman. She can dance with that Viking if she wishes. I could take him in battle with nothing but my fists," Makedewa muttered.

"Then fight him. I will tell him you challenge him on the field tomorrow."

"Fine. Do it."

Makedewa dumped out what was left of his mead as he watched the dancers. Chetan walked up and gave him a hearty shove.

"She dances well," Chetan said.

"Enough!" Makedewa snarled. Winn and Chetan watched him stalk out of the Northern Hall, and the moment he was clear they burst into laughter.

"I have never seen him act this way. Why doesn't he speak to her and be done with it?" Winn asked. Chetan took the drinking horn Winn held and turned it over, examining it as he shrugged.

"I think he should bed her," Chetan replied, "Before he loses his *opomens*."

Winn grinned at the slur. Chetan used many of the taunts Maggie taught him from the future. *Lose his balls, indeed.*

As Chetan went off to fill the drinking horn, Winn looked over to the long table where Marcus sat. Did his customs mean he could not let his brother drink from the horn? Yet Marcus had offered it to both Winn and Maggie on the first night of their arrival, so he could see no error in letting Chetan drink from it. If there were rules attached to the object, his father should have advised him of such before he gifted it.

"Here, *Lord* Winn," Chetan said when he returned, thrusting the horn at him as Winn scowled. "What? The others call you such. They call you *my lord*, as they do your father."

"Enough, brother," Winn said. He looked around for Maggie, who had not returned. It had been long enough to bid their daughter goodnight, so he decided to check on them both. "Hold that for me. I will be back."

Chetan shrugged and took a drink from the horn.

"Find Makedewa. Tell him to stop acting a fool and return. Tell him his woman misses him," Chetan laughed.

Winn shook his head as he left and mumbled a retort to his brother. Rebecca was dancing happily with Cormaic, just as when Makedewa had left. Even if he found Makedewa, the last thing Winn would do was tell him to return.

Winn followed the gravel path through the village toward the Long House he shared with Maggie. The Norse strung blown glass globes from house to house, the orbs filled with lit candles that cast an eerie glow through the courtyard. A crescent shaped moon gave little light overhead, and instead they relied on the candles to illuminate the way. Maggie said it made her feel safe to have the candles burn at night, that it reminded her of streetlights in her own time. It seemed she had known little darkness in the future time the Bloodstone snatched her from.

He slowed his pace as he reached the Long House. The plank door was flung wide, and he heard the murmur of voices inside, one of which was not his daughter.

23

Maggie

"How dare you follow me?" Maggie shouted. Kwetii moaned in her sleep, and Maggie immediately lowered her voice to a seething hiss. "Do you want Winn to kill you? Is that what you're about? I won't stop him, you know, not for one second!"

She stomped her foot for emphasis. Annoyed beyond belief that Benjamin had invaded her space, she did not understand why he could not leave well enough alone. Things had calmed down of late, and Winn appeared to be softening toward the idea of staying. Yet it would take just one stupid move by Benjamin to end her hope, and he was standing in front of her wielding it.

"I dinna come here to fight with ye! I just want a few words with ye, and then I'll leave ye be! I never see ye without Winn at yer side, and I'd rather not cause more strife between us," he said. Benjamin ran both hands through his unruly dark curls, clutching the back of his neck as he stared at her.

Maggie crossed her arms over her chest. Fair enough. She supposed she could hear him out. She did not feel that she owed him anything, after the way he lied and schemed, but since she loved his father and his brother, she would give him a few minutes if it would help things.

"Fine. You have two minutes. I need to get back to my husband."
She saw him flinch.

"Thank ye," he said. He approached, and she stepped back, shaking her head. He sighed and dropped his hands. "It's still strange to me, ye know. Seeing ye here, and knowing yer my brother's wife. But see ye, I must, if I wish to live with my kin, and yes, I do! I do want to be here. Do ye know what it's like, to have no kin?"

"Of course I do. We played together as children. You know I had no parents, that Marcus was my family! Why do you ask that?"

"Oh, aye. I remember that. You were a foul-mouthed thing even then, I think ye told me to go shit myself or some other nonsense before ye kicked me out of yer hiding place," he said.

A grin twisted the corner of her lip, unwilling, but definitely there. Yes, she recalled the last time she saw him as a child as well. Flashes of a curly-headed boy that followed her everywhere snuck into her mind, images of the future life they both left behind. Yes, she knew what it was like, to be displaced, to feel alone in another time. It was one reason she had married Benjamin when she thought Winn was dead.

"Did you come here to talk about that life, or this one?" she asked softly.

"Maybe both. I know not what to say to ye. I wish ye to know there will be no trouble from me. That bloody magic stone is something I never wish to see again, but at least it has returned me to the place I belong. It feels right, to have a place, I mean. A place to belong to. I wish that fer ye, as well."

He coughed, seeming to cover the waver in his voice as he turned to leave.

"I did the best I could fer ye, Maggie. I know I wronged ye, and for that I am sorry. Maybe my heart clouded my judgment, and I'll pay for it fer all my days. But yer wife to my brother now, and a good brother I will be."

He ducked through the doorway and left without turning around. Her mouth hung open at his declaration, and she closed it with a snap. She tucked a fur around her sleeping child as she considered his speech.

So Benjamin wanted to mend fences. She thought back on the short time she had spent as his wife. He had been caring and considerate, treading carefully on the tatters of her broken heart as he tried to win her affection. If Winn had truly been dead, she would still be Benjamin's wife. She looked down on her sleeping daughter and realized that Benjamin would have raised the child as his own. Maggie could not deny that she cared about him, but their relationship was a complicated one. Benjamin was from the future, just as she was, and if not for the Bloodstone magic, they would have grown up together with Marcus on her grandfather's farm.

Yet reality was that the powerful magic served some other purpose, and both she and Benjamin ended up in the past. Reality was that Benjamin served her up to be hanged as a witch in a jealous fit once he knew Winn was alive. Yes, in the end, Benjamin had saved her, but she was not sure it was enough to restore the friendship they once shared.

What would Winn say to Benjamin's declaration? Of course, she would tell her husband of the visit. Maggie kissed Kwetii's forehead and then left to make her way back to the Northern Hall.

Winn was standing with Chetan when she returned, and she noticed Makedewa standing in the corner with a sulking look on his face. She wondered what she had missed. Her husband gave her no time to think further on it, slipping his hand around hers. His fingers twisted into hers, and he squeezed her gently as he raised her knuckles to his lips for a kiss.

"Kwetii?" he asked. She reached over and kissed the edge of his jaw as he pulled her close.

"She's fine. Winn?" she asked. She needed to tell him of Benjamin's visit, but when her husband looked down at her with soft eyes and a curious stare, she decided it could wait.

"What is it, *ntehem?*"

She watched the dancers swirling in circles, their laughter nearly as raucous as the music and drums.

"Nothing," she answered. "I think I owe Chief Dagr a dance."

Winn's lips brushed her forehead and he released her.

"I will watch. But only him. I will share you with no other," he murmured. She caught the hint of strain in his blue eyes, but it was a glimmer quickly passed and replaced with a smile. She turned back and kissed him square on the mouth before she danced away, leaving him with a grin on his face.

***

Maggie left Kwetii in the care of Rebecca the next morning while she prepared to join the women gathering wool. She asked Gwen why they didn't just shear the sheep, but when Gwen took her to the ridge overlooking the valley where they could see the herd, Maggie understood why. The Norse kept no ordinary sheep. The beasts were twice the size of any she had ever seen, with long, stringy hair and thick bulbous heads adorned with curling ram-like horns. It was easier, and safer, to gather the tufts of wool they left behind each morning than to try to procure it otherwise. Gwen said they all came from three surviving breeding stock that made the first time-travel journey with them to Virginia. She clammed up after that revelation, and Maggie made a mental note to take it up with Marcus. She wanted to know everything about their past, and she was fair tired of everyone acting like it was a taboo subject.

She poked her head inside the door to the Long House Teyas and Rebecca shared with a few other women. Teyas was alone in the house, rolling up garments and placing them in a carrying sack, her long black hair falling loose around her shoulders as she worked.

"Are you coming up to the ridge? Rebecca will stay with Kwetii. I thought we would walk together," Maggie said.

"Go without me, sister. I must pack if I wish to say goodbye before we leave."

Maggie bent down and gently took her hand. Tears ran down the younger woman's face, but she would not raise her red-rimmed brown eyes.

"What are you talking about?" Maggie asked.

"My mother and father have arranged a marriage. Winn will take me to the Nansemond village today. Did he not tell you?" Teyas said.

Maggie shook her head, biting down hard on her lower lip.

"He can't do that. He wouldn't," she replied.

"It is his duty, as it is mine," Teyas said softly as she closed the sack.

"But without duty, would you still go?"

Teyas bowed her head. Maggie clasped her hands, and they clung together as she cried.

"I am happy to know I will be a wife soon," Teyas insisted through her tears. Maggie held her as she cried, stifling her own tears in her sister's hair. Not only was Teyas being taken away, her husband had willfully kept that information from her. Maggie felt the surge of anger and helplessness that often accompanied her through such times. Although Teyas knew she grieved, Teyas could not truly comprehend the anger Maggie felt at the woman being forced into a marriage with a man she did not know. To Teyas, it was a part of life. To Maggie, it was unfathomable.

"I'll talk to him," Maggie insisted.

"No! Keep silent, this is no matter for you. You know this!" Teyas said, wiping her eyes with the back of her hand. "I am too many summers to go on without a husband. I am lucky Osawas will have me."

"He is the lucky one!" Maggie snapped. Teyas smiled.

"I hear he is brave. Winn says he has fought with our uncle."

Maggie flinched at the mention of Opechancanough. He was the last Indian she wished to run into again, yet her family remained tied to him as if bound by shackles instead of blood. Even though she shared her knowledge of the future with her husband, Winn still retained his loyalty to his uncle and felt it best to stay in his favor. Maggie suspected this marriage pact was part of keeping that favor with the tribe, and it stoked her anger to see her husband offer his sister up for the taking. She still did not truly understand the way the Powhatan lived, and she stumbled over embracing their traditions, especially when it came to the role of women and men in society. It was just one more issue driving a wedge between them.

"Where will you live?" Maggie asked. She already knew it would not be with them. It was unlikely Osawas would be willing to leave his tribe to stay with their exiled family, so much so that it was not worth mentioning.

"I know not. My mother lives with Pepamhu now at Mattanock, she is first wife since his old wife died, Winn says. But Osawas is Weanock. Perhaps they will send us to live with his people."

"Isn't that far? A five-day ride, at least!"

Teyas made an attempt to smile, but it came out bitter and strained. "Yes, at least that much," she said.

"I'll–I'll go with you. I'll go pack now," Maggie said. Teyas grabbed Maggie's hand.

"He says you must stay here, with Kwetii. He does not trust the Weanock as he does the Nansemond. He fears for your safety."

"Oh, really? He said that?"

Teyas nodded, her eyes downcast.

"Help me pack, sister," Teyas whispered.

Maggie handed her another traveling sack. After they finished, Teyas set off to find the women, and Maggie left her to find Winn. With woolgathering temporarily forgotten, and her temper inflamed at her husband keeping information from her, she struggled to slow her breathing before she confronted him.

Was she angrier with him, or with herself? She still needed to tell him of the conversation with Benjamin, but the longer she put it off, the more difficult it was to bring up. Even more important was the news of the babe growing within her, which she was also at loss to reveal. Now with the issue of Teyas clouding her thoughts, she felt like her control over everything was slipping away.

She found him at the ridge, standing with Erich and Marcus, and surprisingly, Benjamin. The brothers stood well apart, however, and did not appear to be engaging in conversation with each other, but even to see them standing on the same patch of soil was enough to give her pause.

Winn wore a lightweight tunic over tight braies like his kinsmen, his new sword protruding from a harness strapped across his back. She noticed he had new boots as well, knee-high leather bound covered with thick fur, with tough soles that protected his feet better than the moccasins did. Unlike some of the other natives, Winn took easily to trying new things, which Maggie suspected was part of his upbringing. His uncle raised him to be an informant, living among the English and various Indian tribes, learning what he could and acclimating to their ways. Winn had a resultant comfort with change, and although he usually migrated back to his breechcloth and leggings, he was willing to try anything once. Seeing him dressed like the others, especially Marcus, gave her a pang of homesickness.

Winn belonged there with his kin, yet soon they would leave.

"What brings ye up here, my lady?" Erich asked when he spotted her trudging up the hill. She lifted the skirt of her gunna above her ankles as she reached the peak, panting a bit with the effort. It was steep rise. Now that she stood next to Erich, it took her breath away. Swirling below was an inlet, with white-capped waves crashing over silvery boulders and the screams of seagulls warning them away from their nests. She clutched her arms around her waist when a breeze whipped up and her hair rippled back off her face.

"Looking for my husband," she said, stretching her head to peer over the side of the ledge. Winn closed his hand over her wrist.

"You found me. Go back down, I will return soon," he said. His words were abrupt and his grip on her arm was firm. She noticed Winn glanced at the others, and an unspoken word passed between him and the men. Whatever man scheming they were up to, she would hear it, whether now or later. With her curiosity speeding into overdrive, she tried to pull her wrist away from Winn.

"What's down there?" she asked. She stood on her toes and arched her chin over Winn's shoulder, then pulled back with a gasp when she glimpsed the curve of a ship's bow. "Was that a ship down there? Did you build it? What–"

"Aye, a ship, my lady. No need to worry ye, we'll no sail yet. Yer husband here must grow his sea-legs first before we set out," Erich answered. She saw Winn's jaw tighten and he shot a tense glare at Erich. Benjamin remained silent, observing from afar, but Marcus intervened in his typical overbearing manner. She was rapidly losing patience with his new disposition.

"Go back down, girl. This is no talk fer women!" Marcus snapped.

Maggie's fists shook as she clenched them tight against her sides. He had never spoken to her in such a way before, and she did not like it one bit. First Winn had betrayed her by planning to take Teyas away. Then Marcus treated her as if she had no worth at all. It was much more than her pride could handle.

"Did you *really* just say that to me?" she shrieked. "I'm no *girl*, and I'll damn well go where I want to, and I– oh, damn it, Winn! Put me down!" she screamed as her husband scooped her into his arms. He spared her the indignity of tossing her over his shoulder, but being carried like a child was just as humiliating. She uttered a slew of curses at him the entire way back to the Long House, where he deposited her, still screeching, into a heap on their bed platform. When he released her, she immediately jumped to her feet, but he took her by both arms and pushed her firmly back down.

"Enough!" he shouted. "You cannot speak to Chief Dagr like that!"

"Yes, I can!" she insisted.

"Do you have no shame? If you were any other woman–"

"I've known him my whole life, I won't act like he's some–some *King*!" she spat.

"He is! He is Chief to these people! He deserves your respect!" He stared hard into her eyes. "You knew him in a different time, in that future you were born to! That means *nothing* when you stand here, in this time! You are no equal to him!"

"And to you? Am I your equal? Or do I mean nothing to you as well?" she asked, glaring at him as her breath came shallow and rapid.

"You are my wife."

"What if you had been the one to travel, Winn? What if you ended up in my time? Would you just keep your mouth shut and do what everyone else told you, and never ask any questions? I feel like I have no control of anything, like we could all be killed at any moment, and what can I do about it? Sit here like a fool, waiting for you men to give me *permission* to act!"

"Do you think I would let harm come to you? To our daughter? Have I not proved that to you?" he asked. His voice was strained, she could hear the edge of hurt betrayed in it. She had not meant to question his manhood, yet she could see the mere suggestion grated at him.

"No. I didn't say that. I just meant–"

"You think I cannot keep you safe in this time. Is it so safe, where you came from, years from now? Are there no wars, no fighting? Do all men live in peace in this wondrous place?" he asked.

She shook her head. How could she make him understand, without wounding him further?

"No, it's not perfect. But I had a home, one where I felt safe when I slept at night. Men didn't kill each other without consequence. I never saw such things, until I came here, Winn."

"Do you wish to return there?"

"No," she whispered. "Of course not."

"Then stay here, until I come for you. I will be back. Do not leave this Long House!" he warned.

"Why? Why should I?" she asked. Did her words have no meaning to him, and would he ever truly understand her fears? She doubted it as he tossed yet another ultimatum at her, as if he dared her to challenge him. "Once again, more orders! Why can't I go to the ridge?"

"Because I tell you to! You need no other reason!" he roared, punching his fist into the furs beside her. She did not flinch, but she struggled to maintain even breaths as he stared into her eyes. He trapped her between his arms, leaning over her on the platform, his eyes wild.

"What are you men hiding up there?" she whispered.

"It does not concern you."

"Like you taking Teyas away does not concern me?"

She thought she saw a flicker in his gaze, but it was only for a moment.

"Yes. It does not concern you," he growled.

"You're taking Teyas away, to be *married*, and you won't even take me with you? You're an ass!"

He shoved away from the platform, leaving her panting for air. She watched him stalk to the doorway as if he meant to leave, then abruptly turn back to her.

"You. Will. Be here. When I return," he said evenly, advancing closer with each uttered syllable. She could see the fire reaching his blue eyes, smoldering beneath his thick dark brows. She raised her chin a notch in defiance.

"I will leave if I want to," she whispered. He was closer, his chest nearly touching hers when she exhaled.

"Then I will tie you," he replied. She shuddered.

"Try it," she said, her words much braver than she actually felt. She regretted taunting him, and wished desperately to take back their discord, yet the damage was done and they were too far gone to stop. His hands darted out for her and she slapped at him, lurching backward to get away. He was quicker, easily catching her, but she was lithe as well and twisted in his grasp until they stumbled onto the platform with a thud.

She felt her hip strike the wood edge and the sting of tears at the pain as the breath rushed from her lungs, his body pinning hers to the furs. Her legs and arms were useless, since this was not the first time they had battled and he knew her tricks well. Her head, however, was still free, and when she shook it she made contact with his with a sickening crack. He let out a frustrated groan and she took the opportunity to scramble away. She turned onto her belly and crawled further from him, but he yanked her back a moment later, dashing her escape. He tossed her over onto her back and held her with one hand, glaring at her as blood dripped from his eyebrow.

"Are you finished?" he growled. She was panting shallow, trying to catch her breath.

"Get off of me!"

"No," he replied, his breaths coming hard and fast. She felt him shift, his weight full on hers. He was rapidly becoming aroused, she could feel him against her thigh through their thin garments. As much as she would like to end their argument, the thought caused her fury to rise further. Did he think he could silence her with sex? She could not silence the angry words that spilled from her mouth.

"Tie me up then, if you must. Just do it, and go," she whispered. She saw the corner of his mouth twitch, and although he did not smile, his eyes clouded with heat as he adjusted his hips upon hers.

She closed her eyes when he pulled the cord from her waist and used it to bind her wrists, leaving her hands tied above her head with her gunna gaping loose. The breeze whispered on her skin when his fingers traced a shallow path down one breast, and she shivered at the contact.

"I think I should bind your legs as well," he said. He ran one hand down her thigh and then back up, pulling her leg up by the knee toward her chest.

"Stop it, Winn," she said, shifting her hips and feeling a surge of desire spread through her traitorous body. He groaned at her movement and shook his head, and she felt him shed his braies. He plucked at the strings of her dress and quickly gave up, tearing it down the middle so that he could bury his mouth upon her aching breasts. She arched to meet his lips with a cry, her bound hands coming down around his neck to hold him as he paid worship to her. He pummeled the barriers between them with his need, silencing any remnant of protest, until she screamed his name and begged him never to stop.

They fought like that, flesh upon flesh, seeking consolation in release, yet nowhere near satiated as they lay entwined afterward. She rested her bound hands against him, watching the rise and fall of his chest as he lay quietly beside her. Should she breach the silence, or not? She knew no way to mend the tension between them.

Suddenly Winn sat up and moved away from her, resting his arms over his knees as he looked toward the door. She stared at the outline of his sculpted back.

"Obey me, wife," he finally said. "I cannot stay here. They expect me to return."

"Then go," she said softly. She saw his shoulders sag as he let out a shallow sigh. From where she lay beside him on the furs, she could not see his face, but she could see his head bowed onto his knees and the outline of his tense jaw. "Take Teyas away. Keep your secrets. I'm just your wife. I know what that means."

His back stiffened.

"You break me, wife," he said, his voice hoarse and low as he turned back to her. He pulled her into his arms, his eyes shimmering beneath narrowed brows. "You know what it means? It means I want you, as I want water when my lips thirst. As I want food when I have hunger. But this need, this need I have for you–it breaks me. It takes the breath from my chest. It drains the blood from my veins and the spirit from my soul. I cannot be, unless I can be here with you, like this. With our flesh touching and your heart beating here, against mine. I cannot *be*, not without you."

He took her wrists in his hands and slowly unwound the binding. The cord dropped to the furs beside them. His thick lashes lowered over his gleaming eyes as he stared at her hands resting in his.

"Rage if you must. Do it here. I will return soon."

She watched him fasten his braies. He left the Long House without another glance in her direction, closing the door behind him.

24

Winn

He found the men where he left them at the crest of the hill. Erich sat alone on a flat rock, idly grinding a stick into a point as he watched the others. He raised an eyebrow at Winn as he approached.

"Settled things, did ye?" Erich said.

"Yes. What has Jarl Dagr decided?" Winn replied, giving his wife's uncle a nod. He hoped by returning to the conversation at hand, Maggie's behavior would be dismissed. He was certainly in no mood to discuss it further.

"Nothing yet. I think he waits for ye. Wipe yer head, lad."

Winn ran the back of his hand over his brow with a scowl, wiping off the smeared dark blood as Erich grinned. *Damn that woman.*

"She has a temper like her mother, that one," Erich said.

"So I should thank your *MacMhaolian* blood for that?" Winn snapped, his words terse despite the attempt to curtail his annoyance. Eric shook his head as he chuckled.

"Well, perhaps not all of it. Her father had a bit of rage to him at times."

It was the first time anyone had directly spoken of Maggie's parents in his presence. With his curiosity wearing stronger than his frustration, he focused on his wife's uncle. For a man who claimed to love his sister, he spoke little of the woman, and it only made sense to Winn that Erich wished to hide something.

"Esa was your sister, but who was my wife's father? Was he of this tribe as well?" Winn asked. Erich nodded a bit to himself at the question, letting out a long sigh as he considered the ground at his feet.

"My sister was a headstrong woman. I know you see how speaking sense to one like that might not work," Erich said. His gaze shifted to meet Winn's, his green eyes seeming hallowed under the depths of his brows, as if the words pained him. "She met Agnarr at a gathering, but he dinna tell her who he was. By the time we knew, it was too late. She was breeding his child. I should have killed him the day we found out, but I dinna. Dagr and I had too much to think on right then, my headstrong sister the least of it, with yer raving uncle calling for all our heads."

"Did Opechancanough kill Maggie's father?" Winn asked, hungry for more of the tale.

"No. When I sent Esa away with Dagr, he took his people and left, I know not where he went. Better off. We have no need of his kind," Erich muttered. The older man waved at Winn, as if dismissal.

"What kind is that?"

"A worthless *lucht*, that's his kind. Best keep that to yerself, no need for wee Maggie to hear of it. No sense having her chase the dead."

"So you know he is dead?"

"He must be. Or he would have come fer Maggie by now," Erich said quietly. He shook his head back and forth like a wet dog, muttering to himself in his native Norse tongue. "Go see to yer Chief. He waits for your return." The older man ended the conversation, putting a clear obstruction up to further inquiry.

Winn knew there was much more to the story than the few tidbits he gleaned from Maggie's uncle, and he made note to follow through on it with his father. For such a loyal clan, they surely had their secrets. Winn looked toward the peak of the hill where his father spoke with the others.

Marcus and Benjamin stood talking with an older man he did not know. He was shorter in stature, dressed like the other Norsemen, with long muddy brown hair tied back at his nape. Although he differed in stature, he held the bearing of a seasoned warrior as he spoke with Marcus, staring boldly at his Chief in a borderline defiant manner.

"Who is that man?" Winn asked with his eyes fixed on the stranger.

"Oh, Old Ivar? He is the last of Chief Drustan's men. He served yer Da's father well, but I fear he longs too much for the old ways. He wants to sail to Vinland, no matter what the cost," Erich replied.

"He seems angered."

"Aye. He questions the story Dagr tells of the future. He bids to take the ship and sail nonetheless. Do ye think it's all true? Are the colonies really gone from Vinland?"

Both Maggie and Marcus had relayed tales of the future. Winn knew how painful it was to hear of the demise of the life he was born to. Knowledge of the future was a tricky thing, and the tales could not be taken back once told. Apparently, Ivar was having difficulty hearing the Norse colonies no longer existed in Vinland. In fact, the Norse colony in Vinland had been abandoned more than two hundred years before.

"The Chief has no cause to lie. Maggie tells the same story, it is well known in the time they traveled from. Both Vinland and Greenland are abandoned."

"So that means there is no colony to travel to. We've waited too long to return to our own lands, and we have built this ship for naught." Erich stabbed the pointed stick into the ground at his feet and stood up. "Thank Odin Chief Dagr returned. He's a bloody fool fer using that magic, but he saved our people from certain death by it. Without him we surely would be adrift, looking for a place no longer there."

"Will you stay here?" Winn asked.

"If Dagr thinks we must. I care naught as long as our kin is safe and we have food in our bellies. I'm getting too old for new adventures, no less. Aye, I can be a farmer, like the Englishmen."

Winn glanced over at Marcus. The men had listened to his tales of the future, but he could see the unease in their faces as they regarded their Chief. Even Benjamin looked disturbed. When the men had gathered on the ridge to meet with the Chief, Benjamin had kept a careful distance. One son to the right, one to the left. Winn would respect their customs, as he had learned to do throughout the years, yet suddenly it had become much more than regard for another man's beliefs. There was a part of him that wished for the kinship, to have a duty and purpose to his own people again. The last of the Paspahegh had been settled among other tribes, yet Winn and his family drifted from place to place seeking a home.

If not for Benjamin, Winn could see forming an alliance with the Norse. He had grown a grudging respect for Marcus, despite their differences, and Winn knew the man would protect his family to the death. Yet living alongside Benjamin was something he could not do. How could he live peacefully with his brother, the man who had stolen his wife and left him for dead? Even if Maggie had forgiven him, Winn feared he did not have it in his blood to move on.

"Winn, a word with ye?"

Marcus approached, leaving Benjamin with the others. With a glance at Marcus, Erich stood and joined the group, giving them privacy. Winn saw something pass between the two men. It was a quick dip of Erich's chin, and the hardening of Marcus's jaw, slight yet noticeable.

"You will not let them sail, will you?" Winn asked. Marcus shook his head.

"No. The colonies are long gone. We must make our future here, in this land. We've been farmers before, we can do it again." Marcus waved Winn to sit, and then joined him on the log. His father sat with his hands braced on his knees for a moment, staring ahead at the other men gathered overlooking the inlet.

"I must tell ye something of the future, and ye must listen to me," Marcus said.

"Then speak. The men wait for you," Winn replied.

"We took Maggie's mother away to protect her. Maggie bears the last blood of the most powerful of us, she is the key to keeping the blood alive. Old Malcolm and I thought someday she would wed my son, and the Blooded Ones would live on through them."

"A fine plan," Winn snorted. "And the wrong son found her."

"Nay, not the wrong son. It turned out different than we planned, but it was meant for this way. That blasted woman fell through time to find ye, if that is not destiny, I know not what is."

Winn pushed his doubts aside for the moment.

"I told ye I found records. That's how I found ye. What I dinna tell ye was I know when we all meet our end."

"Do not tell me of our ends," Winn said quietly.

"But I must."

"No," Winn growled, glaring at his father. "What good comes of such knowledge?"

"The good of saving her," Marcus replied. "If you take her back to the tribes, even the Nansemond, Maggie will die. Your uncle will see her dead, I know this."

"I do not believe you. My Weroance gave us his blessing. He let her go, when he could have killed her. I have served him faithfully–there is no cause for him to harm her!" Winn shouted, rising to his feet. The others looked back at them curiously, but maintained their distance, the interest evident on their faces.

"You must believe me. I found a story of her death at the hands of Opechancanough. I know not when, but I believe the tale. Leave her here. Stay with these people, make your life here. I beg you, do not return to them."

Marcus stood as well, running a hand through his hair then settling to clutch the nape of his neck. His father's eyes, so similar to his own, were fatigued.

Could his tale be true? Had Winn served his uncle all this time, to see his uncle harm his wife in the end? He would not believe it. Especially coming from Marcus, how could he trust him? Perhaps his father meant to keep Winn and his family close with more lies.

"In the future, family and blood mean very little, not like it does here. Now, in this time, to these people, her blood means everything. To have back that which we always protected, when we thought it lost? It gives them purpose again, something we all must have. Do ye know, son, what power she has? What lies in yer daughter's blood? The blooded *MacMhaolians* have saved our people more than once, and that magic is our secret to guard," Marcus said, his gaze focused like a brand into Winn's.

"There are those that will come for her. I know not when, but I know they will come. They always have, no matter what time our people flee to. I know ye must feel like ye have no choice, son, but ye do. I ask ye to choose us. Take yer place at my side, let these people be yer own."

His father dropped his hands to his sides and turned away, his brows sheltering his stark grayed eyes.

"I will keep them safe. There is nothing for you to worry on," Winn finally answered. "Speak to your men. They wait for your word."

Winn waved his arm at the group of men, and Marcus turned to them. They joined the others without discussing it further.

25

Rebecca

Rebecca spread her cloak on the grass and her bible beside it. It had been a gift from Makedewa back when she first arrived, spoils she assumed he had taken from the ruins of Martin's Hundred. She still recalled the devastation of that day to the place she once lived with her English family, the entire town left in a burned out ruin and most of its inhabitants annihilated. A few days after the Massacre, when she had still been in some sort of haze, Makedewa had brought her a sack of gifts. She cried when she saw the items and he quickly left, so she never did properly thank him for his kindness. She wondered if he would ever try to speak to her again after their last encounter. What man would want such a damaged woman as a wife?

"Why do you walk out alone?"

Rebecca looked up, feeling foolish. Too entranced in her thoughts, she had not even heard Teyas approach.

"Only for some time with my own thoughts. The village is too busy today," she replied with a smile. Rebecca patted the cloak beside her. "Will ye sit with me? I would like your company."

Teyas squinted up at the afternoon sun, raising her hand to shield her eyes against the glare. Her hair was unbound, long and straight down her narrow back, which was a change from the two black braids she usually wore. She was dressed in a peculiar manner as well, with delicately beaded moccasins and a fresh white doeskin dress. Rebecca had never seen her so dressed before. The garb reminded her of the fine ceremonial attire Winn sometimes wore when he traveled to Jamestown on his duties for his uncle.

"I have little time before I must go. I came to bid you goodbye," Teyas said softly as she sat down beside her. Her friend's head was bowed and her eyes hidden under her thick downcast lashes.

"Goodbye? What do ye mean? Maggie said we might stay here, if Winn wishes it so," Rebecca stammered. Teyas placed a hand over hers.

"No, my friend. Only I must leave. My mother and father have arranged my marriage. My brothers will take me to Mattanock today."

"But no man has courted ye!"

"He will court me, when we meet. We will have a few days, I think, before I am a wife," she said.

"Is it always so, for the Indians?" Rebecca asked. "I mean, for you to marry a man you do not know?"

Teyas squeezed her hand, her lips curled up in a smile.

"Sometimes. I hear he is a brave warrior, and he gave many gifts to my mother for this match. I could refuse his pledge, but it would cause my mother shame."

"Oh, Teyas! I don't want ye to go!" Rebecca whispered fiercely, throwing her arms around her friend. They rocked together in a tight embrace, and soon she felt her friend's tears dampen her own cheek.

"Stop it, stop! I am happy to be a wife," she insisted. They drew away from each other, hands entwined in their laps. Teyas patted her hands, as if soothing herself, then wiped the tears from her cheeks. "You will be a good wife as well. I am sure my new husband will allow me to return for your wedding to my brother. I will see you again."

Rebecca swallowed back a sob in the midst of trying to stem her tears. She twisted her fingers together in her lap, clutching a handful of her wool skirt.

"Nay, there will be no wedding for me. I will never be a wife to your brother. I am sure he no longer wants to marry me, after our last parting," she said.

"Rebecca," Teyas said, her voice trembling. "You have a man who wishes to hold your heart. Do not turn him away. I fear you will regret it someday."

Rebecca looked up into her friend's soft brown eyes. Tears glistened on her cheeks, but she was beautiful even so. Rebecca was sure Teyas would make a fine wife. She was strong, confident, and everything a man could desire in a spouse.

Rebecca would regret making Makedewa unhappy more than anything, but she could not admit that to his sister. Teyas pulled her to her feet, and they walked back to the village together.

"Someday, you will see the moon through the trees," Teyas murmured, tucking her arm through Rebecca's. Rebecca hugged her, wishing there was some way to make time stand still.

26

Winn

Winn did not expect her to be in their Long House when he returned, yet she was. His wife and child napped on the sleeping platform, Kwetii curled up against Maggie's breast with one little fist bunched in her red hair, the sounds of their breathing a gentle snore echoing within the confines of the walls. He felt a tug deep in his chest as he watched them, the two he loved most in the world. As he sat down gently next to them, he wondered if Maggie would wake still angry or if she could see reason.

Reason? Perhaps not. It was not the first time they argued over her place at his side, and he knew it would not be the last. He usually liked to hear stories of how she lived in the future, but when it came to her expectations of what a wife was to a man, he had no patience for it. He heard her words and understood her meaning, yet she expected more of him than just listening. She wanted what she knew marriage to be in the future, but she wanted it with him, in their time. With all they had been through, at least that should be witness to why her desire could not be met, but nothing swayed her. Always defiant, never submissive, he had no desire to smother her fire. He only wished to find some impasse, a way to let her smolder without damage.

This time, however, was different. He still had a duty to his tribe, and he owed Pepamhu his respect. Winn would deliver Teyas as requested, no matter how much he would miss his sister and despite how he wished there was another way. Once he settled Teyas in the village, he would ride onto Jamestown to finish his business with the English. There he would meet the Indian translator, Joseph Benning, and escort him safely to his uncle's village. Maggie did not know yet that this exchange would mean the end of his service to his uncle, nor that Winn had cultivated it for months. Although it would ease her mind to know his duty to his uncle would soon be satisfied, Winn held that fact close until he could resolve the rest of their issues.

If Maggie knew his ties to the Powhatan Weroance were severed, she would expect them to settle in the Norse village. Yet that was a decision he was not prepared to make. Between her knowledge of future events, and the prediction Marcus made of Maggie's death, he knew not what path to take. He could only continue to take the risk of their future safety, and that of his family, on his shoulders alone. Seeing his wife bear such responsibility would be intolerable.

Kwetii let out a sweet sigh as he brushed her hair back off her cheek. He felt Maggie stir. Her jade eyes opened, round and swollen from her tears as she stared up at him, and he felt a pang in his belly at the knowledge of her distress.

How he wished he could take her fear away. If only he could banish the uncertainty, give her a foothold, perhaps she would lower her defenses and accept her place beside him.

"Hey," she said.

"I thought you would be with Teyas."

"You told me to stay here," she whispered.

He lowered his eyes as he sighed, nodding.

"Yes. I did," he agreed. She sat up, shifting her weight so as not to disturb Kwetii. As he realized that she had spent the last few hours alone in their Long House instead of with Teyas, he bit back a harsh retort. Yes, she was stubborn, but he had ordered her to stay. For once, despite her bluster, she had obeyed him.

"Come," he said gruffly, standing up from the pallet. "Say goodbye to my sister, bring Kwetii."

He did not wait for her to follow, the hot frustration streaking through him. Knowing he was leaving his wife when things lay unsettled made him bristle. It was difficult enough to honor his duty and take his sister back to the village with the certainty he might never see Teyas again. It was another matter entirely to leave Maggie with whispers of anger between them. He could see the hurt in her eyes, and he knew she did not understand why she must remain behind.

Winn stalked out to the courtyard, where the horses stood ready. Two horses would remain with Teyas, one for her to ride, the other to carry her belongings and to serve as a gift to Pepamhu. Makedewa and Chetan were already mounted, with Ahi Kekeleksu astride his pony beside them. He heard Maggie's footsteps behind him, but he did not look at her as he checked the straps on his mount.

Maggie and Teyas spoke quietly to each other, and Teyas took Kwetii into her arms. The women seemed resolved to the situation, and although he knew how much it pained his wife, he saw the way Maggie channeled her strength to show Teyas a brave face. With a tearful smile and a few stolen kisses, Teyas mounted her pony.

Winn swung up as well. Maggie stood back from the horses, her eyes rimmed pink but dry. Still sleepy, Kwetii rested on her mother's hip, seeming blissfully unaware that her Aunt and Father meant to leave. It was unusual for the toddler to let him go silently, but in light of the events of the day he imagined it was better for them all.

His breath hitched when he looked down at Maggie. Her lips parted slightly, then closed, and he could see her jaw tremble as she met his gaze.

"Before the sun sets on the second day, I will return, *ntehem*," he said, his voice low, meant for only her ears. "This is the last task I carry out for my uncle. When I return to you, my service to him is over."

She stared hard at him for a long moment.

"Be safe, warrior," she finally whispered.

He nodded. His throat was dry, his mouth too tight to speak. He could only acknowledge her with the simple gesture before he turned his horse away.

Those eyes haunted him, as always, seeing through the barrier that shielded his heart. Yes, she was still angry, but simmering beneath that jaded emotion, he could see her fear. When he returned, they would speak on it, find some way to bend the rigid barricade between them before it drove them further apart.

He heard only soft muffled sobs from Teyas as they rode away, yet it was his wife's image that clouded his visions instead.

27

Maggie

Maggie watched the men work on a new frame house adjacent to the Northern Hall. It was built in the English style with two stories and a narrow staircase up the middle, sticking up like an ugly cousin among the litter of thatched-roof Long Houses in the village. Benjamin worked to oversee the construction, and although he labored alongside the men, he clearly directed the efforts. It was easy to convince Marcus a two-story house would be the best use of their limited space in the secluded area, so when the growth of their community demanded it, he approved the work.

Maggie and Rebecca remained in the village to tend the meal-fire, while Gwen joined the others gathering honey. After Kwetii's brush with the bee sting Maggie was still on edge, and although she hoped it was an isolated incident, she was unwilling to risk it by going back to the fields.

The grazing season was nearing end, so the men had driven the herd of cows into a narrow pass above the valley. There they selected which to slaughter, and which to feed throughout the winter. Maggie and Rebecca spent the morning scraping the hides and storing the fat, while the children played nearby. Maggie could see Rebecca found the chore distasteful, but the younger woman carried on with little complaint. She had been even less talkative than usual since Makedewa left with Winn.

"Will they return soon?" Rebecca asked. Maggie tightened the hide over her knee and scraped away in a sweeping motion with her blade.

"Winn said only two days. Maybe tomorrow we will see them," she assured the younger woman. Rebecca looked wistfully out toward the construction, pausing in her scraping with a hide sprawled over her lap.

"Do ye think he will find a bride there, as well?" Rebecca asked softly. Maggie cocked her head sideways at her, stunned at the question. Although it was clear from both their behaviors that Rebecca and Makedewa missed each other, Rebecca had never verbalized it before. Maggie wondered what had prompted her inquiry.

"No, I don't think so. I think he means to return to you quickly," she replied. Rebecca blushed and lowered her head, resuming her scraping with renewed intensity. Maggie smiled.

"Perhaps he should stay. He could find a wife very easily," she mumbled.

"Why would you say that?"

"No matter."

Maggie sighed in frustration. She noticed Cormaic and Benjamin had stopped working, and Cormaic leaned on a spade, looking in their direction. He stared at Rebecca across the courtyard as she continued scraping. Both men propped their tools against the new wood frame and started walking toward them.

"Great," Maggie muttered as the men approached. Cormaic had a mischievous grin on his face, and although Benjamin appeared much less amused, he was still smiling. Both were covered with dust and grime, their skin smeared with the sweat of their labor. Cormaic reached for the bucket of fresh cider Maggie had brought out for the men, but Rebecca jumped to her feet and rationed it out to the men before Maggie could offer it.

"Thank ye, my lady," Cormaic murmured, his green eyes focused on Rebecca. Maggie saw her skin flush from ears to nape, and although she quickly sat back down and ducked her head to her work, she was clearly unsettled by the exchange.

"It looks good so far," Maggie said, trying to break the silence.

"Aye. It'll do fine. I expect the women will like it," Benjamin agreed. Maggie filled a cup and handed it to Benjamin, who took it with a graceful nod. Maggie kept her eye on her cousin, who openly stared at Rebecca as if he had never seen her before.

"Cormaic?" Maggie said.

"Hmm? What, cousin?"

"The house looks quite fine, I said," Maggie retorted. She stuck out her foot and stomped on his toe. Cormaic muttered a curse as his attention was drawn away from Rebecca, and Maggie smirked. He kicked a pile of dust her way in a playful manner, and before she knew it the game was on.

"Aye, ye thorny hellcat, it that what ye are about?" he grinned. The last word came out sounding like *aboot*, and Maggie burst into laughter as she rolled a thin strip of deer hide up and snapped it at him like a bath towel.

"Go on, get out of here! Don't you have work to do?" she admonished him. He roared when she smacked him with the hide, ducked his head, and grabbed her around the waist.

"I think my cousin needs a dunking! What say ye, Benjamin?" Cormaic laughed, picking Maggie up off her feet. He swung around as if he meant to dump her in the village well and Maggie punched him in the ribs, eliciting a grunt but no release.

"Aye, I think so," Rebecca piped up. Maggie glared at her.

"Traitor!" Maggie shot back at Rebecca. The younger girl held her lips closed in a tight line, clearly trying to keep from laughing.

"Come on now, enough," Benjamin interrupted. When Benjamin took her arm and pulled her away from Cormaic, she tried to shrug him off. Benjamin would not be swayed, however, until they had stopped their petty game.

"Ah, let her loose! I fear no simple woman!" Cormaic taunted her. Incensed at hearing Rebecca giggle behind her, Maggie kicked out at her loud-mouthed cousin, causing Benjamin to join the laughter as well.

"Ye should fear this one, she has quite a temper," Benjamin grinned. "She'd let a lad bleed out before she offered a hand to save ye. Mark my word," he said with a twinkle in his soft eyes. Maggie elbowed Benjamin hard in the ribs, and he released her. She stood glaring at the two men in mock defiance as she rubbed her wrist.

"I see no work done here."

They all stopped laughing when Marcus approached, his face stern and not the least bit amused at the antics. Rebecca made a whispered excuse about returning to the Long House, and both Cormaic and Benjamin straightened up as Marcus reached them. Maggie crossed her arms over her chest as she waited for his criticism. It seemed Marcus had turned into some high-handed stranger since they settled in the village, and she did not care for it at all.

Cormaic took a swig of cider as his eyes followed Rebecca. Benjamin dipped his cup for a refill and turned his attention to Marcus.

"Leave the women be, ye have plenty of work to do before nightfall," Marcus said.

"Aye, just having a drink, no harm," Cormaic said. Maggie shot him a scowl. If his intent was to impress Rebecca, he had come away looking like a playful fool, and she was glad of it. Rebecca had enough to think about without Cormaic vying for her attention.

Marcus stared hard at Benjamin, who met his gaze with measured return. Maggie sighed and sat back down to her work as Cormaic walked back to the frame-house. Marcus appeared annoyed as he sat down beside her, taking the cup from her hand and pouring himself some cider.

"Well? How's it coming?" Marcus asked, directing his inquiry at Benjamin, who stood in front of them. Benjamin drained his drink and then wiped his mouth with the back of his hand. At that moment she was struck by the resemblance, and she wondered how she had not realized it long ago. With his dark curling hair plastered along his neck, and round slate eyes staring at her, Benjamin was the image of his father.

"It goes well. It will be finished in two days time, if the weather holds. Gwen thinks a storm is brewing, so we shall see," Benjamin answered.

"Good. I expect we will need the space when yer brother returns. Go on, get on with it then, son."

Benjamin nodded, and she saw the muscles of his throat contract as he looked down at the dirt.

"Aye, well, enjoy yer drink. I'll see ye at the meal," Benjamin murmured.

Maggie took the cup Benjamin held out. The corner of his mouth lifted in a grim smile, and then he turned and left. She heard Marcus let out a deep breath beside her as they watched him leave.

"Ye seem to be getting on all right," Marcus commented. Maggie was taken aback at the implied accusation in his tone.

She dipped her own cup into the cider bucket and took a drink, ignoring his prompt. She did not want to discuss Benjamin with him.

"He dinna trouble ye, did he, Maggie?" Marcus commented.

She looked sideways at him as she drank.

"No. It's okay. He means no harm," she replied tersely.

"Sure, he means none."

"Spit it out. What do you want to know?" she asked, seeing through his fumbling attempts at conversation. It had been a long time since they spoke as friends, and she was certain his inquisition was more than just concern.

"I just worry, that's all. I have two sons, more than I ever had to lose in my life. And you, and Kwetii– I want ye all here, with me. But I think it might be too much to ask of ye."

"Why do you say that?" she said softly. Suddenly, as his shoulders sagged and his forehead creased over his thick brows, he looked like the old Marcus again. She felt a pang of regret over her rash anger.

"Can you stay here, with yer husband's brother looking at ye like that?"

They both glanced across the yard at Benjamin, who was using a hatchet to split a log. As if on cue, he looked over at them, and when he saw Maggie he flashed a smile before he bent back down to work.

"He said he would be no trouble. He promised me that," she said.

"Well, then, if he promised," Marcus said, his words trailing off with unspoken doubt.

If she did not forgive Benjamin, how could she expect Winn to do so? Surely it was the only tangible way to move on, for all of them. Yet discussing her feelings for her former husband was too much to share with even Marcus, so she turned the topic to one they could be in agreement on.

"How is Finola today?" she asked, intent on changing the course of their conversation. She knew he had visited his mother several times since the older woman's arrival, yet Finola had not spoken a word to him.

"Gwen is convinced she's trapped in her visions. She must see something dreadful, the way she sits there." He sighed. "I fear she will never be sane again. In our future time, she'd be locked away, fer sure."

"She might come through. We can't give up on her," Maggie said quietly. She placed a hand on his arm, and he covered it with his own briefly before he stood to his feet.

She intended to reassure him, but the pounding of hooves invaded the village. Astride a horse much too large for his boyish frame was a tow-headed youth, who galloped the horse into the courtyard where he came sliding to stop as the animal buried his haunches in the dirt. The boy looked younger than Ahi Kekeleksu, no more than six or seven, but he handled the massive animal with surprising grace considering his diminutive stature. Dressed in linen trousers and a vested tunic, he was clearly English, and despite the lack of risk associated with his presence, she saw several of the men reach for their weapons.

Although Marcus growled a warning for her to stay put, she followed him anyway. What harm could the boy bring, no matter what people he hailed from?

"Are ye lost, lad?" Marcus asked. The boy shifted in the saddle, his eyes darting around the camp as his fingers gripped the reins. The whites of his knuckles gleamed like little white pearls across his fists.

"I'm looking for kin of the savage Winkeohkwet," the boy said. His horse pranced nervously in a circle, but he kept his eyes sharp on Marcus.

"Who asks?" Marcus replied. Marcus took hold of the horse's rein to steady the beast, who snorted at the action, but calmed.

"I'm Morgan White, ward of John Jackson. He sent me with a message, but I will only give it to yer leader. Would that be ye, sir?" the boy said as he thrust his chin out in an insolent manner.

"I am. Get down, and tell me yer message," Marcus answered evenly.

Cormaic came forward unbidden, and pulled the lad down off the horse. Marcus handed the horse's reins to another man, and she saw Benjamin bend down to inspect the youth.

"I know ye. Yer were friend to my father," the boy said.

Benjamin put a hand on Morgan's shoulder with a nod. It was then that Maggie recognized the boy. The memory of that terrible day rushed back to her. It was the day Winn was shot by Thomas Martin, setting into motion events that had changed all their lives.

Yes, Maggie remembered that day, and by the hollow look on Benjamin's face, she was certain he recalled it as well.

"Aye," Benjamin said quietly to the boy. "What news do ye bring, lad?"

Morgan looked up at the men towering over him. Maggie thought he must be afraid, with the semi-circle of brawn surrounding him, but the youth held his stance and glared defiantly at them.

"Ye need to come for yer savage if ye want him to live. There's men planning to kill him when he leaves town with Joseph Benning. They say they will hang him in the square."

Maggie felt a swaying beneath her feet. *No. Not Winn.* He had been faithful in his task, served the English and Indians fairly. How could they turn on him?

"Gather the men from the fields, send them to the Northern Hall. Boy, ye'll stay here with us," Marcus ordered. No one moved for a moment, until Marcus swung on them in a fury.

"Go!" He bellowed. The men scattered, and Maggie followed Marcus through the courtyard.

***

They gathered in the Northern Hall, yet Maggie did not understand why they did not immediately leave. Cormaic and Erich roused the others, demanding a quick response to aid Winn. Maggie grew frustrated as Marcus stayed silent, listening to the others argue on the best plan. Finally, Marcus threw back his shoulders and stood up, and the hall fell silent as attention shifted to the Chief.

"We will make two groups. I will take two men into town. The others will wait outside the palisades. If we show them he is not alone, they will not dare follow him," Marcus announced.

Maggie hung back away from the others, poised at the door to the Northern Hall. She crossed her arms over her chest and closed her eyes as she listened to the men, their words blending into a senseless fog to her ears. There was only one thing she wished to hear, that they would immediately ride out to find Winn. Panic washed through her with each moment that they delayed.

"What if they already attacked? We must take them by surprise. It is the only way," Cormaic argued. Erich placed his hand on his son's shoulder, shaking his head.

"We have not enough men. And they have many more guns, we only have a few."

"What of the Nansemond? Send a rider for help, the warriors will come fight with us," another man suggested. The hall erupted with murmurs, discussions of what course to take trailing off between men.

Benjamin remained silent through the exchange as he sat at his father's side. Tense through his shoulders, wearing the fur mantle of a Chief's son, Benjamin glanced over at her. She met his eyes briefly before she left the hall.

Damn them for not leaving right away. Every sliver of her sense screamed it would be a mistake, but all she could think of was getting to Winn. After all, she had snuck into Martin's Hundred to help Benjamin. It might be more sensible for a woman to try to go in. The English would not expect it, and she was fairly sure no one would recognize her, since she had not been near any English towns since the Massacre.

She needed a plan, but she would have time to make one on the way to town. Rebecca would keep Kwetii without alerting the men, giving her time to take one of the horses and slip away. She entered her empty Long House and took stock of her supplies: one rifle with half a bag of gunpowder, her bone-handled knife, and one of Rebecca's English style dresses. It would have to do.

Her hands were slippery with sweat as she clutched the rifle and grabbed a traveling sack to pack with supplies.

"You're not going anywhere."

At the sound of Benjamin's voice behind her, she bit down on her lower lip. She kept her back to him and continued shoving items in her bag.

"Leave me alone," she replied. He placed a hand on her arm and she shook it off, turning on him in a fury. She slapped his second attempt to reach for her, until he stepped back with both arms held wide to give her space.

"All right! Stop yer fighting! I willna touch ye! But yer not going anywhere, I canna let ye leave!"

"By the time the others decide what to do, he could be dead. I have the best chance of sneaking in without notice, and you know it," she countered. "I saved your hide once, didn't I?"

"Yes, ye did. At too much risk to yer own blasted neck. Jamestown is different than Martin's Hundred, Maggie, ye'll be caught. Even if ye get in, ye canna get him out. Did ye think of that, or do ye wish to sit in the cell with him?"

"I won't lose him again." She swallowed back a sob as the sting of tears blurred her vision, and he reached for her again, but then dropped his hands when she backed up.

"What of yer daughter? Who will see to her if ye end up dead?" he said quietly. It was that notion that finally rattled her, and she felt the tears streak down her cheeks. He was right.

She sat down hard on the bedding platform and dropped the sack onto the floor. He kneeled down in front of her, his tousled locks falling over his face as he bowed his head. She could hear each breath he took, slow, controlled, as if he meant to speak but could not. When he finally looked up, his fingers were clenched into fists and his slate eyes were round and thoughtful.

"Do ye remember that day, when we were children? The last time I saw ye?" he said softly. She nodded. She could recall it well.

She placed her raven on the ground as she played on the floor of the old barn. No one would bother her there. Grandpa had no use for the space, but she liked it. It was a secret place, her hiding spot, a place to call her own among the world of adults.

Hinges creaked, and she saw the wood plank door open. A pair of round blue eyes peered at her between the slats.

"Can I come in, Maggie?" he asked. She rolled her eyes. It was the boy, Marcus's son. He wasn't so bad.

"Oh, I guess. Hurry up and close the door."

He slithered in and plopped down beside her.

"Ach, crap, I cut my finger on the stupid door. Gimmie your sock, will ya?"

"No, I'm not giving you anything! Go get a band aid, or keep bleeding, I don't care!" she sniped. He shrugged.

When he saw her raven sitting solitary in the dirt, he fished in his pocket for a moment until he produced his own treasure.

The boy held it up, a wide toothless grin stretching across his face.

"See? Da gave you the raven, but I have the eagle. It's better than the raven," he bragged.

"No it's not!" she hissed.

"Aye, it is! My Da said so!"

"You're a liar, and I'm telling!" she shrieked. She jumped up and left him in the dirt.

It was the last time she saw him. Grandpa said not to speak of it, poor Marcus could not bear it. His little son, disappeared without a trace. The police said the mother must have taken him.

"You followed me everywhere, you were such a pest," she laughed, wiping a tear from the corner of her eye. His eyes softened and he nodded with a wry smile.

"That I did."

They both laughed, a nervous, strained interlude in an otherwise uncomfortable silence.

"I think I knew who ye were, when we met again. The day Winn brought ye to town, even with yer hair in braids and dressed like a squaw, I thought it was ye," he confessed.

"Why didn't you tell me?" she whispered.

"Those memories were buried down deep. I had to keep them silent, lest I fear I was mad. I was only a boy when I traveled here, not like ye, a woman grown. And then ye turned up, and I started to remember things. I knew where I came from, where ye came from."

He thrust his fist into his pocket, pulling out his eagle figurine. She was shocked it was still in his possession, but it was the same as when she'd last seen it. He placed it gently in her hand and closed her fingers over it.

"You may be right. One man could get in, and warn him, much better than all of us," he said.

"What are you saying?" she whispered.

"Ye'll stay here. If the others know I've left, they will follow, and I will lose the chance to get into town. Let no one know I've gone."

Her eyes followed his as he stood up, his face a steady mask betraying no sign of fear. He took the rifle from her hands and turned to leave.

"Why would you do this?" she asked. He paused at the door, without turning back.

"I have only one brother in this world. And he has only one wife."

He closed the door gently as he left.

28

Maggie

When Marcus learned of her role in helping Benjamin leave the village alone, he descended on her in a fury. He slammed the door of her Long House, his face a mask of heathen rage she had never witnessed before, even the first day he had helped save her and Winn from attack.

"Are ye out of yer mind?" he hollered. She stood shaking before him, more at the shock of his response than fear of him. They had suffered through many a heated argument over the years, and despite the violence clouding his blue eyes she knew he would never harm her.

"He wanted to go. He has a better chance being alone–" she tried to explain.

"He chances being killed!" Marcus shouted.

"I wanted to go. He wouldn't let me!"

She heard the sharp intake of his breath, and watched him wave his hands at her in dismissal.

"What would ye do, save him yerself? Dinna I raise ye to have more sense than that? Jesus, Maggie, sometimes I think ye haven't the good brains ye were born with!"

"You can go to hell, Marcus! I am sick and tired of being treated like I have no say in things! I'm sick of all you stinking men, running around like a bunch of idiots, making all the decisions! I'm sick of this stupid time, the stupid English–and–and you bloody *men*!" she shrieked.

She threw an empty bowl at him and watched him duck to avoid it. He glared at her, eyes widening in surprise before he closed the distance in two strides. He grabbed her arms before she could launch another missile, shaking her like a child.

"In this time, you have no say in it," he shouted as she tried to twist away from him. He shook her roughly by the arms, his face contorted. "This is the time ye were meant to be born to. Ye live here now, and ye cannot change the ways of men. Do ye want to see them dead, for want of yer stubborn pride? For you to say ye saved him, like a woman of your time might do? Yer foolish plan will get him killed. Both of them this time. Both my sons."

She felt her anger slipping away as he glared down at her, the sounds of their ragged breaths the only murmur between them. His fingers loosened on her arms, and with a sigh his frown deepened.

"I know ye think ye have no power here, Maggie. But ye have it all, ye just don't know it yet," he said softly.

"Do you mean as a *Blooded One*? I still don't understand."

"Aye, there's that. But more than that. Ye have the love of two brave men, who each would move the earth itself to see ye happy. In this time, my wee hellion, that power is the most fearsome of all."

She felt her throat constrict as tears smeared her cheeks. She had no answer for him. Her heart was filled with the love of one man, yet she knew in some part that his words held truth.

"I bid ye keep yer arse here while we fetch my sons. I've never had cause to take ye over my knee, but if I find ye up to any more trouble, I'll tan ye good, grown woman or no. Agreed?"

She nodded. He kissed the top of her head before he left the Long House, slamming the door behind him.

***

The village was quiet without the men. The women gathered in the Northern Hall to prepare for the eventual return of the warriors, yet a veil of unease hung thick among them as they worked. She sat next to Gwen, who was focused in a dedicated manner pounding dried stockfish with a mallet. Maggie idly stirred the thick butter mixture they would soak the fish in later for the night meal as she stared off toward the doorway. She felt the eyes of the other women upon her as she worked, her skin prickling with the unsaid accusations. The men were gone to battle to retrieve her husband, and there was nothing she could do but sit by and wait to see if they all returned safely.

"Do you think they will return soon?" Maggie asked. Gwen continued to pound the fish, her mallet sliding off the slippery table edge as she worked.

"They'll nay be long, worry not." Gwen answered. "And ye would be dead right now if ye'd gone to town," the older woman added.

Maggie dropped her ladle and looked up.

"I know," Maggie replied quietly. She had already endured being chastised by Marcus. As much as Maggie knew she deserved it, she felt a heaviness in her chest at the thought of Gwen being angry with her as well.

"Ye dinna mean any harm, I can see that. But fer want of your foolish acts, our men might die," Gwen said as she clenched her mallet. "We've survived here peaceably until today. No one bothers us, and we keep to ourselves. Some of these women willna forget if the men do not return."

"Gwen, I'm so sorry," Maggie whispered, her voice trembling. "They'll all come home safely, they will–"

Gwen cut her off, pointing the mallet at Maggie.

"Ye need to take yer place here, girl, and remember who ye are. Ye cannot act alone as ye did today. Winn will be our Chief someday, and he needs a strong wife. Not a spoilt girl who thinks only of herself."

Maggie could not answer. The breath caught in her lungs and tears coursed down her cheeks. Gwen was right.

"I–I'm sorry," Maggie said. Gwen clucked her tongue and shook her head, laying down her mallet. Maggie put her face in her hands and brushed away the tears, trying to keep from falling apart as the painful truth roared in her ears.

"I know ye are. I know yer sorry," Gwen replied quietly.

Maggie knew Gwen's words were true, and the implication of her actions tore through her. If some of the men did not return, it would be her fault. She had made a foolish decision in a heated moment, and as a result, the lives of many men were put at risk. How would anyone ever forgive her if something terrible happened?

"I can't sit here like this. I'm going to check on Kwetii," she said. She avoided looking into Gwen's face. Maggie knew she would break down in front of all the women if she stayed any longer.

"Go on then, have at it," Gwen muttered. "Yer no help fer me here, with ye staring off and no work done."

Maggie left the Northern Hall and made a brisk walk back to her Long House. There was no way she could concentrate on anything but worrying over Winn and the others. She knew better than most how ruthless the English could be, and how bloody a battle between them might turn out. As she entered the space she currently called home and reached for her sleeping child, it was all she could do to lay beside her without crying.

Maggie nestled down beside Kwetii, the child's unique toddler scent comforting amidst the fear that threatened to suffocate her. Kwetii's long lashes twitched as she slept, her bow-shaped lips making a sweet snoring sound as she breathed. Maggie suspected her daughter would be through with afternoon naps soon, but for now she watched the last remnants of her childhood slipping away too fast. Kwetii was born to the seventeenth century, and as such, her childhood would be a short one before she was thrust into the reality of life. Lying beside her and holding her close, Maggie wished she could shield her from what was to come. She prayed that Winn would be there to guide them.

It was impossible for her to rest, knowing the men she loved were in danger. After watching Kwetii sleep for a few minutes, Maggie decided to busy herself with tidying the Long House.

Since their arrival in the Norse village, they had acquired many more items than they were accustomed to owning. Winn found it strange to have personal possessions since the Indians regarded supplies as belonging to the community instead of individuals, yet even he had adapted to the change. She folded his braies and tunic and placed them in a basket hanging along the wall, and put his spare boots there as well. He must have worn his breechcloth and leggings into town, and she was not too surprised to see he had worn his native attire to conduct his business.

After she arranged his clothes in the basket, she turned to the corner he piled his belongings in. Sitting there, propped against the wall, was his sword. It gleamed in the flicker of the hearth fire, the amber light bouncing off the smooth metal. She ran one finger down the long, thick handle, which was carved deep with a tangle of runes. The symbols were meaningless to her, but a part of both her blood and Winn's. A grandfather he had never known, Chief Drustan Neilsson, had held that sword in his hands as he fought those who meant him harm. So many tales, so many legends. Would she ever sit with her husband and children, and listen to the stories?

She looked up when Kwetii made a tiny mewling sound. The child did not wake, and for that she was glad. Maggie preferred to spend her desolation alone.

Winn's second pair of leggings was still damp from washing, so she decided to lay it out in the sun to dry. Fall was upon them, and winter would arrive soon, but still they had the last remnants of summer sun in the afternoons and she preferred to take advantage of it. She draped the doeskin leggings over a bench and sat down, letting the warmth of the sunshine caress her face. She wished it was his touch on her skin, his fingers in her hair, instead of her own hands raking over her face as the tears fell.

What if the last words between them were those said in anger? If there were Gods in his time, did they listen to requests? If she asked for forgiveness, would it be granted? Perhaps if she promised to be a good wife, an obedient wife, a wife that Winn would not need to fight, it might be enough to please the Gods. Whatever Gods looked over the Powhatan, or the Norse, she would do anything to appease them. Even if it meant denying the time she was born to and all that she was.

She heard a stifled cry from the Long House and hurriedly wiped her hand across her face. It sounded as if Kwetii were in the throes of a nightmare, and with a wry smile she thought of how both Winn and she had suffered the same as children. As she turned to retrieve the child, her attention was distracted by the scent of smoke in the air. Across the courtyard, the storehouse was in flames, its roof alight like a torch against the blue sky. Maggie could see the other village women gathered outside the burning structure. She raced back into the Long House for Kwetii.

Crouched over her child was the misshapen back of a man. At the sound of her footsteps, he swung around, his fur cloak swirling around him as he snatched Kwetii into his arms. It was an older man she had never had words with, but she recognized him from meal times. Was his name Old Ivar? She could not recall.

When she took a tentative step forward, he stepped back and held up one hand straight out. Her stomach made a sickening leap when she saw he held a knife.

"Sir, I–I think my daughter must need me, if you please," she said softly, her voice trembling. Kwetii hung from the crook of his elbow, her round eyes wide as she uttered a grunting cry. Her dangling legs kicked out. Maggie held out her arms. What on earth did he want with her child?

"Keep yer distance, ye bloody devil!" Ivar said. "Move away, or I'll cut her, I swear it!"

She noticed his arms shook, the knife quivering in his unsteady fingers. She kept her eyes on his instead of Kwetii, afraid seeing her child's terror would cause her own fear to take over.

"What do you want with her?" she asked.

"You're the ones with the power to send our ship through time. I won't stay in this blasted place anymore, I'm going to Vinland, no matter what yer Chief says!"

"I don't understand. Truly. Please let her go, we can talk about this –"

"No! It's too late fer that! I'm going back without them, let them rot here with the Indians and the English, I'll nay be part of it any longer. Git out of my way, woman, now, I have a ship waiting fer me. All I need is the magic of a Blooded One, and I can return to my true time."

"Then take me," Maggie pleaded. Was this it? Was this her punishment for her crimes, for her rash actions? Would the Gods take her child as penance?

She slowly dropped to her knees before him, bowing her head, her body wreaked with tremors as he gripped her crying child. If it was Kwetii's blood he wanted, she shared it as well. She did not understand what he meant, or how he meant to time travel, but the sight of a man holding a knife to her daughter lent to desperate measures no matter what the reason.

She felt his hand on her shoulder and she thought he might relent, but instead he thrust her aside and brushed past her with Kwetii in his arms. As she pushed to her knees, she saw a flash of yellow hair by the doorway, and then heard the hollow twang of a bowstring plucked.

Ivar fell to his knees with a muffled groan. A single arrow protruded from his chest, and Kwetii rolled to the ground beside him.

"A warrior woman once told me to strike swiftly, when I meant to kill a man," Rebecca said. Her chest heaved against her snug shift, her bow poised in readiness for another shot as she glared at the fallen man. "I meant to kill that one."

Kwetii burst into a panicked howl, and Maggie gathered her into her arms.

29

Winn

Joseph Benning seemed like a competent man, and Winn thought he would serve Opechancanough well. Born to the Powhatans, Joseph had been sent to live with the English as a boy, and had even traveled across the ocean to England with the *Tassantassas* on several occasions. He was a slight fellow, slim in build with his Indian coloring typical, but his manner and dress was purely English. Winn suspected they were of similar age, yet Joseph had a solemn disposition that made him seem much older when he spoke. Like Winn, he was versed in several languages, trained from boyhood to be useful to his Weroance. Winn felt little regret at turning over his duties to Joseph. In fact, he could hardly finish the journey fast enough.

Although leaving Teyas had been difficult, he knew she was in good hands with Makedewa and Chetan at her side. They would see her settled with her new husband and escort her traveling party to her new home. He was not certain yet what village that would be, but his brothers would bring word of it when they met again at the Norse settlement. Finally, he felt their struggles were nearing end; perhaps they could settle in peace, as Maggie wished among the Norse. Knowing now what Marcus predicted of the future, Winn knew he could not settle with his family among the Powhatans. He would make his wife happy and keep her safe. Although it was in a different way than he envisioned for his family, it was the path they must take. It was all he could ask for.

Winn waited for Joseph outside the apothecary shop, where the other man had stopped for supplies. The sky overhead darkened with dense clouds, the signs of a storm moving in from the bay. He could see the pale underside of leaves as the wind whipped up the trees, and could smell the scent of salt in the air. Yes, a storm was brewing from the water, and it would likely be a harsh one, all the more reason to complete his task without haste.

Winn checked the strap on his horse and patted the animal's neck as he looked across the wide thruway. It was a quiet evening in town. John Jackson stood outside the smith's shop, absently rubbing down the barrel of a gun with a rag. Winn met his gaze and lifted his chin in acknowledgement. He had not spoken to John during his visit, and it was likely the last he would see the man for some time. Instead of a wave or nod, John looked away, beyond Winn's shoulder, and Winn suddenly felt the presence of others walking up behind him.

"The Governor will see ye before ye leave, Speaker."

When he served negotiation to the townsfolk, they called him Speaker, but Winn did not miss the inflection in the Englishman's tone. He did not recognize the man who spoke, but when he turned his head slightly to the side he spotted Thomas Martin among the group. He counted six men total. With a quick glance at the shop for his companion, he determined two additional Englishmen detained Joseph inside as well, and he stiffened his shoulders as he realized he could not fight six men alone.

"I finished my business with the Governor. Tell him I will call on him another day. It grows late, and I am weary of talking." Winn spoke his words, slow and even, as he turned back to his horse.

One of the men raised a musket level with Winn's chest.

"Ye'll come now, or have a hole in yer hide," the one with the musket said.

He heard Thomas Martin make a wheezing nasal laugh. Winn turned to the men, making a purposeful effort to relax his tense back as he surveyed them. The street was eerily empty except for the group surrounding him, with not even an English soldier in sight. It seemed the Englishmen had planned well.

That one, he thought, glancing at Thomas Martin, *that one he would kill last.*

He saw John Jackson watching, unmoving as he stood by his shop. Winn squinted up at the sky and considered mounting up. He could get away, but he would not make it out of the palisades, which remained closed and guarded.

"Go then. Take me to the governor," Winn said. He knew he was not being returned to the fanciful dwelling the Governor enjoyed within the settlement, but he complied nonetheless.

He left his horse tied to a post and followed the men.

***

Winn twisted his wrists against the rope binding, but the jailer had done his job well and they would not loosen. He sat upright with his arms bound behind him, and his ankles tied to the wooden legs of a chair. The English did not have a large space for detaining men, so they used a storehouse adjacent to the Governor's dwelling. It was a simple one-room structure fit for no more than housing vermin. His shoulders ached from the strained position, and his head throbbed from where he had been struck with the butt of a rifle near his temple. Apparently, the English had more in mind for him than simply speaking with the Governor. He suspected Thomas Martin had much to do with his detainment.

"If ye tell us where the village lies, perhaps we will kill ye quickly," Martin said. Somehow, the English had knowledge of the Norse colony up in the hills, and they wanted it taken for their King.

When Winn did not acknowledge the taunt, Thomas grabbed Winn's hair and yanked his head up. The man's squat, flushed face looked about to burst as he shoved it close to Winn, his breath nearly as rancid as the stench littering the storehouse.

"Nothing to say? Yer not so hard to kill now, are ye? Why, if a musket dinna finish ye, maybe this will," Thomas said, letting Winn's head drop. As his chin hit his chest and his gaze clouded over, he felt the burn of a rope twisting around his neck. He summoned all the strength he could muster to fight then, wrenching his body away from the men as they cut his ankle ties and pulled him to his feet. His muscles failed him as they looped the end of the rope over a low-hanging rafter and stretched his body upward until only the tips of his toes touched the ground.

Tighter it pulled, the pain of the rope burning like fire as he gasped for air, straining with all his might to keep his neck stiff against the hanging. His hands and legs fell numb and useless, like pins sticking him over every ounce of his skin, and when he thought he would take his last breath, they dropped him to the floor.

"We know they live near the Nansemond! Tell us where, save yer own life, ye filthy fool! We know it's a bunch of Spaniards or worse up there, hiding in the hills! Why do ye protect them?" Thomas shouted as he kicked Winn in the ribs. The impact of the boot was a dull strike, yet an effective one, knocking the breath from Winn's lungs. He knelt over on both hands, gasping shallow breaths against his screaming chest as he struggled for air.

He would not tell them. Let them hang him, let them take his life. He would not give up the last place his family could be safe.

"There is no village in the hills," Winn said, spitting the blood from his mouth onto the dirt floor.

The Englishmen strung him up once more.

***

It was well into the night before Winn's captors tired of the game. Finally they closed the door to the storehouse and left him in the shadows, the only light a glimpse of the moon from between the slats of the window shutters. He pressed his face to the earth as he lay on his belly, his arms still bound behind his back. The packed clay felt cool upon his skin, numbing the swelling of his jaw as he closed his eyes to the sensation. He considered the Bloodstone pendant still hanging from him neck, crusted into the wounds on his raw throat. If his hands were free, might he have used the magic to escape? It was better to have no choice, he imagined, rather than risk leaving his family. As he felt the wings of sleep take him into the darkness, the door burst open.

"Wake up!" A voice whispered. He felt hands on his wrists, and the smooth metal of a blade as it sliced through the rope. Unbound after hours of torture, his arms fell to his sides, limp and tingling. Winn kept his face flat to the floor, wondering what further punishment they sought to inflict at such a late hour.

"Can ye stand? Hurry, before they find us both!"

Winn opened one swollen eye, the one that was not plastered to the floor. He knew that voice, and he knew that face. It was Benjamin who kneeled over him, shaking Winn by one sore shoulder.

He had little enough strength to protest as Benjamin hauled him to his feet and looped Winn's arm over his shoulders. His legs failed him at first but he gained his stance quickly. They had no time to lose, and for whatever reason his brother was there, it would likely be his only chance at survival. As Winn stumbled beside Benjamin through the door, his foot hit something soft and large lying on the ground.

"Lucky they left only one man to guard ye. It seems they dinna expect a rescue tonight," Benjamin muttered. "That one was full in his cups when I came upon him."

Winn was shocked that Benjamin had killed the Englishman, but would not dwell on it further. They had more pressing matters to deal with at that moment.

"The gates are guarded," Winn said, his voice strained through his dry throat and cracked lips. He took in a breath and then bent abruptly over at the sharp pain in his side, coughing up a froth of bloody mucus. Benjamin held him by the shoulders to keep him upright as Winn heaved, and then pressed a flask to his lips. Winn took a gulp of the rum, spit it out, then took another.

"Ye ready?" Benjamin asked. Winn nodded as Benjamin pressed a knife into his hand. He rose up on shaking legs and followed of his own accord as they left the building.

The streets were dark and quiet. A sliver of a crescent moon still graced the purple sky, assisting their escape, but daylight would be upon them soon. Instead of making toward the gates as Winn expected, Benjamin led him behind the storehouse where there was a rope coiled in a heap on the ground.

"Can ye climb? The only way is to go over."

Benjamin threw the looped end of the rope over the pointed tip of the palisade fence and gave it a yank. It held. Facing Winn, Benjamin could not see the Englishman sneak up behind him, but Winn did. Winn snatched the knife from his belt and threw it at the intruder, narrowly missing Benjamin's head, but hitting the man squarely in the throat.

His brother slumped back against the fence, holding the side of his face where the knife had sailed past him.

"Could ye warn me, next time, ye think?" Benjamin snapped. Winn made a harsh snorting noise as he nodded.

"Yes. Next time," he agreed. He bent to the fallen man and pulled the knife from his throat. Winn wiped the blade with his fingers. As Benjamin watched with his eyes narrowed and his lips pressed tightly closed, Winn placed the palm of his bloodied hand flat against his face. There the sticky, hot blood left a mark, one he would wear until he repaid the English in kind.

"Good Christ, man," Benjamin muttered, shaking his head. They scaled the fence and made off into the woods behind Jamestown.

***

There was only one way out of town. Since Jamestown was almost completely surrounded by water, travelers to and from the town always took the same path. Benjamin, however, knew the area well, and he had used an unchartered trail through the dense forest that would be less likely to draw attention. It might delay an English search party, but Winn knew it would not deter them for long.

They walked for more than an hour before they found the place Benjamin tied the horses. The two men spoke little. He was not so dense as to be ungrateful for the help, yet Winn wondered why Benjamin had taken the risk of freeing him. Even more so, how did his brother know Winn had been detained?

Benjamin tossed him the flask as they sat down by the horses.

"How did you know?" Winn asked quietly. He took a sip, and passed it to his brother.

"Old Morgan's son rode to the village for help. Sent by John Jackson."

Winn considered the response, and it made sense. He recalled John Jackson watching from the gunsmith's shop, and the lack of surprise the man showed when the English surrounded him. It seemed John had helped Winn in his own way, without the risk of showing involvement to the other Englishmen.

"We will be followed. Are you ready to fight?" Winn asked, tilting his head as he looked at the man who was his brother. Benjamin let out an insulted sigh.

"Ask yourself such. I'm the one that saved yer bloody arse, didn't I? I can kill a man, the same as ye."

"So you've learned to kill?" Winn answered.

"I've changed a bit," Benjamin said. "As have ye, brother."

They fell silent at the use of the title aloud. It hung there heavy in the air between them, waiting for acknowledgement, for either of them to broach the damage that had been done. Benjamin cleared his throat with a cough and took a swig of the rum.

"I'm not like ye, Winn. I thought ye were dead when I sent ye back on your horse that day. I knew not what else to do. As for her," Benjamin said, his voice lowering an octave as he referred to Maggie. "I did the best I could. I had no people then, no man to stand by my side. I know I wronged ye, and I will pay for it all my days. There was no way for me to keep her safe unless we wed."

"It meant more to you than that," Winn answered. He felt the old anger rise, the sting of betrayal knowing his friend had stolen his wife. As Winn lay feverish and wounded near death, Benjamin had taken everything from him. Was his brother asking for forgiveness as he made his excuses?

"Aye. I wanted her. I willna deny it. But if I thought ye lived, I would have returned her to ye. Believe it, or not. I tell ye now as the truth of it." Benjamin passed him the rum. "She suffered much with Martin. To make the marriage contract he asked for twice the bride price, and I gave him all I had. I couldna see her treated so poorly."

Winn raised his head.

"How so?" Winn asked. Maggie had hated living with the English, but she had not spoken of any mistreatment.

Benjamin sat up as he squinted at Winn's question.

"Martin saw her run to ye when ye were shot, and she tried to take the gun from him. He dinna care for the sting on his reputation, I suppose. The man hates the Indians. Maggie would not tell me what had been done to her, but I saw her wounds. I couldn't leave her there."

"What wounds?" Winn asked. His chest tightened as he realized what Benjamin spoke of, and his heart sank with the knowledge that Maggie had kept it from him.

"He beat her. I feared the babe would not survive. There was scarce an ounce of her skin without mark."

Winn stood abruptly to his feet. He strode a few paces away, his hands tight at his sides as he let out a low groan.

Why would she hide such a thing from him?

He knew the answer immediately, of course. Maggie knew Winn would have killed Martin, and it was the fighting and death that his wife feared the most. His chest ached as he drew in his breath, and he did not know if it was due to the trauma to his ribs or the fist that clenched his heart. She was a stubborn one, he knew that well, but keeping such a thing from him? He could only imagine how she must have felt. Trapped alone in his time, carrying his child, with no way to care for herself. It was no wonder she fought so hard to stay with the Norse. Perhaps it was the only way he could make her feel truly safe.

Benjamin stood.

"Winn-"

His words were cut off by the roar of a rifle. As Winn turned, he saw Benjamin thrown to the ground with a wound to his shoulder. Winn's eyes darted to the periphery of the clearing to find the source of the shot, but in the cover of darkness even his sharp eyes were of little use.

He grabbed hold of Benjamin's good arm and dragged his brother into the trees for cover.

"Quiet!" Winn hissed when Benjamin let out a groan.

"Help me to the horse, we need to leave!"

Winn shook his head at Benjamin's plea.

"I don't know where they are. Stay down."

Winn took a few precious moments to tear apart Benjamin's shirt and put pressure on the wound. Although it surged with blood, it was not deep, the flesh only torn by the graze of the shot. It would not kill him, but Winn was sure it was painful. Benjamin pushed Winn's hand away and applied pressure to his own wound as he tried to sit up.

"Come out, Speaker! You'll fare no better for hiding!" an Englishman called out from somewhere beyond the tree line.

Winn looked down at Benjamin. The wounded man might be able to make it to the horses, if the English had not scared them off. If Winn distracted their attention long enough, perhaps his brother would succeed in getting away. There was no time to think of a plan, nor regret that they had stopped for rest instead of continuing on. Although Winn did not yet know whether to trust Benjamin or not, the man had saved his life, and for that he could not let him be taken by the English.

The English came out of the trees, and Winn could see that they had gathered more men before they pursued the escaped prisoner. Winn crouched at the waist and shifted his stance so that he stood between Benjamin and the approaching English. He adjusted his grip on his knife as he eyed them. More than a dozen settlers all held muskets, a show of firepower against the single knife Winn held and the flintlock rifle tied to Benjamin's horse. Winn weighed the probability of winning the fight.

No, he might not win it, but he would take many of them with him when he fell.

Winn saw one man raise his musket, wavering as he pointed it into the trees near where Benjamin lay. Instead of waiting for the sound of the shot, he dug his heels into the soft earth and took off at a run toward the man. As Winn uttered a guttural scream, the startled man fumbled the weapon and nearly dropped it, leaving Winn the opening to launch himself at the Englishman. Chaos exploded around them as he tackled the man to the ground, and he heard the scuffle of bodies and shouts behind him, yet all he could focus on was the one lowly man he held in his grasp at that moment. His gaze became a tunnel, seeing through his opponent, yet narrowed on the prize, and as Winn thrust his knife into the side of the man's shuddering chest, he could see only blood cloud his vision.

Winn took the gun from the dead man and used it to smash into the head of the next Englishman who dared challenge him. Winn dipped his shoulder and rammed it into another, slicing his knife upward across the next throat with a shrill scream. The remaining English seemed to recover from their panic at his distracting warrior bellow, and from the corner of his eye he saw Benjamin grappling with two men as Winn crouched to face yet another attacker.

Two attacked the wounded Benjamin. If he could kill three more that stood circling him, he might help his brother.

His fist slipped when he clutched his knife, holding it out in front of him, and he was perplexed to see a smear of blood trickling down his arm when he glanced at his palm. He had not felt it when the Englishman sliced his skin, and he did not feel it now, it was only a semblance of distraction at losing his grip. He tossed the knife to his dry hand and wiped the blood off on his bared chest. His blood or that of another, he would wear it until he ended them.

Thomas Martin lifted his flintlock musket, standing no more than a few paces away. Winn lurched for the man, grabbing the barrel of the weapon before the man fired it. The shot rang out close to his ear, but Winn found Martin's neck with one hand and squeezed it as he felt his strength begin to fade. His damaged ribs screamed with each breath as Winn thrust his knife up into the man's chest.

Martin glared back at him, his black eyes forming a look of defiant surprise as Winn held him.

"I should have made sure ye were dead," the man groaned.

"Yes," Winn muttered. "You should have."

Winn dropped him to the ground, and the remaining Englishmen closed in. He refused to retreat as he felt Benjamin scramble up behind him.

"We should run," Benjamin said.

"No," Winn replied evenly, his eyes on the advancing men.

The decision was suddenly taken from them. He heard the bellows before they came into view, the sound of the pounding hooves and fierce war cries piercing the air and causing even the English to shudder. Norse and Indians rushed upon them amid a clash of metal and bodies, and suddenly the upper hand in the fight changed. Winn heard the shout of his father and the screams of his brothers as they ran into battle.

The English were outnumbered, and although most continued to fight after the initial burst of surprise, a few tried to run away and were quickly cut down. Makedewa and Chetan fought alongside each other, cutting through men who challenged them. Crouched down beside Benjamin, Winn watched as Marcus brought his *bryntroll* down with a sickening thud across the chest of a fleeing Englishman he knocked to the ground, and then calmly wrenched it from the fallen body as he surveyed the scene.

"Is that all of them?" Marcus called out. Cormaic approached, his face flushed like a ripe cherry and his reddish blond hair hanging streaked with blood. His breath came rapid, but Cormaic nodded, a smug grin on his face as he looked to his Chief.

"And that one?" Erich asked, nodding toward the man fallen next to Benjamin. Benjamin tried to rise, but faltered with the use of only one arm.

"Aye, he's dead," Benjamin said.

Marcus gave a few curt orders, and the men scattered around the clearing gathering up weapons from the dead. Winn moved to join them, but Marcus put a hand on his arm.

"Are ye all right?" Marcus asked, the words coming out part choked, half-whispered. His father stood before him, his face creased, his blue eyes hooded with rancor. Yet Winn could see the gleam of fear there as well, and as Marcus darted a glance at Benjamin, Winn knew what that fear felt like.

It was the fear Winn felt when smoke rose above the trees the day deserters attacked his family. It was the fear Winn felt when his scheming uncle stole his wife and child. It was the fear Winn knew every time he thought he alone might not be enough to keep his loved ones safe.

It was the fear of a man for the life of those he loved.

"Good timing, father," Winn replied. Marcus stilled, his hand clenched on Winn's arm, and his eyes widened before they softened. He placed his calloused hand on Winn's cheek, gripping his hair, and his mouth thinned into a grin as he nodded.

"Aye. I'll help Benjamin to the horses, you go help the men."

"I will help my brother," Winn replied. He turned back to Benjamin and extended his hand, helping him to his feet. Benjamin's face was careful, his expression relieved yet sheltered. Things were not mended between them, but they had a start of it, at least.

Winn grimaced when Cormaic thumped him heavily on the back, and Erich made an offhand comment about the state of the Englishman's ballocks. They all joined in the laughter, a welcome reprieve as they gathered in the clearing among the dead. Englishmen littered the ground in various states of demise. Their defeat was due to their own insatiable need of conquering the land, and Winn knew it would not be the last time they fought the settlers. Although Winn would kill any man that threatened him and he had taken the lives of many an Englishman, he did not view it in delight, rather as necessity. It was simply survival, and suddenly he was glad to have the men at his side that would ensure it.

He helped Benjamin mount, and suddenly a shot rang out through the laughter. The horse reared, but Benjamin held on, and Winn grabbed the reins to steady the animal as he turned to look toward the explosion.

The Englishman whom Benjamin had thought dead sat up, perched on one shaking elbow with a smoking musket jammed against his shoulder. Winn reacted with a swift motion, sending his knife through the air to land in the man's chest, ending his life for sure with the blow. As Winn stalked back toward the body to retrieve his knife, the sight of a Norseman lying too still on the ground stopped him quick in his paces.

Blood pulsed from a spreading wound to his belly. Winn sank down to his knees beside his father in the dirt.

30

Maggie

Smoke filled the yard from the remnants of the storehouse fire, the breeze a hazy curtain as the men filtered into the yard. Old Ivar had set the storehouse aflame to distract everyone from his crime, and it still smoldered even though the fire had been doused hours before.

Winn stood apart from the others. Covered in grime, his face stained with the crimson mask of a dried handprint, Maggie trembled to see him meet her eyes across the courtyard. She had seen him in such a state only once before, and that had been when he painted his body in war grease and arrived to slaughter the English on the day of the massacre.

Winn walked toward their Long House, but when he saw her, he stopped. Although he had returned safely to her, she could see something was terribly wrong. His grey eyes seemed to stare through her as she approached him, and she saw his fists clenched at his sides in unspoken rage. The despair in his face should have made her afraid to approach him, but she had tamed her warrior husband before and would do it again if needed. If she had power over nothing else in their life together, she had that. She refused to fear the sight of his berserker eyes and rigid muscles.

"Winn," she said softly as she joined him. As he stared down at her with haunted eyes, she could see the handprint on his face was blood, and if it belonged to him or another lost soul, she did not know. She braced her own trembling as she reached for him, running her palm over his chest, then up to his shoulder. He stood straight, unyielding, until finally he let loose and pulled her into his arms. She felt her breath leave her chest as he squeezed her, and she let out a little cry when she felt him shudder.

"*Ntehem*," he said. He took her face in his hands and kissed her, then buried his lips in her hair as he clutched her to his chest. The torn skin on his neck bled as she felt the sticky blood of her husband on her hands, but it did not sway her as she cried and he whispered sweet words in her ear. "I am so sorry," he murmured.

"For what?" she asked. "Here, come inside, let me help you, you're bleeding–"

"No, not now," he said. She pulled back so that she might see his face, yet when she saw the echo of despair in his eyes she was not reassured.

"Come to the Northern Hall. The others are there," he said.

It was then that she saw it. The litter was carried by four warriors, one at each corner. On it was the still body of Winn's father.

Time halted to a blur as they followed the litter inside. Among the sounds of weeping, Maggie and Winn kneeled down by his side. Marcus was not yet gone, but it would not be long. She watched as Gwen peeled back the torn tunic to reveal the injury. Across his navel was a deep, jagged wound, pulsing with each staggered breath he took despite the pressure one of the men held on it with a makeshift bandage. Maggie felt the hot tears on her cheek as Gwen pulled away with a grim shake of her head.

"I will bring him a drink to ease his journey," Gwen said as she left and pushed through the gathered crowd. Maggie heard Gwen shout a barrage of orders, and soon the others moved away. Erich and Cormaic stood nearby. Winn put his hands on her waist as she sunk to the ground beside Marcus, steadying her as if she would fall.

His skin had drained to a grey pallor, the hollows of his eyes standing out like shadows on his face. She could see he still breathed by the occasional rise and fall of his chest, but with each movement his face winced and he uttered a groan. When Gwen returned with a cupful of liquid, Winn helped him sit up to take a sip. As Gwen pressed the cup to his lips, Marcus opened his eyes.

"Is this the drink of the Gods?" he asked. Gwen nodded, tears in her eyes.

"Yes, my lord," she said.

"Good then. Help me rise, so I may take it."

Gwen helped him drink, and then she placed a series of rune stones on his chest when she laid him back down. They were round and flat, lying stark against his pale skin as he struggled through each breath.

Maggie bit back a sob as she watched him drink the thick honeyed liquid. As her eyes darted to those watching, she realized with a sickness in her belly that they all knew what it was.

They were sending their Chief on his way. They eased his journey with a sweet nectar drink, a gift to lighten the load he must bear.

"No," she whispered, starting to rise. Winn held her tight, refusing to let her move from his father's side. Marcus finished the last swallow, some of it leaving his mouth in a drip to stain his cheek. Maggie reached for his face to wipe him with the edge of her gunna apron and he smiled, closing his hand over hers. Her fingertips tingled where the nectar smeared her skin.

"No crying, lamb. Ye know I canna stand it, not from ye," he said. "Here, lay yer head down. It's been awhile since ye were a bairn, but I see ye as that, always."

She did as he requested, placing her head gently on his chest as he gripped her hand. The sound of his heart was far away, a slow thud that would not be chased, its message fading with each breath he took. She felt his hand on her hair, and the soft touch of his chin on her forehead. Whether it was the strength of the drink or the despair in her soul she did not know, but at his touch, numbness seared her skin. She hoped that same numbness gave him comfort as the last of his lifeblood drained away.

"Yer grandda would be happy to see ye with yer kin again. It's where ye belong, make no mistake," Marcus murmured. He tried to push himself up again, but fell back down at the effort with a strained moan, his hand moving to his wound. His fingers were stained with blood. "Go now, Maggie. I must speak to my sons for a bit. I'll see ye later."

Her teeth closed tight over her lower lip at the attempted jest. They both knew quite well there would be no later, yet they were the parting words they had shared her entire life.

When she left for school each day. When she took her first drive in their farm truck as a reckless sixteen-year-old. When she left on her first date as a teenager in the car of a boy he did not like. It was a promise between them, one she always knew he would keep.

"I'll see you later," Marcus promised.

"All right, then," she whispered. She leaned up and pressed a kiss to his cheek, and her lips immediately felt numb. "I'll see you later."

She left him there, tears hot on her cheeks, even as she did her best to hide them. Winn and Benjamin knelt down at his side, and as she walked away she could hear the murmur of his last words, fading like the whisper of sunshine on an autumn evening as he spoke softly to his sons.

31

Winn

Winn stood at the doorway of Gwen's house, watching in silence as Maggie took hold of Finola's hand. His grandmother sat motionless in her chair by the hearth, her grey eyes wide open, yet staring off at the wall as if something entranced her. She had spoke little since her arrival in the village, and he feared the outcome should she chose to finally find her voice again. The Pale Witch would not find any consolation in the truth of her predictions this time. He could see now why such things drove her to madness.

"Finola, it's me. Maggie," his wife murmured. Maggie brushed a stray lock of yellowed hair from the older woman's forehead and gently shook her shoulder with her other hand. With her chest rising in a deep breath, Finola closed her eyes, and then turned toward Maggie.

"I know why ye come here. I see my son in Valhalla, waiting to feast with the Kings," Finola whispered, her voice surprisingly steady. It was if she possessed her old strength on simple impulse, finding some purpose in the grief of the Chief's passing.

Maggie's eyes opened wider, and she moved back away from Finola to stare at the older woman. Finola's face was a flat slab, an empty canvas as to what her true feelings might be. Winn recognized the sudden light in her eyes, the way the blue eyes glowed like tepid orbs beneath her fair brows. The spirit of the Creator had returned to her, and he was glad for it.

"Take me to him, my Chief," she whispered. The voice was not her own. It was the voice of a priestess, the commune of the magical host within her, a welcome intruder that would use her earthly body for the duty ahead.

They escorted her to the Northern Hall. The space was filled with the villagers, each tending a task to send the Chief on his way. Winn did not fully understand the ways of the Norse, yet from what Erich explained it was the only way to send Marcus to the afterlife. Women were busy at tables, preparing food for the journey. Fresh honeyed mead and the scent of charred lamb filled the air, mixed amongst the smoke of the funeral pyre sneaking in from the courtyard. Someone had sparked it when Marcus took his last breath, and from what information he gleaned from the Norse, the fire was meant to keep burning until the Chief was sent on his way.

The hall fell silent when they entered. In the few days since his father had passed, Winn felt a growing discomfort with the sudden title thrust upon him, and the further reverence others showed him. They called him Chief, and Jarl, and waited for his command on all things. What once had been a source of amusement for his brothers to tease him with was now a stark reality. His father had fallen, and now Winn was expected to take his place. There was no fight over such a position; it was his by right of blood, the blood of the first born son.

The heads of men bowed when he entered the hall, and women bent low at the waist as he passed. He could feel Maggie tense beside him, also unsure of her new role, her fingers entwined tightly in his as she walked at his side.

Gwen and Erich approached and Winn grimaced when they behaved in a similar fashion. He placed his hand on Erich's shoulder.

"Will it be today?" Winn said.

"Yes, my lord. The fire burns, and his vessel is ready to receive him," Erich replied.

"The other men are in agreement?" Winn asked. Erich's eyes squinted down, darting toward Gwen for a moment. Gwen took Finola's hand and led her toward the other women, and Maggie followed them after giving Winn's hand a gentle squeeze.

"The decision is yours," Erich answered. Winn tightened his grip on the older warrior's shoulder, looking him in the eye.

"I wish to know if the men agree. They have labored long to make the ship. I would not allow it if they object," Winn insisted. He did not fully understand the Norse ways, and it seemed wasteful to him to burn a ship for a dead man. Yet, if it was what the people wished for the fallen chief, Winn would agree to honor the tradition.

Erich sighed.

"Winn, I know ye have doubt in leading these men. But this is not the time to dwell on yer fear. Send yer father to Valhalla on the ship, give him the respect he deserves. We saw his own father buried the same, and his father before him. Our Chiefs deserve such a reward when they have given their very lives in battle. It is an honorable way to die."

"I was not born to this life, as you were. If I lead them, it will be in my way," Winn replied. "And my way is to know what the people I serve wish of their Chief."

"Then give me yer trust, as yer faithful man. I tell ye, yer people wish it so. It will give us all great pleasure to see him sent off as such."

"And my brother? What does he say of this?"

"That, I cannot tell ye. He made his offering this morn, and I have not seen him since. I would not worry on it. He is like ye, born of another place, he does not understand our ways."

Winn was aware Benjamin had been absent from the funeral preparations. In fact, Winn had not spoken with him since the day they knelt down at his father's deathbed and heard the Chief's last words.

"Benjamin...my son," Marcus said. They could see the strength leave his limbs as he lay prostate on the platform, the rune stones lying over his scarred skin like brands on his flesh. The scent of death surrounded him, a dank fog amidst the echo of his fading spirit. His color fell gray, his lips tinged blue as he spoke, and Winn was glad Maggie was not there to see him falter. Benjamin

slipped his hand around that of his father, and bowed his head down, his dark curls falling over his anguished eyes.

"I'm so sorry, father," Benjamin whispered, low and strained.

"No. Say nothing of the sort. I am sorry fer leaving ye lads like this. There is much I meant to tell ye," Marcus said. He grimaced then, uttering a stifled groan with a deep sigh, after which he was silent for a long moment. He opened his eyes again once more, however, and this time he stared at Winn.

"I failed ye both, as I was never a father to either of ye...for that I have suffered. But by right of our blood, I served our cause, as my father did, and his father before him. You must both bid me promise that ye will do the same."

"I do not understand," Benjamin said. Winn felt no power to answer, knowing exactly what his father meant. Marcus had tried to tell him of the old ways, many times, and each time Winn had let his anger rule him and refused to listen. How curious it was that he now understood. He knew the power of the magic in Maggie's blood, the magic in his daughter's blood. Even before now, he would have protected them with his own life, yet now he understood there was a much greater duty upon him than that of a husband to his family.

"The blooded MacMhaolian, our most powerful one," Winn answered, his eyes meeting those of his father. Marcus made a small nod, staring back at him with those ice-laden blue eyes so like his own.

"It was the blood of a Chief Protector that brought us here. Only great magic can send a Longship through time. The power of time travel must remain our secret, and ye are sworn to protect it. Put aside yer quarrels, for the good of your people. I left my family, and all those I loved, to see it safe. Do not make it for nothing. Keep them close, see that they live on. I was born to protect them, and so are ye. I ask ye both, as my sons, to make it so."

"Father–" Benjamin said. Marcus shook his head.

"No. Give me yer oath, as protectors of our blood. Give me yer oath!"

The choked demand strained Marcus, and he fell back onto the furs. Winn took his father's hand and bowed his head to him.

"I give it to you, father," Winn said. Marcus clenched his hand, a slight gesture, yet enough for Winn to know his pledge was accepted.

"As do I," Benjamin agreed.

"It may take ye from this time. It may take you from yer own people. But it is yer duty now, and I expect ye to honor it. I tell you now, be ready. Others will search for her, as they have always searched for her kind. No other King must ever take her from us, lest all will be lost. The secret of Time Travel is ours to bear, ours to guard. Give me my knife."

Winn handed Marcus his dagger. He had tried to learn the meaning of the runes and did not expect to recognize the markings, but when he looked down at the weapon he felt his chest tighten. His father's dagger bore a familiar twisted knot on its hilt, a deep carving on a weapon meant for the Chieftain Protector of the Blooded Ones.

Winn did not flinch at the cut, nor when Marcus sliced Benjamin as well. Marcus clasped their bleeding arms together, brother to brother, their blood bound now more beyond what time or family could envision. Marcus seemed satisfied at that, and he lay back onto the furs with a long sigh.

Death took him. In the shadows of the Northern Hall, Winn saw them descend. The Norse called them Valkryies; he thought them only messengers of the Great Creator. Across the divide of time and the separation of their lives, they came together in that moment, two sons and a father, as they watched his lifeblood slip away.

"See to the final arrangements. We will send my father to Valhalla tonight. I will speak to Benjamin," Winn said. Erich nodded and left to join the men. Winn went in search of his brother.

***

Winn searched the village for Benjamin without a hint of his whereabouts, finally checking on his wife again in the hall before he looked in one more spot. In his travels he had seen nearly every person in the village, and none knew of where Benjamin might be. There was only one place Winn had not thought to look, and it was that place that he finally found his brother.

The door to the Long House he shared with Maggie was ajar, and Winn could hear the murmur of Kwetii's laughter inside. She was a cheerful child who reveled in any attention shown to her like a hungry scamp, taking it all in with her greedy little smile. Although she likened to most adults with ease, it made his chest heavy to see her so enthralled with his brother. She sat perched in Benjamin's arms as they stood by the hearth, speaking softly and pointing to the figurines on the mantle. Benjamin handed her one tiny sparrow, which made her coo with delight, and then he carefully returned it to its spot so they could consider the next one.

There was little resemblance between Benjamin and Winn, other than the peculiar blue berserker eyes and their physical size. With Kwetii, however, Winn could see the Neilsson blood. Her small, round tipped nose, her thick brown brows, and the shape of her high, flushed cheeks. Did her heart-shaped face come from them as well, or was that a feature of her special blood? Yet it seemed to no longer matter as he stood watching his brother hold his daughter, and Winn knew with a sickness in his gut it would be the last he saw of Benjamin.

Winn cleared his throat, more in defeat than meaning to disturb them, but Kwetii quickly perked up, distracted from her quiet conversation with Benjamin.

"Da!" Kwetii cried. She held her arms out to Winn.

"Go on, then, ye fickle one," Benjamin chided her, handing her over. She smothered Winn with a wet kiss, and he smiled.

"I thought Rebecca watched her," Winn commented.

"Makedewa walks with her to give her his farewell."

Winn took in that confession, the ache in his chest growing stronger. He had suspected it of Benjamin, but not Makedewa, yet he was hardly surprised by the revelation. Both men were damaged. Perhaps they would find peace as they journeyed together.

"Must I order you to stay?" Winn asked. He saw a wry smile twist his brother's mouth.

"Aye, order me, then, my Chief. And I will disobey you. Then what? Will you take your sword to my neck?" Benjamin shook his head. "Nay, give me no order, brother. It is better this way, surely you know it."

"If it is for the sake of her," Winn said, unwilling to speak Maggie's name, "Then put it from your mind. She wishes you to stay, as I do."

Benjamin shook his head.

"What part would I play in this life here? It is our father's blood that stains my hands, just as surely as if I dealt the blow. It was my mistake that ended him. I cannot see the faces of these men every day, knowing what I have done. I cannot see yer face, each day.... knowing what I have done."

Winn knew his meaning ran deep. Benjamin had not forgiven himself, and for want of the truth Winn was not sure he had forgiven him, either. He did not blame his brother in the least for the death of their father; that was a separate thing, more of an excuse to give him more strength of resolve. No, the thing that drove his brother away was the love Benjamin still held for Winn's wife, and they both knew it.

"Then find peace once more. Go. Be safe, my brother."

Benjamin clasped his arm, and he returned the gesture in kind. As he held his brother's embrace, Winn looked into the eyes so similar to his own. It was then that he could see it. A glimmer, a hint, a sliver of hope that someday he would return. After all, they had made a blood vow to protect the Blooded Ones. It was a vow Winn was certain Benjamin would honor when he was needed.

32

Makedewa

Makedewa did not touch Rebecca as they walked quietly through the village. People bustled in every direction, making the last of preparations for the burial of their fallen Chief. He was glad for the distraction, since he did not know how to tell her what he planned to do.

"You were brave to save Kwetii," he finally said. Perhaps if he started off with a compliment, it would ease the way for the rest of what they must discuss. She tilted her head a bit to the side and looked gainfully at him with her soft round eyes, her hair falling back away from her face.

"Thank ye. My teacher was quite skilled," she said. Her shirts rustled with each pace, her hands swaying at her sides instead of tucked up in fists. He took a chance by catching her fingers, entwining them in his own. He was glad for the risk when her lips curled into a shy smile.

They walked together to the edge of the village, where the clearing opened up to the meadow. He stopped her when she started to take the path toward the ridge, afraid of betraying too much of himself should they be alone so far from the others. The sounds of the villagers behind them reminded him of his intent.

"I wish to say goodbye," he said softly, pulling her to a stop. She turned quickly back to him.

"Another task, for yer uncle? I thought ye men were through with doing his deeds," she said, uttering a sharp sigh as if his statement made no sense.

"It is no task for my uncle. I leave with Benjamin today."

His chest tightened as her face crumbled and her mouth formed a half-opened denial. Her cheeks flushed crimson as she struggled with her response.

"But why? Is it because…" she said, her words trailing off unsaid. Her fingers clenched tight around his.

"No, little bird, I do not run from you," he replied. He cupped her face gently with his hand, running his thumb over her lips. He smiled when she turned her face toward his touch and closed her eyes.

"Then why?"

"Because I am not ready to be a husband to you. A man should have a great journey before he takes a wife," he whispered. A tear spilled down her face, and he brushed it away. They both knew it was a lie. "So you must wait to be my wife. When I return, I will be much stronger. I will be ready to be a good husband."

He closed his mouth gently over hers as her tears fell, holding her face his hands, his body trembling at the touch of her skin against his.

"*Nouwami, chulentet,*" he whispered. *I love you, little bird,* he thought as the realization of leaving her felt like a stake piercing his chest. He had never considered his heart before, but as he looked down on her, he suddenly felt it breaking. Yet he knew it was what they needed, what they both needed. Soon, when she was ready to spread her wings, he would return, and she would welcome him.

He kissed her urgently once more and then pulled away. It took strength he did not know he still possessed to leave her, but thankfully, it was enough. As he walked away he heard her voice, only a whisper, yet still resilient, and he smiled through his pain.

"I love ye too," she said.

It was enough for now.

33

Maggie

Maggie placed a bundle of fine linen into a deep thatched basket for Gwen to add to the burial pyre. Although she was painfully aware of her new role in the community, she leaned on Gwen's strength to finish the task ahead. Hearing the bustle of the villagers prepare the feast, and the roar of the fire in the yard as Finola muttered a pagan chant was near too much to bear. It was expected of Maggie to attend and oversee the details, yet she deferred to the others not out of obstinacy, but of grief. She simply could not look at the lifeless body of her beloved friend without falling apart.

Maggie clutched her thick fur mantle up around her neck with two fists, rubbing her chin against the lush white pelt. It was new to her, an exorbitant gift from her husband to wear to the ceremony. Looking around at the others, her vision began to blur and her heart raced, so she decided she had enough. They could do without her for a short time.

She spotted Winn walking toward her across the yard as she left the Northern Hall. His pace was brisk, his eyes troubled, and she hoped there was no more trouble for him to bear. Her husband had already borne too much.

"What is it?" she asked as he reached her. He did not touch her, keeping his hands loose at his sides. His pulse danced rapid on his neck, his veins standing out like cords across his skin. She put a soft hand on his cheek, relieved when he did not flinch away, but instead covered her hand with his own.

"Benjamin is leaving," he said.

"Oh," she murmured. She was not shocked by the news, but stunned that it was Winn who spoke the words to her.

"He watches Kwetii now, while Rebecca speaks with Makedewa. It seems Makedewa will join Benjamin on his journey."

She searched his gaze for a hint, anything to guide her in what Winn expected of her. She sighed with the realization that she had never been any good at doing what he ordered, and now was not the time to fret over it. Her husband was hurting, despite whatever had transpired between him and his brother, and she could plainly see he was troubled over the impending departure.

"You should go see to Kwetii," Winn said quietly, his voice low and hoarse. He drew her close then, pressing his lips gently to her hair, his voice meant only for her ears. "Go. Go see to our daughter now. I will wait for you in the Northern Hall."

She closed her eyes to his words. No, this was not her husband sending her to tend their child. It was her husband sending her to say goodbye to his brother, in the only way he knew how, the only way he could accept.

"Go," he whispered. He swept the hair back off her face and kissed her roughly, his lips harsh with possession, although they both knew she belonged only to him. She tried to cling to him, but he gently peeled her hands from his face and placed them at her sides. He turned abruptly and walked away.

She folded her arms across her chest, her breath coming fast as her heart pounded in her ears. How could their lives have taken this turn? To finally find safe haven, a family, for Winn to have a father? Now they stood on the edge of losing it all. His father had fallen, and now he would lose two brothers as well. For all they had suffered, she could not watch it end this way. Instead of a goodbye, there would be a different conversation.

Kwetii was asleep when she arrived, snoring peacefully on the bedding platform. Benjamin sat beside her, swaying gently in the new rocking chair Erich had made for her. His eyes were closed, but he opened them and stood up when she approached.

"She's sleeping sound, I bid ye she'll stay like that for some time. Give ye a spot to yerself," he said, as if he did not guess why she was there. She knew him better than that, and she resented his games.

"How can you leave like this? Now, of all times?" she asked.

Benjamin placed his hands on his hips, in that way he did sometimes when he had no answer, giving himself time to say something meaningful in return. She could recall him making the gesture as a child, and later as a man. He looked like Marcus then, his blazing eyes shadowed by a furrowed brow. Suddenly he flinched and turned his back to her, as if to shield himself from her accusations.

"How can ye ask me to stay? You, of all of them. Ye who know me best," he replied.

"Marcus wanted you here, with your family. He risked his life using that damn Bloodstone, just to come here to find you!"

"Aye, he traveled far to find me. But it was ye he meant to see safe, on his sworn vow. I know now what it means, to be the son of such a man. In yer blood lies the power of the *Blooded Ones*, and mine is bound to protect ye."

"You can't protect me if you leave," she said.

His shoulders stiffened.

"I think my brother will serve ye well in my absence."

She put a hand on his arm.

"But you can't leave," she whispered. "What can I say to make you stay?"

He swung around, his hands shaking in closed fists at his sides. He came so close they nearly touched, staring down at her with a mixture of despair and sadness she had never seen in him before.

"Your words would not make me stay. Nay, woman, get ye gone. I have no more for ye, except goodbye."

She wanted to comfort him, to give him something. For all he had given her of his heart, she could not keep it, yet looking into his red-rimmed eyes she was flooded with grief. Grief for what he had suffered, for what pain she had caused him. Anguish at the truth that lay between them, as thick as the smoke from the burial pyre burning in the courtyard. He had given, and she had taken. She knew he could not stay.

"Where will you go?" she asked quietly. He lifted his head, his tousled hair falling back from his face. Stark blue eyes faded to dull glimmers as he looked at her.

"I don't know. I shall know when I get there, I suppose."

Her breath slowed as met her gaze.

"Your family is here," she insisted.

"Aye. And they will be here someday, when I return."

"Benjamin, I–"

"No," he whispered, his voice hoarse. "Say nothing more except goodbye. Bid me farewell, as your good brother."

"I cannot."

"If ever a woman could bear such things, it is you. Look at me, with a smile on your face, so that I might remember it." He looked at her for a long moment, his eyes hard yet searching, until he dipped his head down. She felt his hand brush over her hair, and then the soft touch of his lips near her ear. He brushed past her, close, but without further contact as he headed for the door. She heard his voice behind her, low and strained with the last few words he might ever speak to her.

"I know ye never truly belonged to me," he whispered. "But I loved ye once, and I loved ye well. I do not regret that part of it."

The tears came unbidden as she heard him walk away and the door flapped shut behind him. She settled there, wishing there was another way to keep him close, not for her selfish heart, but for his family and all those who loved him.

But even the asking of it was too much. She could not bear to wound him further. He was right, she could see it then.

She looked down at the twisted scar on her palm. As she closed her fingers around the time travel brand, suddenly things seemed clear. Had

Marcus not said her blood was powerful? That it was so dangerous it must be protected? That the secret of time travel lay squarely in her hands?

"Maggie? Are ye here?" Rebecca called. Maggie swung around, her hands shaking with the realization of what she meant to do.

"Would you stay with Kwetii until I return?" she asked the younger woman. Her shimmering curls bounced as Rebecca nodded.

"Of course. But will ye not come to the Northern Hall?"

"I will. I have something to do first."

Maggie avoided looking into her friend's searching eyes as she brushed past her, clutching her mantle around her shoulders. A dampness in the air betrayed the upcoming storm, and as she made her way to the ridge, she felt the sprinkle of cold raindrops on her face.

Yes, she thought, as she climbed to the peak. Her legs ached from her rapid gait and her lungs felt the stress of the journey as she reached the clearing. As she stood, trying to slow her breaths, she looked down upon the ship below. White tipped waves splashed into the vessel, rocking the final resting place of her beloved friend as the men below filled it with gifts. She could see the line of warriors and women, even the children, and although they were small at the distance she stood from them, she could see their arms filled with treasures intended to ease his journey.

None of it needed to happen. She had the power to change it, didn't she? Winn had suffered without a father his entire life because of her blood. Countless others unknown had given their vow to protect the Blooded Ones. Marcus had given his life.

"I know ye think ye have no power here, Maggie. But ye have it all, ye just don't know it yet."

She took the bone-handled knife from her waist. No, she did not know how to control it. If her Bloodstone could take her to another time, could spilling a greater amount trigger the magic? She recalled Harald's story of Chief Drustan, and how he said all the blood of a Chief Protector, or that of a *Blooded MacMhaolian,* could send a ship through time. She knew the others feared the magical power, but Marcus had believed enough in her blood to spend his life in service of protecting it. Perhaps it was as simple as draining her vein and demanding her wishes be done. Then they would all wake up, together again, before death took Marcus.

She lifted her chin against the wind, the rain now needles spiking her skin. Her shift was soaked through, sticking to her skin, her cloak feeling heavy with the dampness over her shoulders. She shrugged the cloak away and it fell to a heap at her feet.

"Listen to me, Odin! God! Whoever you are! I want him back, do you hear me! I want him returned to me! *Take my blood, and bring him back!*" she screamed into the rain. A crash of thunder rolled close overhead as she drew the knife across her forearm. She felt no sting as she watched the blood trickle down her wrist and drip to the ground. *"Bring him back!"*

The wind continued to howl, whipping her hair back off her face as she confronted the storm. She felt the fight leave her body as her demands went unanswered. As she covered her face with her hands, she heard his footsteps behind her on the wet grass.

Winn pulled her into his arms and slipped her fallen cloak over her shoulders. When he spotted the blood he uttered a sigh. He ripped the edge of his tunic and bound her wrist with the strip of fine cloth. It seemed fitting that he stemmed her bleeding with the garment of a Chief. Had they not already died to protect it? Her precious, useless, magical blood?

"You'll catch your death up here," he said softly, his blue eyes gleaming sadly down at her.

"I want to bring him back. Get Finola, or Gwen, and make them show me how," she demanded. She grabbed hold of his tunic with fisted hands. "Please. Please, Winn."

"No, *ntehem*," he said.

"This is something I can do! I can make this right, I can bring him back! I'm the one who has this power, right? I'm the only one left to do it!"

"Yes, you can. You can bring him back," he said softly. "You can travel back in time to stop it. You can take us all to another place. But you must not."

"I must," she replied.

"How would you change things, Maggie? Would you change the day I was born, or the day the Norse came here? Would you change the visions of my uncle, or bring back the men he killed? Would you change the day you bloodied your hand and came through time for me? Is that what you would change? Our future lies here. Death is part of it. Living is more of it. This life here, this is our future. Yes, you can change it if you wish…but I know that you must not." His hand slipped down over the gentle swell of her belly. *No, she had not told him yet.*

"I don't know what will happen. I can't see the future like Finola can."

"I see it. I see our son, here with us. He laughs at his foolish father, and loves his brave mother so very much," Winn answered. He sank to his knees before her on the sodden ground, placing his forehead to her belly. "Tell your mother to give me her hand, my son. Tell her I will stand by her side in this life, and always."

She wrapped her arms around him and pulled him close, sinking down beside him on the damp ground as she closed her eyes to the tears and pain that tore through her soul. The scent of his skin, of earth and of her tears, sent her deeper into his embrace, his lips closing over hers. She savored the strength, and took hold of his hand, twisting her fingers through his.

"I love you too, warrior," she whispered, both to her husband and to their unborn son.

***

Maggie felt numb as they joined the others on the sand. The villagers stood on the beach as Finola lit the funeral pyre with a torch, setting the Longboat aflame. The fire quickly rose high above, snapping and roaring like a beast unto itself as it consumed the last essence of the Chief's earthly body, the heat of its fury licking their skin. Winn's arm tightened on her waist and she leaned into him as Gwen began to sing. She had a beautiful voice, the sweet trill echoing in the smoky air as she cried her song of sorrow.

As the ship drifted out toward the ocean, a glimpse of movement caught her eye. High on the ridge up above where she had tried to change the course of their destiny, Benjamin and Makedewa sat mounted on their horses, watching those below. Rebecca saw them as well, her eyes glistening as she stood beside Gwen.

She felt Winn adjust his hand on her hip as he followed her gaze upward. He stood motionless for a moment, staring at the two men, and then slowly unsheathed the sword at his side.

It had belonged to his grandfather, and it shimmered in the remnants of the pale sunlight as he raised it high above his head. She heard the sounds of metal weapons drawn, and around them, the remaining men copied Winn's gesture, pointing their swords toward the ridge.

Makedewa and Benjamin echoed the salute, thrusting their swords above their heads. The two travelers gave a silent acknowledgement to the new Chief, and then they turned their horses towards their journey.

Winn squeezed her hand, and she held his tight.

"Return soon, my brothers," Winn whispered.

PREVIEW: OF VICE AND VIRTUE

1

Elizabeth City, Virginia Colony
1626
Benjamin

Benjamin emptied the last of his ale and set his tankard down, his eyes scanning the inn for a glimpse of the brown-haired serving girl. She was a feisty lass. He had watched earlier in the evening as she waylaid the clumsy attentions of several Englishmen, swatting their groping paws as she busied about her duties. With more than a bit of annoyance he wondered where she had gone off to, and why she was not refilling his drink.

"Enough yet?" Makedewa asked. Benjamin looked up at his Indian companion, shaking his head despite the glare of contempt the lean warrior bestowed upon him.

"No. I'll have one more," he answered. He lifted his hand to beckon the serving girl near the stairwell, pleased when she nodded an acknowledgement in his direction.

"Ah, *kemata tepahta!*" Makedewa cursed. Instead of pulling up the bench beside him, Makedewa muttered a few coarse words in Paspahegh and then left, swinging his fur-lined cloak around as he stalked away. Benjamin watched him shoulder through a few teetering Englishmen as he made his way to the door.

"Fine then," Benjamin sighed. They both needed a break after traveling together so long. Benjamin adjusted the long handled axe harnessed on his back with a sigh as he sat back in the rickety chair. Although it had been less than a year since they left the Norse village it seemed like much longer, yet not long enough to chase her memory away in a permanent manner. Even as he sat there, allowing his mind to wander to that forbidden place, he knew it was better to leave those things buried. The feel of her soft pale skin beneath his fingers, the honey-kissed scent of her auburn hair close to his lips... those were things he needed to forget. It was the reason he left the only true home he had ever known, and it was his mission to bear.

Forget Maggie, the wife of his brother. A simple thing, yet one he was not ready to do. At least not until he had another drink.

"More, sir?" the girl asked, pausing with a jug of fresh ale perched over his tankard.

"Fill it. Took ye long enough," he muttered. The utterance seemed to come from some dark place he did not recognize, the voice of a fallen man he did not wish to know. Apparently, she did not care for his tone either, and she slammed his mug back down on the table with a thud, spilling most of it in his lap.

"Bloody sod!" she snapped. He had enough good sense left to be somewhat ashamed of his behavior, so when she turned to leave he grabbed her hand. Her mantle of brown hair fell across her face when she swung on him in a fury.

"My apology, mistress," he said as she yanked. He was about to let her go when suddenly her hand went limp and her tawny eyes softened. He regretted his clumsy attempt at chivalry as she stared down at him with a curious look on her face.

"No, sir, no need. I've been busy, and I dinna see ye needed more," she said, her voice barely a whisper. He tried to drop her hand but then her second hand tightened around his as well.

"Well, no harm, then. Carry on with ye," he replied, a bit unsettled but willing to brush off the uncomfortable episode.

"Sir, might I ask a favor of ye?" she said. Her eyes darted briefly toward the tavern bar, where the innkeeper stood watching them. Benjamin saw the pulse throbbing in her throat and she suddenly appeared afraid.

"A favor?"

"I've not made enough tonight for my employer. Might I take ye upstairs to earn a bit of coin? I'm quite good at my job, sir," she murmured.

Benjamin stared hard at her. So that was her game? Only a whore, picking her customers? Well, he might be tied down by memories of what he had lost, but he was not that far gone to buy the affection of a woman. He leaned forward and looked her in the eye.

"No thank ye, mistress. I'll be on my way now," he snapped.

"Please. He will beat me if I don't take ye upstairs. He's a fearsome man, I'm barely healed from the last time!" she pleaded.

He paused in his attempt to flee, looking down at her hand on his arm. A memory of the beating Maggie had endured at the hands of an Englishman entered his thoughts, the remembrance of her bruised and battered skin tearing through his resolve. No, he would not wish such a thing on any woman, even one who earned her living peddling her body for coin.

Funny, he thought, as he nodded his consent. *She did not look like a whore.* He had not known any, but she certainly was not what he envisioned one might be. She was a tiny thing, barely reaching his shoulder with the top of her head. A full mane of russet brown hair graced her narrow shoulders, and by Odin's tooth he had to admit her snug corset was filled out in a pleasing manner.

"Fine. I'll go with ye. For show," he agreed. He followed her up the stairs, avoiding the stares of the men and the assortment of laughs that accompanied them. He prayed Makedewa would not come asking for him anytime soon.

He rented the first room at the end of the hall, so he opened the door and shoved her inside. It should be sufficient enough to please the innkeeper and save her from a beating. He paced away from her and cleared his throat, and when he turned back to her she had a smile on her face that did not reassure him in the least. She threw herself into his arms, knocking them both forcefully back onto the narrow bed.

"Get off me, woman!" he barked. She ignored his request and settled astride him, her hands pressing him back into the feathered mattress.

"I just want to thank ye, my lord," she insisted, fumbling with the buttons of his breeches. He placed his hands on her waist in order to forcibly remove her, but she snuggled down over him and ran her mouth over his neck. *Great Odin. Sweet Jesus.* What was she doing?

"Stop it, lass," he croaked, his voice completely unconvincing.

"Ye wear a strange pendant, sir. Might I see it?"

He stiffened at the request. Yes, he wore a copper-wrapped Bloodstone around his neck, but surely she could not see it. His shirt fell open a bit since he'd loosened it in his cups, yet it was not enough to see the pendant that lay against his skin.

He rose up to a sitting position, taking her with him. As he tried to shove her away she clung like a snake, her eyes fastened on the twisted scar upon his palm. She grabbed hold of his hand. Her jaw dropped open, and he felt his blood drain to his feet.

Whoever she was, whatever she knew, he would not stay to find out. He jerked his hand from her grasp and pushed her onto the bed, running one hand reflexively over his hip to assure himself his knife was still sheathed there. With that confirmation he made for the door.

"Wait!" she called out.

The squared outline of a man blocked the gleam of moonlight from the doorway, and with a sliver of sickness streaking through his gut he knew he was correct on his earlier assumption.

She was undoubtedly no whore.

~END PREVIEW~

About the Author

E.B. Brown enjoys researching history and genealogy and uses her findings to cultivate new ideas for her writing. She grew up in Gibbstown, New Jersey, and is a proud graduate of Paulsboro High School and Drexel University. Her debut novel, *The Legend of the Bloodstone (Time Walkers #1)*, was a Quarter-finalist in the 2013 Amazon Breakthrough Novel Award contest. An excerpt from another Time Walkers novel, *A Tale of Oak and Mistletoe (Time Walkers #4)*, was a finalist in the 2013 RWA/NYC We Need a Hero Contest.

E.B. is a proud supporter of Special Olympics New Jersey and works multiple charity events throughout the year to support the cause. She loves mudding in her Jeep Wrangler and likes to cause all kinds of havoc the rest of the time. She resides in New Jersey.

CONNECT WITH ME ONLINE:
FACEBOOK www.facebook.com/ebbrownauthor
GOODREADS www.goodreads.com/EBBrown
OFFICIAL WEBSITE: www.ebbrown.net

Also by E.B. Brown

TIME WALKERS
The Legend of the Bloodstone
Return of the Pale Feather
Of Vice and Virtue
A Tale of Oak and Mistletoe

TIME DANCE
Ghost Dance
Season of Exile
Through the Valley
Song of Sunrise

TIME WALKERS WORLD
The Pretenders
Time Song

CPSIA information can be obtained
at www.ICGtesting.com
Printed in the USA
BVHW041335110720
583345BV00021B/109